THE WOMAN WHO KILLED MARVIN HAMMEL

THE WOMAN WHO: BOOK TWO

C.K. CRIGGER

WOLFPACK
PUBLISHING
— EST 2013 —

WOLFPACK
PUBLISHING
— EST 2013 —

The Woman Who Killed Marvin Hammel
C.K. Crigger

Paperback Edition
© Copyright 2020 C.K. Crigger

Wolfpack Publishing
6032 Wheat Penny Avenue
Las Vegas, NV 89122

Paperback ISBN: 978-1-64734-327-9
eBook ISBN: 978-1-64734-326-2

Library of Congress Control Number: 2020941468

THE WOMAN WHO KILLED
MARVIN HAMMEL

CHAPTER 1

SHAY BILLINGS REACHED TOWN A LITTLE EARLY FOR HIS MEETING with Albert Sims, the president of the Selkirk Trust Bank. Seemed a waste of time, riding all the way into town when he ought to be harvesting his oats, but with the final payment on his property's loan contract soon coming due, he wanted to be certain everything was in order. Every i dotted, every t crossed and verified.

Not that he didn't trust Albert Sims, but . . . yeah. He didn't trust Albert Sims.

Because Hoot, his gray gelding, had been frisky after being stuck in the corral for the last week while Shay repaired and sharpened his mower teeth, tightened bolts on the binder and greased the threshing machine, they'd made good time. That's why he spotted the woman emerging from Sims' inner office which, he suspected, was a pure bad accident. On her part.

The woman wore a veiled black hat with a long pheasant feather, also dyed black, set atop her blonde puffed up hairdo. Wrapped in a voluminous black cloak, she appeared the epitome of a sorrowing widow.

Recognizing her right off, Shay knew her for a widow,

all right. Sorrowing, though, that he wasn't so sure about. Mad as a half-drowned hen, he knew for certain.

"Mrs. Hammel," he said, tipping the brim of his hat. He'd rather have ignored her, but folks there in the bank were watching, their gazes avid.

"Mr. Billings," she said in return after a fraught pause.

Both of them polite as could be, but going by the woman's icy green glare, if her eyes had been guns he'd be dead. Or maybe have a knife slashed across his gullet.

Shay figured if he'd been one of those watchers he'd be doing the same as they were, which was waiting to see what happened next. That would be nothing if he had anything to say about it. But, he had to concede, it wasn't every day a woman met face-to-face with the man who'd killed her son—the son who'd tried twice but barely failed to kill the man. Then there was the fact Shay's wife had killed the woman's husband, who'd been trying to kill her at the time.

Confusing? No doubt. And not a pleasant situation any way you looked at it.

More confusing to Shay was the curled-lip smirk on Mrs. Hammel's face, like she knew something he didn't. Something that didn't bode well for him.

Then they were past each other. Shay eyed Sims who stood, mouth agape, at the entry to his office holding the door open.

"Come in, come in." The short, stout, bank president smoothed sparse hair and jerked into speech. "Thanks for being so prompt, Mr. Billings. Something has come up we need to discuss. A serious matter indeed."

Shay's brows drew together. If the fat man had spoken any louder, he might as well paraded down the street and hollered through a bullhorn so the whole dang town could hear.

"Don't know what it would be," he said, "but that's why I'm here."

Sims smiled, an insincere lift of the lips over a pair of canine teeth that stuck out a little farther than they ought. They gave his round face a peculiar porcine effect, like one of those wild boars with long tusks a feller sees down south.

"Sit down, Mr. Billings, and I'll explain the situation to you." Sims ushered Shay into the office, closing the door and cutting off the sounds as people began to whisper. Knees creaking under his considerable weight, he sat in the cushioned chair behind the desk where some papers had been laid out.

Shay, in seating himself across from the man, noticed his name showed in an obvious position on the top page. So obvious, in fact, he had no doubt Mrs. Hammel had had the privilege of viewing it too. What's more, it didn't take much to read the top document even upside down. It was a duplicate of the papers in Shay's possession. The loan papers regarding his property.

"What's going on, Sims? What's that doing out where the Hammel woman could see it?" Eyes blazing, Shay nodded toward the desk, his expression hard.

Sims shifted in his chair. His smile turned sickly as he opened one of the lower desk drawers. "Woman?"

Shay stared at him.

"Oh, you mean Mrs. Hammel? Oh, no. No. I just put these papers out when she left the room."

"Do I look like a blind fool to you, Sims? I was standing here when she came out, you with her. The papers were already there."

Shay reached forward and snatched up the documents, beating Sims, who tried the same thing, by a hair's breadth. With another dark stare at the banker, he started reading. Bare seconds passed before he looked up again. "What is this?" The sharp edge to the question could've sawed through ice.

Sims squirmed his fat butt a little deeper into the leather of his chair. "I . . . ah . . . in getting ready to sign over the deed, I noticed an irregularity. Something that needs seen to before the due date on the loan. We don't want this deal going awry, now do we? Not at this late stage."

"What irregularity? I've been paying on my land for six years the end of this month. On time and in full according to the agreement. *The original agreement.*" He put heavy emphasis on that part. "All signed, sealed and in duplicate. There is no irregularity. What're you trying to pull, Sims? You and Mrs. Hammel?" Shay didn't often lose his temper, but he knew it was going south fast. Not wise. With an effort, he reined himself in.

"I don't know what you mean," Sims said. "In anticipation of your final payment due . . ." He made a play of checking his calendar. ". . . on October first, just two weeks from now, I made a final check through the papers."

Shay heard the unspoken *and* at the end of Sims' sentence.

When he remained silent, Sims continued. "I discovered that apparently, whoever surveyed the area made an error."

"An error, you say?" Shay's mouth twisted into a doubting half-smile. Not, from the look on Sims' face, the reaction the banker had expected.

Sims cleared his throat with a rattle of phlegm. "Yes. It seems you've fenced in twenty acres you're not entitled to. Now I've talked with the executor of the Ordurf estate, the original owners, and provided you pay the extra money for the acreage, everything will be fine."

"Or?" Shay knew the man lied. Anger pounded at him but he wanted to hear what kind of tale he spun. How big of a moron did he think Shay was, anyhow?

"Or, I suppose you could remove your fence and settle for the allotted acreage. The land you've illegally taken runs down by the river. If you do build the fence, it will shut off your water access." The rasp of throat clearing came again. "There is just one more thing."

Here it came. Shay's jaw clamped down so hard he almost broke a tooth and waited for the banker to drop the bomb, one sure to be full of gas and smoke.

"No matter which way you decide," Sims said, "everything has to be final by the note's due date. That means either the fence moved or payment made for the extra twenty acres, plus interest on the value for the six years you've used the land, plus a fair rent."

Shay figured it was a good thing he didn't have a gun on him right about then, or he might've been tempted to use it. Fortunately, he made it a habit to go unarmed in places like the bank, especially in these last few months. There'd been enough gunfire in his life.

"Just out of curiosity, what number are you putting on this value and rent and what not?" he asked.

"Oh, I think two thousand will about cover it." Sims smiled and folded his hands over his paunch.

Shay figured the man knew to the penny how much he had in the bank. It wasn't that much. He'd never be able to come up with that kind of money within two weeks, even if he owed it. Which he didn't.

Having removed his hat and set it beside his chair, Shay picked it up. At last he looked at Sims. "I see you've added a falsified page to the contract. A page my copy doesn't contain. Now, I suppose I could get a lawyer and we could wrangle this, me fighting the addition, you denying acceptance of my final payment until it is in arrears."

"A false page?" Sims grinned like a gargoyle. "No, no. If there is a discrepancy, it seems clear to me that you must've subtracted a page."

Placing the hat on his head, Shay stood up. "One thing maybe you didn't count on, Sims. Six years ago I had a notarized copy of the contract made. See, I'd heard about some shifty deals coming out of this bank even before I walked in. I figured I best plan on somebody trying to rock the boat."

Sims, face flushed, hissed a breath from between his teeth like an angry cat. "We'll see about that."

"We will," Shay said. Turning on his heel, he left the banker's office, closing the door softly behind him. But not to leave the bank. Stopping at the teller's window, he presented his contract.

"Howdy, Jim," he said to the man behind the half window. "Gonna pay off my loan a couple weeks early, if that's all right with you."

Jim peered around at Sims' closed door and shrugged. "Sure enough, Mr. Billings. So that land of yours will be free and clear, after today. Congratulations. That's real fine."

"Thanks, Jim." Shay, digging a seldom-used checkbook from his pocket, wore a broad grin as he wrote out the correct sum—minus any unnecessary fees and fines and rents. *This'll work. Sim's can't stop me now.* "All mine, just like the contract states."

His account covered the payment without a whole lot left over, but the receipt and his original loan papers, both stamped *paid in full* came as a relief.

Sims had made a mistake when he took Shay for a backwoods nobody who'd never bothered to read through his contract.

"All yours," Jim said and reached under the half-window to shake Shay's hand.

Business finished, to Shay's mind in a most satisfactory manner despite the run-in with Sims, a celebratory drink seemed in order. That, and he had a letter to write before he left town. Tying Hoot to a handy rail in front of the Barefoot Saloon, Shay got his letter written and mailed, treated a circle of friends with a shot of the Barefoot's best stuff, and in turn, had his good news saluted by a couple of those friends. It was already nearing dusk when he started for home.

In a good mood, the fine Kentucky bourbon still sending a glow through his innards, Shay was whistling some little ditty a man had been playing on the Barefoot's ill-tuned piano. In truth, he could've sat down at the keyboard and played it better, but his whistle suited him well enough. And Hoot, too, who seemed to pick up his hooves in rhythm with the tune. The thought tickled Shay. Old Hoot dancing. Who would've ever figured such a thing?

That may have been why he didn't at first notice the buggy with its lone occupant parked under some trees at the side of the deserted road.

His blurry eyes—or blurred good sense—may have been the reason, even when he and Hoot were close enough to identify the person in the buggy, he felt no real cause for alarm. Not until the buggy rolled out in front of him, the single horse throwing its head and rattling the bit.

He had an intimation then, all right. The flashing eyes, the jaw working as though on metal hinges, the colorless cheeks, all clues as to the driver's state of mind. Well, that and the pistol, a small revolver, held in a gloved fist.

"I'll take that contract." The voice shook more than the hand.

Shay huffed his disgust. "Won't do you any good. Like I said earlier, I took the precaution of making a copy. All anybody has to do is look in the records to see the right of it. Besides, you're too late. I stopped at the teller's cage on the way out of the bank. Paid off the loan then and there, all right and legal. Plenty of people saw me do it."

Did his ears deceive him? Did he hear a sob?

"I don't believe you. Either give me the contract or I'll shoot you."

"Listen," Shay started, only to have the buggy roll and veer into Hoot, who shifted aside.

"Give it here, I said." The harsh whisper sounded half-crazed. The pistol barrel followed him as though drawn by a string.

Thinking to buy a little time, Shay reached toward his pocket, but just then the buggy horse, no doubt sensing the tension in the air, jolted forward again.

A single shot cracked into the dusk.

Shay's hands flung into the air. He grunted once, then fell toward his left side, toppling slowly from the saddle as though reluctant to meet the earth. Hoot jumped as Shay thudded to ground.

"I told you. I said I'd shoot." Gun still in hand, the driver started to get down, but then the buggy lurched again.

Because of Hoot. The silvery gray horse lunged toward the buggy horse. Toward the person who already had one foot on the ground. The foot shrank back.

"Get away." The brandished weapon lashed out, catching Hoot a smack on the cheek.

Then, for a moment, it looked as though Hoot wanted to climb into the buggy, his forefeet climbing all the way onto the driver's seat before he dropped back down.

"Hyah." A terrified, high-pitched yell set the buggy horse into action. A whip flicked and the animal ran. Away, this time.

Hoot trotted a few steps after the buggy, then stopped and watched them go. Standing off a short way, he paced around his master's still form, whuffling Shay's face every so often as to awaken him. Shay didn't move.

An hour passed, then two.

At length, one of the Inman sisters' ranch hands who'd been out sparking a young neighbor lady, chanced by. Due to the ghost-like horse standing protectively over it, he didn't see the body on the ground at first. But then he did. He saw the blood stain spread across Shay Billings' shirt, too. The ranch hand, Ezra by name, swung down from his saddle.

Hoot, calmed enough by now to allow the wrangler close, made no protest when pushed aside for the rider to get a better look. "Mr. Billings," Ezra said. "Hey, Billings, wake up."

But that, as he found a moment later, wasn't ever going to happen.

Gathering his reins, Ezra swung aboard his horse. "You," he said, pointing at Hoot. "Take care of him. I'll get the sheriff."

CHAPTER 2

January Billings, nee Schutt, completed mortaring the last stone of the foundation into place and tossed her trowel into the empty bucket. It landed with a satisfying dull *thunk*. At first she thought that's why Pen, her old dog, woke up and whuffed. The dog, mightily bored by watching her mistress work at such a monotonous task, had slept for most of the afternoon. But from the way the dog stood and looked off down the road, she may have anticipated something more exciting than setting stones in place

Shay should be home in time for a late supper. Pen may have sensed his imminent arrival and that's why she'd awakened. January glanced toward the road. She admitted to anticipating that first sight of him, too. Most certainly even more than the dog. She doubted Pen got a tingle that stirred all the way through her body the way her mistress did.

Smiling, January stood back to survey the results of her labor and stretched, easing tired back muscles. Shay would be surprised when he saw how much she'd accomplished while he'd been gone. They'd made a start on the new house together, making a detailed plan, digging the half cellar and lining the walls with some of the round stones so plentiful to the area—and which had taken her months to gather even before she met Shay—then started on the above ground part. That foundation is what January had finished today. A job well done.

He'd kissed her before he left for town. January blushed thinking about it.

"Sure you'll be all right?" he'd asked, one of his work-worn paws moving over her trouser-clad bottom. "You'll be careful, won't you? Don't try moving anything too heavy. A little lady like you could hurt herself."

He seemed to have forgotten she'd built a whole bridge and shored up a falling down barn—not to mention collected all those foundation stones—by herself. And yet, here she stood, hale and hearty.

"I'll be careful," she promised, because that's what wives said.

He'd kissed her again, lips trailing over her scarred cheek. "Sure you won't come with me? We could eat dinner at the café in town. You deserve a day out."

She was sure, all right. January thought of going to town as an ordeal, not a treat.

So he'd climbed into the saddle and ridden away, turning once to wave.

Tomorrow—or no—tomorrow her husband would need to check his livestock, mend any fences, and begin threshing the twenty-acre patch of oats growing in the creekside meadow. Afterward, he'd get back to helping her build the house here at the Kindred Crossing bridge.

The bridge she'd built in the spring and that had brought them together. Well, that and Shay getting shot and having to lay up in her barn where she'd carved out a place to temporarily live.

Shay Billings. Her husband. January shivered with delight, with gratitude, with joy. Scarred face and all, he loved her anyway. She'd never believed she'd find love.

Slapping dust from her hands, January thought she'd better clean up before Shay arrived. He might not mind a little grime, but she did. She didn't like for him to see her dirty and sweaty. It just didn't strike her as ... romantic .. . for lack of a better word. They'd only been married four months and were still new to each other.

"C'mon, Pen," she told the dog. Instead of riding the two miles back to Shay's small two-room house where they lived now, she'd go down to the deep pool formed by a curve in the stream and bathe. Although mid-September had arrived, the days were still warm and the water would be refreshing. Not freezing like in winter. Anyway, she hadn't grown so soft in just four months, had she? She'd bathed here all the time weather permitting, when, in a single room fixed up well enough for a hardy soul to survive, she'd lived in the old barn.

Walking the path down the hill and across what had been a pasture, January spared a glance for the barn, now a burned-out scattering of mostly consumed timbers, some metal parts, and heaps of sooty debris. The fall rains and winter snows most likely would cleanse the area fairly well by next spring, she thought. And good riddance. Who wanted to recall what had threatened to become a war, or the men who'd set the barn afire with the intention of cremating her and Shay inside it?

She shuddered, remembering despite herself. She'd prefer *never* to be reminded that she'd killed a man here. Maybe more than one. Self-defense, but still. Because of her scars, she'd never liked to show herself in town, back then. Now, because of Shay, she found it possible to ignore the scars, but not the people who looked down their pointing finger and called her "the woman who killed Marvin Hammel."

Most of them added, "He deserved it."

But not all. And those pointed fingers disturbed her. Shay somehow managed to shrug off the cruel things people said. Or maybe he only put on a good act. She hadn't made up her mind about that.

Ablutions finished, hurried because she found the water more chilly than the anticipated refreshing, she donned a fresh shirt over the men's britches she wore. Tying her shoulder length brown hair at the nape of her neck, she and Pen walked along the riverbank to the bridge. She'd wait for Shay there.

An hour ticked away, each second a beat of her heart.

To while away the time, January counted the nickels in the can that had served to help pay for the toll bridge she'd built. Once she'd made her investment back, she'd thrown the can away, but someone, she had no idea who, had replaced it.

She stowed the money away in a pocket, leaving the can on a post. After that, it took a full half hour, a pry bar, and the efforts of her horse Molly to move a large rock that high water from a violent summer thunderstorm had lodged against the bridge pilings. The stream's current kept the loose stone knocking against the timbers. After so much had gone into building the bridge, she didn't want it battered down. Not when people had grown dependent on it.

But still Shay didn't return. What on earth could be keeping him so long?

Disappointed, she waited until dusk before she gave up and mounted Molly. Calling to Pen, who seemed reluctant to leave the bridge, she urged the horse toward Shay's place. Well, their place, his and hers. Home. Just like her homestead was hers and his. The melding brought a smile to her lips. A smile that didn't last long, especially as Pen whined and lagged behind.

"Pen, come," she urged the dog. More than once.

They went slowly in the hope Shay would overtake them. After all, his gray gelding Hoot covered the ground at a much faster pace than Molly.

But no matter how many times January turned in the saddle to look, the road behind remained empty. They rode into the ranch yard where Brin, Shay's brindle hound bayed a welcome. Even older than Pen, the dog spent most of her days sleeping in the sun, but now she came looking for Shay, groaning disappointment when she didn't find him. A good scratch behind the ears did little to assuage the dog's unrest.

Worry hovered at the edges of January's mind. Worry she did her best to ignore, although the dogs' odd behavior kept it right there. What might they know that she didn't?

As she went through the motions of unsaddling and brushing Molly, hand-feeding Shay's prized colts and their mamas, milking the cow and scattering grain for the chickens, a tenseness, like a knot in a rope, stayed with her.

What is keeping him so long?

She had no appetite for supper, though her stomach growled with emptiness. Even the dogs showed no particular interest in the scraps she divvied between two bowls.

At ten o'clock she went to bed, though not to sleep. She'd grown used to him at her side, sometimes snoring softly, but for the most part, Shay was a quiet sleeper. He teased her that she wasn't. Teased!

Smiling into the dark, she finally dozed.

PEN'S COLD NOSE SHOVED A WAY INTO JANUARY'S EAR, startling her awake. She'd left the bedroom window open to the night and now her senses told her it must be around midnight. Her hearing sharpened. Hyper-alert, the sound of a horse's hooves in the hard-packed yard came clearly.

Shay at last.

But no. Not *a* horse's hooves. At least two, maybe more.

A man's voice spoke quietly. "His missus is asleep."

And another replied. "A shame, but we'll have to wake her."

"I guess it's up to you, Schlinger," a third said.

January shot upright and tossed the blanket to the side. *Schlinger.* The new sheriff, after Elroy Rhodes got thrown out of the office and incarcerated down in Walla Walla. *Why? What are these men doing here?*

Heartbeat a frantic thudding in her ears, January slid out of bed. It took only seconds to pull on her britches and a shirt. Barefoot, Pen pacing by her side, she passed through the house to the window where she could see out.

Three men sat horses, their shapes dim in the moon-less night. Three men, sitting erect, but a fourth horse stood with them. A gray horse, his coat shining out from between the darker colors, bay, brown, chestnut. The three were using this horse as a pack animal. A bulky burden lay across the saddle.

January's heart stopped. She knew it did. Stopped, then ran like one of foals in the pasture, jumping and skittering and shying at shadows.

The gray horse was Hoot. And the burden— *No. No.*

Although she didn't utter a sound, the word screamed, filling her head and the whole room. Then the scream stopped. Barefoot, she went to the door and slipped outside, so quiet the men in the yard didn't notice her standing there.

"Who's going to tell her?" One of the men asked, whis-pering, but January recognized his voice. Bo Cobb. Their neighbor and a friend.

"Schlinger, you have to do it. That's your job." She knew this voice even better. And of course, she recog-nized the big brown horse that belonged to Bent Langley. Immeasurable sadness wafted from Bent. "I just can't."

The sheriff dismounted, his knees stiff, and leaned against his horse. His curse, though softly spoken, carried to her. "Wish I hadn't signed on for this job," he muttered. "I'd druther face a gunslinger."

"Ain't many gunslingers these days," Bo said.

"Well, there's sure in hell one left." Bent's bitterness came clearly.

January wanted to shout at them. Why didn't they just get it over with? But then she realized they still hadn't seen her. That they were avoiding looking at the house, at Hoot and his load, at anything but the dirt under their feet. She could almost feel sorry for them. Or would have if it hadn't been for her heart shriveling to nothing in her chest. She didn't know how it managed to keep blood flowing through her veins.

She didn't know if she wanted it to.

After a while, her voice croaked a question—the question—and to a man, they flinched as if she'd been loud as a cannon and the sound a missile that passed too closely among them. "Is he dead?"

Schlinger turned to face her and swallowed with an audible click. "Yes, ma'am. I'm afraid so."

January forced words past the dry lump in her throat. "How? What happened?"

"Don't know exactly what happened except . . ." He brushed at his flowing mustache as if to wipe away the words. The awful, awful words. "A hand from the Inman ranch found him a few miles from here with his horse standing over him. Shot dead. Must've died instantly. The hand raced into town to fetch me, but there wasn't anything I could do. I'm sorry as I can be."

Bo and Bent added murmurs of condolence.

Meaningless, hardly registering.

Bare feet padding in the dirt, January descended the porch steps. Hoot nickered as she came near and nosed her when she patted his neck. He knew the burden he carried.

"Who did it?" Maybe she was asking the horse as he tossed his head. If so, his answer made as much sense as the sheriff's. Which meant nothing at all.

"Don't know," Schlinger said. "I've got a deputy staked

out where we found him. It'll keep anyone from tramping over the site tonight. Come daylight I'll look around, see what I can see. Maybe the killer left some sign."

"Yes." So far, January hadn't been able to look at Shay. The men had tied his body over his saddle, hiding his face. Without his hat, brown hair flopped forward, hiding his features. His beloved features. But when she did look, what stood out all too clearly even in dark of night was his blood-stained shirt and the raw edges of the wound under his left shoulder. Almost the same place as he'd been shot before. Maybe an inch of difference. An inch that meant life or death.

Swaying as the night closed around her, January swallowed bile.

The men waited, silent, no doubt expecting her to break down and cry. Scream. Wail. But, not being the kind of woman who did such things, no sound escaped.

Rage swelled in a firestorm like to consume her. She physically couldn't speak. Couldn't move. She stood at Hoot's shoulder, still as a mortuary angel.

"Ma'am?" Schlinger said. "Mrs. Billings? What . . . what do you want done with . . . with his remains? We'll do whatever you say."

Remains. Shay is dead. His body is 'remains.'

No. How could that possibly be?

But even as the unreality of the situation struck anew, her mind worked, turning over what she knew like a plow turned soil in a field.

"Murdered," she said aloud, although she believed it only a thought until Schlinger nodded.

"Yes, ma'am, I reckon so," he said, and the other two men's heads rocked up and down as well.

Now, finally, she put her hand on Shay's cold back and drew in a breath. "We'll take him in to Hannon's Funeral Parlor. But before Mr. Hannon touches him, I want Doc LeBret to take a look. I will be there too, and probably you, as well, Mr. Schlinger. Perhaps there will be something that tells us who did this."

Schlinger reacted with horror. "You, ma'am? Oh no. That wouldn't be right."

"Wouldn't be right? *Wouldn't be right?* Why not? What's not *right* is that my husband has been murdered." Her fury ran red hot. If she let go for even one little moment, January thought sure she would burst into flame. That mustn't happen. Not to these good men who had brought Shay home. Resolve wreathed itself around the anger. She'd save her rage for the one who'd pulled the trigger.

The men were silent, Bent Langley nodding his agreement. He'd know how it felt, to have a loved one's body returned home lying across his saddle. His fifteen-year-old son had been murdered a few months ago, just like this.

Just like this.

The phrase stuck in January's mind and refused to move.

Marvin Hammel is dead, his schemes and quest for power checked.

And yet, who else could have a grudge, a killing grudge, against Shay?

When she spoke again, her voice was quiet, under control. "I'll be with you in just a few minutes, gentlemen. Let me get my shoes and saddle my horse." She'd have to put Brin and Pen in an area Shay had fenced with chicken wire to prevent the dogs from following them. Best they stayed at home.

"I'll fetch Molly for you." Bent started off toward the barn where January's buckskin lounged in the adjacent corral.

"Thank you." She felt frozen in time. Stiff and icy.

They didn't talk as they rode, each man wrapped in his own thoughts. January hardly thinking at all. Only a murmur of thanks—strange to thank someone for bringing your dead husband to you—as first Bo Cobb, then Bent dropped off and headed toward their ranches by the river. Bo wasn't married, but Pinky, Bent's wife was most probably worried sick about him.

January and the sheriff continued on. They and Shay's *remains*.

Once they pulled up, where a man sat nodding at a small campfire. He jumped up at their approach. "All quiet," he said. "Nobody's been around."

The sheriff just nodded and hurried her past.

"Here?" January asked. There wasn't anything obvious about it. Simply a spot on the road.

"Yes."

They rode on.

Sheriff Schlinger, who'd been quiet and apparently deep in thought, finally broke the silence. "Missus Billings . . ."

He paused until she, as though rousing from a dream—or a nightmare—said, "Yes?"

"Somebody must've thought they had a reason to kill your husband. Frankly, it doesn't seem like an accident. Do you know what reason that might be? He have any enemies you know of?"

She'd been waiting for this question. Was almost relieved to have it asked even if she had no real answer.

"I can't think why anyone would want to kill him. Not

now. The people who tried this spring are either dead or in jail. You know Shay. He was a good man. Honest. Didn't cheat. Helped his neighbors." She choked. Even as she made the denial, a face rose in her memory. A face pale and furious. Of threats made and discounted.

Schlinger winced. "I do know that. I just can't figure why anybody would do this."

"Except . . ." she said, drawing it out.

"What?" Sheriff Schlinger asked. "Who?"

"There are still Hammel people here."

"Hammel's wife? His girls?" The sheriff scoffed. "Nah. I don't think so."

There didn't seem to be anything else to say. Neither spoke the rest of the way to town.

CHAPTER 3

JANUARY'S FINGERS CLENCHED UNTIL THE BONES FELT READY TO SNAP.

The three of them, Doc LeBret, Sheriff Schlinger, and January stood around a table in the doctor's surgery. Shay's body, still in death as he never was in life, lay upon the table. Doc's full supply of lamps hung overhead, their harsh light revealing details of her husband's present state.

He was just as he'd been found. Nothing added and nothing taken away. Blood dried on his clothes. Dirt ground into his curiously empty face. Even the faint smell of the liquor he'd drunk before leaving town.

She wanted to yell at him. To tell him to get up. She wanted him to be warm.

The darkness outside had been better, January thought. It had hidden some of the ugliness of his death. Maybe Schlinger had been right. Maybe she shouldn't be here for the autopsy. She didn't know how she could bear it. Unaware, she slumped and leaned against the table as though to be closer to her husband.

But she had to bear this next part. For Shay.

I'm strong. Whatever I have to do, I'll do. Whoever

did this will pay.

Her inner talking to didn't do much to buoy her, especially when Doc frowned and said, "We can do this without you, January. Whatever we find or whatever we don't, I promise to tell you and I won't lie. Neither will the sheriff."

Schlinger nodded.

But it just didn't seem right to abandon Shay, to let his body lie stiff and lonely on the cold metal table while Doc cut into him. He was already turning rigid with death. Gray as ash, except for his face and hands livid from hanging over the saddle, the curve in his body had made it difficult for Doc and Schlinger to get him off Hoot and into the medical office.

"I'll stay." January straightened. Swallowing, she gagged on the hard lump in her throat.

"Well, I know you for a stubborn woman." Doc shook his head. "If you feel faint, my dear, find a chair, sit, and put your head down between your legs. Better yet, take yourself outside and put your head down. I'm not going to do a full . . ." He hesitated.

"Go ahead," she said. "I know the word. Autopsy." Most people, even men, were squeamish about the process.

He nodded. "All right then. We'll just see what we can find."

"Get it over with, Doc," Schlinger said. "It's been a long night."

So Doc LeBret began. As he started to remove Shay's vest and shirt, January stepped forward to help. Fingers trembling, she gently undid buttons and lifted and tugged, until her husband's naked torso lay revealed under the lights.

"Did you notice the powder burns on his shirt?" Doc held the garment for Schlinger's inspection and pointed at the hole. "Means he was shot from close up."

Schlinger, leaning over the see better, nodded and made a contribution of his own. "Shows he was taken off guard."

Doc murmured agreement and handed the garments to January. "There's some papers in his vest pocket, Missus. You'd best take them in hand."

January glanced. "They're the documents for the property. Shay paid off the loan today."

"Good on him," Doc said, bending over the corpse again.

But January was stuck on one question. "You said close up. That he was shot from close up. What does that mean? One foot, two. Six?"

"Certainly no more than six. Probably less." Schlinger had the answer.

"Which infers that he knew whoever shot him."

The sheriff grimaced. "Knew, or at least didn't think he had cause to defend himself."

LeBret made verbal observations as he worked, waiting occasionally for the sheriff to agree or to make comments of his own. Finally, he took up a thin rod, then sent a searching look at January before poking it into the hole in Shay's chest.

Gasping, she had to turn away, but only for a moment. When she looked again, the rod, protruding from his chest at a slant, stood quivering. Thick and darkened blood seeped from around the instrument.

"Well," Doc said. "That's interesting."

"What does it mean?" Schlinger's question came before January got her dry mouth working.

"For one thing, it means whoever shot him stood, or maybe even sat below his level. I think he was probably astride his horse when the bullet reached him. See the rod? It's at a very acute angle. An angle impossible, or at least unlikely, to have come from anyone either taller or even across from him."

Schlinger frowned. "So, what? We're looking for a short man, or maybe one laying at ambush?"

The doctor studied the rod's position before shaking him head. "More likely the short man. Lying at ambush would've made the angle even more acute. As it is, the bullet went in through his lung, hit a rib and traveled up into his heart." He looked at January. "Woman, you're white as milk. You shouldn't be ..."

A sharpish shake of her head stopped him.

He stared at her a moment before he continued. "It would've killed him almost instantly. As you can see, there isn't as much blood as when the heart keeps pumping for a time. If he'd lived a while, his body would've emptied. In this case, you can be glad for that. I doubt he knew what hit him. He wouldn't have suffered."

Oh, she hoped he hadn't. Better this way, if there was any "better" to be had. "Is there anything else?" she asked.

"Maybe. Help me turn him, Schlinger, and I'll dig out the bullet."

January hated the way he savaged Shay's body in the procedure. Hated the small sounds the process made. The uneven in-and-out of Doc's breathing enough to make her flinch as though she felt the cut of the scalpel in her own living flesh. She could only be relieved that Shay was beyond feeling the probe of the knife and forceps, unlike the other time, when Marvin Hammel's son had ambushed him. Yet that time Shay had lived.

Edgar Hammel. But he's dead. Shay killed him. The thought ran on a track through her brain. *And I killed his father.*

And a moment later, *just females.*

"Looks to be about a .32-calibre," Doc said at last, tossing the recovered bullet into a pan. "Smaller than I would've thought for the damage it did." He looked up at the sheriff. "Either somebody knew just where to aim or he got in a lucky shot."

"Lucky for him, maybe, but not for Billings," Schlinger said.

"Know a man who carries a pistol of that size?" Doc asked.

Schlinger shook his head.

"A woman's gun," January said, her mind racing.

Both men turned to stare at her.

"A woman?" Schlinger seemed doubtful, as though he'd forgotten her mention of women earlier. "Why a woman? I've never heard of Shay having any trouble with women."

A faint smile quirked Doc LeBret's lips. "Only getting you to marry him, January. I remember he avoided the Inman twins whenever he could. Think he was afraid he'd be saddled with the two of them if he took up with one. Happiest day of his life was when you said yes."

Her breath caught. The words felt like a bullet to her own body. Tears flooded her eyes.

Both men shifted their glances away.

After several long minutes, Doc set aside his tools and, his stitches quick and neat, sewed the opening in

Shay's chest closed. "I can't see anything else that'll be of the slightest help to you finding who did this." He turned out the brightest of the lamps. "I'll get Hannon over here to take care of the rest."

Hannon, the undertaker.

"Hope to God there's something to be found where the shooting occurred." Schlinger went to the window. "Something to point to the killer. It'll be daylight soon. Missus Billings, I'll let you know if we get a lead on whoever done this."

"When," she said. "When you get a lead. I'll come with you. Help you look. If there is any trace, we'll find it."

"You won't." Doc shook his head. "Leave it to Schlinger and his deputy. You've got other things to do."

For a moment she didn't understand. Then she did. A funeral. There'd be a funeral to plan and people to notify. Decisions made on where he should be buried. Would he rather be laid to rest on his own place, or would the town cemetery make a better spot to lie for eternity? What should she do about the ranch? What would he want her to do? God knows it was all too much for one lone woman.

Eternity. A lifetime without him.

BY THE END OF THE DAY, the only moments January'd had to herself were on the ride back to the ranch. No time to think, really. Not enough time for the reality of her loss sink in or for the heat of her rage to cool. Those plans Doc had mentioned had to be . . . well . . . planned. Chores had to be done, the animals fed, come what may.

The future must wait.

At home, one of Bent Langley's sons, who Bent sent over to help, had already finished the milking and wanted to know where to find the cream separator. January's little cow was renowned for the quality of her butter. It made up some part of January's independent income and she made sure the separator was washed and rinsed with boiling water every day.

Then Shay's best clothing—the suit he'd married in—had to be supplied to the undertaker for the funeral, which would take place the day after tomorrow. The other of Bent's boys lifted that chore off January's shoulders, conveying the suit in to Hannon's.

While riding home, she'd made up her mind where to put Shay to rest. What would Shay want? Such was the question she posed herself. A favorite quiet spot where he'd often stood of an evening watching his horses, that's what. As if he were either a mind reader or a man who knew his neighbors, Bo Cobb sent over two of his hands to dig the hole. *The grave.*

And the women. Lord love the women. By the next day, so many she didn't know them all, young and old and in-between, gathered in groups talking behind their hands, murmuring the words people always say in the face of death. And whispering too, wondering why. Wondering who.

Apparently, they didn't recognize her building rage. Except maybe Pinky Langley. January thought she might understand.

Murdered. Shay murdered. Why?

At least Pinky knew who'd murdered her son. And why, if you could call pure avarice a reason.

Before the afternoon had passed, the Billings kitchen table groaned under the weight of the roasts and hams and pots of stew the ladies brought for the funeral the following day. Breads and pies and cakes, and even a gelatin dessert flavored with what was supposed to be strawberries, graced her pantry and the ice box.

January wished they'd all go away and leave her in what peace she could find. And finally, promising to return the next day, before dusk fell they all departed in a rush, like a flock of birds taking to the sky in formation.

In the quiet, something, she didn't know what, drew her to the barn. Perhaps just to reassure herself, as Shay had done every night they'd been married, that all was safe and buttoned up tight.

Lantern in hand, she found Shay's saddle draped atop one of the saddle stands he'd planned and she'd built. They were the best way she knew of to dry the sweaty underside of the saddle and cinch, and help prevent galls on the horse's skin.

Shay, she thought, managing a small smile to herself, would never allow such a thing to sully Hoot's fine silver-colored coat.

It was there she found a slip of paper stuck to the open space between the saddle fork and the gullet with a spot of dried blood. Shay's blood? Maybe. Maybe not. Probably not.

The paper had four words written on it.

You're next, you bitch.

A skull and crossbones had been drawn, and drawn well, as punctuation to end the sentence.

She'd been meant to find it. She didn't even know who

had taken Hoot in hand when she led him home after the autopsy in town. Probably the Langley boy. Had it been there when he racked the saddle? Or had an enemy come with the crowd today? People she knew. Her neighbors.

She blew out her lantern and stood in the dark, trembling.

The skull and crossbones, should she consider it a sign of intention? Poison? Of what? The livestock? The dogs? Her?

After a while, the trembling eased. Outwardly, at least. Not inside.

Shay's horse nickered to her as she stopped by his stall on her way out of the barn, the sound striking her as lost and lonely. Leaning into him, January patted his neck and caressed his velvet nose. "He's not coming home, Hoot."

He rubbed his head against her chest and blew his warm breath over her.

Not coming home. Loneliness settled over her like a leaden mantle. Loneliness and rage combined.

"Who did this, Hoot? Who murdered him and wrote that note? You know."

But Hoot remained silent.

AFTER A NEAR sleepless night with the note's threat running an endless loop through her mind, January barely had time to bathe and dress before people began arriving. Bent's boy came to do chores again, but before she could ask about the note, others interrupted. The Inman sisters were on hand early to instruct Bo Cobb's men on where to set up tables for the food and to arrange a place for the preacher to stand. They'd brought flowers, most assuredly robbing their own gardens of the last of summer's blooms to arrange on Shay's grave.

Grateful beyond words, January let them handle it.

Hannon, the mortician, with Shay's body in his black hearse drawn by four dark brown Morgans, pulled into the yard about ten o'clock. After that, the drive in from the road held a steady stream of neighbors come to pay their final respects, many having made use of the bridge January had built.

They all blurred together, although Pinky Langley and Ruth, one of the Inman twins, both complimented her on the dress she wore. It was new as the barn fire had consumed all of her old possessions.

"I don't think I've seen you in a dress since your wedding," Pinky said, then looked stricken at the reminder of how short a marriage this had been.

January didn't mind. Or rather, she didn't mind being reminded of her marriage, just that it had been so short. An all-consuming fury was building in her soul, moment by moment.

Later, January couldn't have quoted a single word the preacher spoke at his carefully prepared service. Every sympathetic word of condolence bounced off her brain without leaving a mark. She couldn't bear to look at Shay, his brown hair stiff with pomade as it never was in life, looking like a stranger in his coffin. Something kept insisting it wasn't really him. Finally, after those who desired had walked past for a final viewing and the mortician closed and locked down the casket lid, she found it almost a relief to hide his changed face from the world.

Next came the trek up the hill to where dirt, piled in a high mound, rose next to a casket-sized pit dug into the earth. Into Shay's own final piece of the earth.

January hardly breathed as she followed the hearse. Hardly wanted to breathe. She felt as if something inside her bore the same lock that secured Shay's coffin. The preacher's eulogy went unheard, his final prayer a relief. The mourners murmured a last amen, and it was over. The Cobb ranch hands grabbed shovels and began filling in the grave, a sight that shriveled the edges of January's heart. Brin, Shay's old dog stayed with them.

She caught up with Sheriff Schlinger on the way down the hill. "Have you discovered anything worthwhile that points to whoever killed my husband?"

Her bald question may have put him back a bit because he took off his hat and cleared his throat before answering. "No, ma'am. Not a thing. I'd hoped for footprints, a matchstick, maybe even the unburnt end of a cigar, but there wasn't anything but horse and wagon tracks. No telling what belonged to who."

She had to agree. "His killer was careful. I'd bet he planned this well ahead of time."

Schlinger's expression seemed uneasy. "You might right about that, ma'am. On the other hand, could've been someone just riding through. Someone already gone from here. It's going to be hard to find a cold-blooded killer."

January didn't think of the killer as cold-blooded. She had a notion that blood ran plenty hot and wild. As hot and wild as her own ran, right now.

"Whoever did it is here," she said so firmly that Schlinger blinked in surprise.

"Here?"

"Yes. Shay wasn't robbed. A stranger would've robbed him."

His jaw hardened as he nodded thoughtfully.

She'd kept the slip of paper in her pocket to show him and, drawing it out, proffered it. "And there's this."

He took the note. "What is it?"

"I found it last night, stuck to Shay's saddle in the barn. Stuck with blood. He . . . they . . . someone meant for me to find it."

Brow deeply furrowed, the sheriff read the four little words. Read them again. Looked up. "If it's a joke, it ain't funny."

"No. None of this is a joke. Shay is dead." She had a hitch in her voice as she said, "There must be a reason beyond blind bad luck."

"Yes, ma'am. Have you thought of anything since we last talked?"

She shook her head. Not an idea she wanted to repeat, at any rate, since he'd so firmly discounted what she said then.

Silent for a moment, he said, "You seen any strangers around here, Missus Billings? Anybody you thought was sneaking around where they ought not be?" He peered at the folks filing past as though a killer might jump out and identify himself.

"A good many of these people are strangers to me." The muscles in January's jaw felt tight, as though she needed to open her mouth and scream. "I'm not well acquainted with many folks."

Schlinger, as she was well aware, knew part of her history. She'd kept almost totally to herself—until Shay. Her

scarred face brought too many questions. Not everyone
needed to know her own grandfather, crazy as a rabid
dog, had done the scarring.

Understanding this, he nodded. "I don't see many
strangers here today, either. But why would any of these
folks do such a thing in the first place? Motive, ma'am.
That's what I can't figure. If not robbery, then what?"

January could think of only one motive, and it was a
reason that included her. Shay had killed Edgar Hammel,
the son. She had killed Marvin Hammel, the father. Neither of them had regretted that they'd done so. Only that
they'd had to do it.

While Sheriff Schlinger and the good people of Stevens County had evidently forgotten the threats Mrs.
Elvira Hammel made back then, when it first happened,
January had not. And something about that note shouted
"female" to her. *And the gun, a .32.*

She'd only seen Mrs. Hammel once, at the hearing after
what almost became a war. The woman had appeared
wearing the black of mourning and a stylish veiled hat that
hid her face. January had no certain way to recognize her.

Eyes narrowed, she scanned the women who'd gathered around the tables where folks had begun lining up
to fill their plates. One stood out. A woman, of an age
to have a son as old as Jr. had been. Well-preserved and
better dressed than most, she looked a little bewildered
as the line swirled around her. She had blonde hair, too.
Mrs. Hammel, she remembered, had blonde hair.

Just as January took a step forward, Pinky Langley
smiled a welcome and took the woman's arm, leading
her to the head of the food line.

January relaxed. If the woman had been Mrs. Hammel, Pinky would have chased her off with a stick. After all, one of the Hammels had killed her young son.

Or, she reminded herself, if not pulled the trigger themselves, had paid a killer to do it for them.

Maybe history was repeating itself. The idea struck like a cloudburst.

January surveyed the crowd another time. Woman clustered together like a band of sheep. Men milled about, grim-faced and speaking in quiet growls. Several of them made no secret of taking nips from shirt-pocket flasks. Younger men, or maybe she should call them older boys, had their own groups. So did the girls.

Except for the one girl wandering from group to group alone. Young, sharp-featured, she wore clothing that seemed unfitted to her, as if the attire were a disguise. Her thin lips curled up, as though in disdain for a man's funeral.

January's nerves tingled.

She touched the sheriff's arm. "Mr. Schlinger, who is that girl? The one wearing the floppy gray hat and the leather vest over her blouse? I think she rode up alone."

Schlinger peered around a drifting trio of younger girls. "Don't know, Missus Billings. Looks a little like . . . " He stopped. "Maybe you should ask the Inman ladies, or maybe Missus Langley. Why? Surely you don't think she's who shot Shay, a youngster like that?" A laugh, or maybe just a "hah" burst from him.

No need, she thought, in mentioning her thoughts to him. He wouldn't take the idea seriously.

But January, staring at the girl, didn't rule her out. She didn't rule anybody out.

CHAPTER 4

DAYS PASSED. January wandered from one thing to another in a fog, beginning one project before abandoning it and starting another. Everywhere she went, from the pasture, to the fields, to the barn, into the house—the bed at night—it was as though Shay must be waiting for her just around the corner.

Except, he wasn't.

The dogs followed her through the daily chores with their tails dragging. Hoot nudged her away when she tried to pet him. The silver-coated colt Shay had been working took a bite out of her arm and before she thought, she slapped his nose hard, making him shy away. Her actions made her ashamed.

The field of oats Shay had intended to start harvesting drooped on the stalk, heads dry and heavy to the point of shattering at a touch. Winter feed for the horses, along with the timothy grass and alfalfa hay he'd put up in mid-summer. January knew she had the work to do. She just couldn't summon the will to do it.

Then, on a Thursday, Bo Cobb dropped by, riding into the yard accompanied by a couple of his men. The youngest she recognized as one of the gravediggers. The other was considerably older. She didn't remember having seen him before.

January, interrupted at washing two days' worth of soiled dishes, an unprecedented act of slovenly housekeeping, walked out onto the porch to meet them. "Mr. Cobb, gentlemen." Even the short greeting took effort.

Cobb dismounted and, tossing his reins over the hitch rail, climbed the steps before speaking. "I come over to see how you're getting along, Missus Billings."

January didn't know what to say. *I'm empty inside? I'm heartbroken? I'm furious?* All those things and more.

She managed a small smile, a twitch of the lips. "Thank you, Mr. Cobb. That's very kind of you." She raised her voice to the other two, who remained astride their horses. "Would you gentlemen care to get down? There's coffee on the stove. Or water."

Sensing the older man's eyes on her scarred face, she held herself erect and didn't turn away. Let him look. The S-shaped scar her grandfather had carved there when she'd been a terrified child ran from cheekbone to jaw, but it didn't matter to her anymore. It hadn't mattered to Shay, ever, or only for the pain it had caused her.

"We're fine, Missus Billings. Don't mean to put you out." Cobb claimed one of the two porch rocking chairs and gestured toward his men, who remained where they were. "I brung Johnson—think you know him—and Rand along to see if they could help get that oat crop of Shay's into the barn. Weather ain't going to hold good much longer and you don't want to leave it in the field. Snowberry bushes are heavy loaded. It's apt to be a hard winter and your stock will need the feed."

Rand, old enough to be a little stooped, with a cluster of wrinkles around the eyes, nodded.

January gathered herself. "I know. It's just . . . I just haven't . . ." Her voice dried up and she trailed off, weary beyond measure.

"No, ma'am, I reckon you haven't." Cobb sent her a sympathetic look. "It ain't a women's job anyhow, but Rand can take care of the work. He's got experience and don't need bossed." The older man tipped his hat as Cobb kept talking. "And Johnny can do whatever else needs done. I know you ain't well acquainted with all the folks around here, so I figured to steer you on to men you can trust."

A woman's job? For the first time in days, January truly smiled. It seemed Mr. Cobb had forgotten that not only had she built the bridge he and his men had used to cross the creek and get here, but also the porch on which he sat.

"That is very kind of you, Mr. Cobb, but won't you need their labor yourself? I expect you're still getting in the last of your crops."

Cobb shrugged. "We'll get along. Might take us an extra day or two, is all. Rand has worked for me the last couple seasons, after he has his own place buttoned up. He says he finished yesterday. I figure this year he can work for you."

The man, Rand, nodded. January noticed he was already scanning the oat field, bleached almost white under the sun, as well as the barn and corrals and horses. Then his eyes stopped on the silver colt cavorting in the pasture and she saw his smile as he turned to her.

"You got the equipment and the horses, ma'am?" he asked. "Or do you need me to bring my own team over? In fact, I'd druther. I'm used to them and they're used to me."

He was taking employment for granted and for a moment January resented his surety. *If only Shay—* Swallowing hard, she pushed the memories aside.

A worried thought ran through her. She would have to get some of the horses sold in order to pay these men's wages. She and Shay had talked about his intentions for the ranch. Horses were his main business above the farming, and he'd wanted to share his expertise with his bride. She had been an eager pupil, soaking up his teaching, so she knew what to do. He'd planned in this month to sell three of the horses he had in training. Two to work cattle and one, a stallion possessing a fine turn of speed, to race in the local fall meets. A team of draft animals had already been spoken for, with the county paying top dollar. Once the sales went through, she'd be set for the year. Summoning the grit to do the needed was the hard part.

And what then?

"Ma'am?"

January, her attention snapping to, became aware the man Rand had been asking her a question. What had he said? Then, like an echo, it came to her.

"I understand your preference for your own team, although I have a top-notch four-horse hitch of Shire breeding. And of course my husband is—" her thoughts drifted for a moment, to when she'd loved saying those words. *My husband.* "—was the best trainer in this part of the country. Aside from the horses, he has the necessary machinery, a binder and threshing machine. They're stored in a lean-to at the back of the barn. He'd worked on it, sharpened the cutters. Everything is set to go."

"That's real fine," he said. "I'll start tomorrow, then, if that's all right."

"Billings kept his equipment in top condition, Rand," Cobb said. "You'll see."

With a nod, the man started off toward the barn leading his horse.

To check for himself, January assumed.

The youngster, Johnson, looked a question at his boss. Cobb cocked a thumb, indicating he should follow the other man.

When they were out of earshot, Cobb leaned forward in his chair. "I ain't been to town in a while. Not since—" He started over. "I wondered, Missus Billings, if you've heard anything from Schlinger. If he's made any progress in finding Shay's killer."

Shay's killer. *Why, why, why?* The words stabbed at her and as though to form a defense against the pain, her stomach muscles knotted. She couldn't even guess at what showed on her face. "Not a word, even though he said he'd keep me informed."

Cobb's frown wrinkled his features into something resembling a dried brown apple with hair. "Nothing?"

"Nothing."

He appeared to search for something to say. "Well, I expect he's still looking. Looking hard. He ain't like Rhodes. There probably ain't anything to find and he won't want to make a mistake."

"I imagine you're right." January made no attempt to keep her bitterness at bay. "Whoever did this had a well thought out plan. Even to guessing—or knowing—when Shay would be in town."

Sometimes she had to prod her own memory to think why he had taken the time when his plans had called for harvesting the oats, then working on their new house at the crossing. Thinking back, the reason seemed flimsy. Manufactured.

It had come about because Albert Sims, the banker, had sent a letter asking him to consult about an irregularity in the contract regarding the last payment on Shay's ranch. Shay, upon reading over his copy of the contract, hadn't found any reason for concern, but, as a gesture of goodwill, had gone to meet Sims on the appointed day.

She had the papers here, removed from Shay's jacket pocket and stained with his blood. but hadn't looked at them yet. Hadn't even thought of them until now. The will—*the nerve*—to do so failed her. It had all seemed so unnecessary.

Her eyes opened wide. "Oh!"

"Ma'am? Miss January?" As if alarmed, Cobb set down his coffee cup and stared at her. "What is it?"

"A set-up. A set-up between Albert Sims and someone else." For the first time, a hypothesis that made sense. Had to be.

Bo Cobbs cocked his head. "Sims is a hard man to deal with, but my impression is he ain't a murderer. Or even too awful dishonest as a general rule. He's just one of those fellers who likes to get away with small, niggardly things so as to feel bigger than other men." He hesitated. "But see, there's something else. Something one of my hands picked up on in town the other day. I come over to find out if it's true."

Belly twisting in apprehension, January knew from his sad look that what he'd heard couldn't be anything good. She steeled herself. "What is it?"

That hesitation came again. "Said he heard you'd be leaving here right soon. That someone else would be taking over the property."

January, her eyes opening wide, nearly choked on her own spit. It took her a long moment to find her voice. "An odd rumor, wouldn't you say. Who started it, I wonder?"

"It ain't true, then?"

"Certainly not."

Cobb, shaking his head, pondered the question, then said, "Good. Since we're talking about Sims, it sounds to me like something he'd say, just casual like. But why?"

January didn't have to think too hard on this. "Maybe he wants to feel a lot bigger. Signs point that way. I think he might've been, or might still be, planning to get his hands on this place. Trying, anyhow."

"What?" Cobb's mouth dropped open. "How could he do that?"

"Sims sent Shay a letter and asked for a meeting. He said there is a problem with the pay-off and set a date and a time for Shay to be at the bank. That's why Shay went to town." She was surprised this hadn't occurred to her sooner. "In other words, he set a trap."

"Even so, he'd know he ain't big enough to take down Shay Billings. Not after what Shay and you and that Deputy U.S. Marshal did." His eyes glinted at her.

"I'm not saying Sims pulled the trigger himself."

"You're saying he paid someone?"

"Possible. But no. Maybe not that, either. I don't know. But I'll wager he's in collusion with whoever did."

Cobb shook his head. "He ain't got the guts. Besides, why would he do that? Or how? Everybody in the country knows Shay about had this place paid off. We talked about it last time I saw him. So why would Sims mess with a good customer?"

Clasping her shaking hands together, January's chair rocked in time to her thoughts. "Maybe for that very reason. Maybe because Shay did have only one last payment to make."

Cobb's gaze drifted out over the pretty property. A fine bunch of horses grazed in the pasture and meadow where a windmill pumped water from the stream into a galvanized trough. The thick stand of oats in the fertile, cultivated acreage, the well-built barn and shed, and even the small house added to the property value. Beyond the open land nearest the river that watered his cattle, a white pine forest in the distance turned the rising hills blue. Timber fit for cutting.

"Well, Missus Billings, I can't deny it's a property worth having. Shay near about worked himself to a nub these past five or six years making it so." The concession came slowly. "Now I think of it, Sims palled around with Marvin Hammel. Them and their wives together. And I know Hammel tried to coerce Shay out of the ranch, but with Hammel dead, what would be Sims' reason now? He's no rancher."

"Neither was Hammel, in the end."

"Huh. I reckon that's true."

"I'm sure you can think of several reasons, Mr. Cobb. Although maybe not as many as I can." Hammel's wife and Sims' wife together. And Elvira Hammel had vowed revenge. She couldn't forget that.

"Needs looking into, for certain." Bo Cobb nodded as

he got to his feet. "I reckon it fits, sort of, with that story about you leaving the ranch, too. So how are we going to prove it, Missus Billings?"

We. A flush of gratitude brought a small lightening to January's heart. It took a very good neighbor to want to take a hand in solving her husband's murder. "I've got an idea, sir."

Cobb's hand rested on the handgun riding his hip. Something new to him since Shay's murder and just now noticed. "And what would that be?"

"I'll begin by paying a visit to Albert Sims first thing tomorrow morning. See what kind of lies he tells me, or if he tells any at all."

Slowly, Cobb nodded. "Good idea." He smiled with a show of teeth. "He won't be expecting you."

January's expression hardened. "That's what I'm counting on."

Rand and Johnson returned from their inspection of the equipment and Shay's team, with Rand nodding his head in satisfaction.

"I'll be around in the morning, young missus," he said. "I'll stay in the barn then 'til I finish the harvest. Looks," he added just a tad grudgingly, "to be a heavy crop. You got a fair piece of ground here. Think you could use another roll of twine for the binder."

She nodded. "All right. I'm going into town in the morning. Thurston's mercantile stocks twine."

Rand nodded.

"I'll be staying here, too," Johnson said, not to be left out.

Blinking, January nodded at him. "You'll be welcome."

Gratitude came in a rush. These were good men, good

neighbors, unexpectedly so to a woman who'd been stared at and pointed to—scorned—for most of her life. She didn't know how relieved she was until a calming sense of peace settled around her heart.

"Your meals will be furnished," she said. "I trust you'll have no cause for complaint." She hesitated. "And men, thank you."

To her amusement, the first she'd felt in the two weeks since Shay was killed, Johnson blushed so brightly she almost felt the heat.

That night, after a preparatory cooking frenzy of pies, cookies, fresh bread and a stew to sit and meld its flavors, she drew the loan papers from the envelope and studied them by lantern light. She'd forgotten the payment was on the verge of coming due until she and Cobb talked of it. Shay had kept those details from her, merely saying he had it all in hand, with the money in the bank to take care of the pay-off.

He'd been so proud. So happy to bring his wife home to a place he owned, to provide for her, for the family they'd never have.

Her anger burned afresh, her pain rubbed raw once again.

Something had happened at Sims' office, she judged, because here was a receipt and paperwork stamped "paid in full" with a notary seal and signature. Otherwise, he wouldn't have cleaned out his bank account before the payment's due date.

But why kill Shay? Was this document what the killer had been after?

If so, she had best have a care of the signed and sealed pages. Put them away where no one could find them.

And she knew just the place.

Wrapping the papers in a waterproof oiled packet, she went out and deposited the small bundle in one of the cottonwood trees in back of the house. An odd hollow had formed there when two saplings met and grew, almost, but not quite together.

As she tucked them away, she wondered at herself. The years since childhood had made her distrustful of people and their motives. Even these men of Bo Cobb's. Even Bo Cobb himself. Shay had trusted him; she didn't forget that. Him, and Bent, and Doc LeBret.

But still, she wasn't Shay.

CHAPTER 5

RAND AND JOHNSON—Johnson more commonly called Johnny—arrived the next morning as they'd promised, just as the sun rose above the hills to the east and spread a luscious pink across the sky. From the orchard the scent of old apples, a cider-like smell, wafted on the breeze as she stood on the porch.

True to his word, Rand had brought his own team of big mismatched bays. He rode the smallest of the four and led the other three. One carried a well-arranged pack on its broad back that January heard give off a metallic rattle.

Men, January reminded herself as she identified the pack, always seemed to have tools they relied on, much like a housewife with a favorite cooking pot, generally her cast iron spider. In this case, a hand scythe stood up like the grim reaper's hook.

January had already gathered eggs from her Buff Orpington and Shay's White Langshan chickens, milked her cow, and finally, checked the hiding spot in the twisted cottonwood tree in daylight. Satisfied as to its well-hidden safety, she prepared for her most important work. That of discovering who had killed Shay. Even after sleeping on the idea, January considered Albert Sims the first person on a short list of people she intended to interview. A very short list. Right now it existed only of Albert Sims and the bank clerk who'd stamped the loan papers paid. Because, when she considered the paperwork in her possession, it indicated skullduggery on the bank president's part.

Rand, as Cobb had assured her, soon had the binder hitched behind two of his bays. Johnny, with the other pair, walked beside a wagon and prepared to toss in the tied oat sheaves to carry to the stationary threshing machine.

"I'll trade off the bays with your Shires at noon," Rand told January when she waved the two in for a second breakfast. "Keep both teams in prime condition."

It sounded like something Shay would say. She appreciated Rand's care for the animals and his straight-forward manner. On Bo Cobb's word and her own observation, she had no qualms about trusting Shay's team to him. And entry into her house, too. Before the men returned to the field, she gave the two instructions on how to fix their own dinner if she wasn't back from town. Not difficult, after all. Stir up the fire in the stove and set a pot, meaning *her* cast iron spider, on to heat. And to blamed well set it to cool when they were done! She didn't want to contend with burned on stew.

In the normal course of things, and given her impatience and upset, she would've ridden Molly into town. But, as long as she was going, she thought to stop at the springhouse at the bridge and load up her little Guernsey cow's rich butter and take it in to T.T. Thurston's general store to sell. With hired men to feed over the next few days, provisioning her larder seemed in order. Johnny had a healthy appetite, as she'd discovered at breakfast, with Rand not that far behind.

Turned out that Pen's begging eyes and a softly whimpered entreaty fuzzled her into taking the dog along. Why not? Pen was always good company. Besides, putting together what had happened to Shay with that note she'd found, Pen just seemed like an extra layer of caution.

January harnessed one of the horses Shay'd been training to the buckboard. Better keep the learning going, she figured, before the horse forgot his lessons. Shay would be so disappointed in her if she neglected his work now. The thought sent a pang through her whole being.

They reached town at nine o'clock, just as the bank opened. With Pen at her heels, January jumped from the buggy in perfect time to follow Albert Sims' squat figure not only into the bank, but on into his office. She closed the door behind them before Sims even realized he had company.

He turned at the soft snick of the door and eyed her with a raised eyebrow and a snarling upper lip that caught on a protruding tooth. "Who the devil are you? What do you mean, bursting into my private office?"

He acted as if he didn't recognize her, a lapse she knew must be a lie. Not, perhaps, a good beginning.

She remembered him well enough from the judge's hearing after the lawlessness in the spring. He'd sat on a front-row bench and objected when Ford Tervo, the governor's specially assigned deputy who'd helped Shay and her bring down Hammel's gang of gunfighters, stood up to say his piece. Sims had been on the Hammel side of the courtroom. He and his wife and Elvira Hammel and her girls, the latter three all veiled. There'd been a few others, mostly out-of-towners, or so she'd heard, none of whom she recognized. They'd all stared at her, the woman who killed Marvin Hammel. She thought it unlikely he didn't know her now after the way he's stared at her then. If nothing else, the scar on her face made her memorable.

Too late, it occurred to January that she should've worn her Sunday-go-to-meeting clothes, not a worn split skirt, faded shirt and scuffed boots. Some people judged others by their clothes and possessions. A mental shrug calmed her. She suspected him of murder. What he thought of her and the way she dressed didn't matter.

She sat down and motioned Pen to sit beside her. "You know who I am. I'm also sure you know why my husband was murdered on his way home from this office."

He gave a start, seeming to shiver. *Goose walked over his grave, did it? Good.*

"Yes. Murdered. It's an ugly word isn't it?" She wanted him to know she'd noticed his reaction. "An ugly word for an ugly act. But I suspect you know all about that."

He found his voice. "I don't know what you're talking about. What I do know is that you, or perhaps I mean the Shay Billings estate, is in arrears in paying off his loan. I'm taking action to have you removed from the property."

Lips feeling numb, January forced a smile. "That won't work. I know my husband paid off the loan on the day of his murder, well ahead of the deadline."

The banker's eyes shifted. "Not quite. He owed more than he paid. It's obvious he altered the papers in his possession in an attempt of what amounts to downright theft. Now, I don't—"

"Altered the papers?" At the intensity in January's softly spoken words, Pen put a paw on her knee.

Sims didn't appear to notice the narrowing of her eyes or the quiver in her eyelids. "That's what I said." He hefted his well-fed bulk to his feet and turned to a file cabinet behind his desk. Unlocking the top drawer, he rustled through some papers and withdrew a thin folder, which he tossed onto the desktop. "Let me show you. These are the original documents right here. Now, did Mr. Billings explain any of this to you? Or no. I don't suppose. You hadn't been married long had you. I'm sure other activities occupied you." He chuckled as at a dirty joke, seeming very sure of himself. "If you need help reading them, perhaps one of my clerks can help you out. I can explain anything you don't understand."

"I am—" she started, but he flung open the door and bellowed at a mousy looking woman using a typewriter at a desk outside the office. "Mrs. Filmore. Get in here."

The woman jumped, her chair scooting back. Face pale, she hurried into the office. "Yes, sir?"

He pointed at the papers. "Read this document to Mrs. Billings, if you please, and let's hope she understands. I'm afraid she isn't up on all the legalese, but she needs to hear the terms."

The woman glanced quickly, sorrowfully at January, her eyes wide, took the papers and began. There were three pages. *Three.*

Words of hot denial rose up in January's throat. Words she fought down. The years when she and her father had fled from place to place, worried all the time that her dad would be accused of killing his own father, served her now in good stead. She kept her face expressionless. Best to hear what kind of fakery Sims presented, so she'd know how to fight. She scratched Pen behind the ears as the dog leaned against her leg. Pen's presence was all that kept her from erupting in a frenzy.

Clearing her throat, Mrs. Filmore read the beginning clauses. She got through the first page and turned to the second. The woman darted a quick, startled look at Sims. Her voice took on a drone-like quality, leaden and a little shaky. This is where January's ears perked and, for as long as it took the woman to turn to the last page, she barely took a breath.

Sooo.

Mrs. Filmore, as if she were handling dead mice, re-tuned the documents to Sims. "Will that be all?" she asked.

"You may go," Sims said grandly. "Unless..." he turned to January, "you didn't understand all that. I know it was a great deal of information."

January's lips pursed. "No. I understood everything. It's all very clear to me."

"Good, good. Then when I say you must vacate by the end of the week, you understand that time is of the essence. Oh, and be certain you only take what you brought into the marriage. Everything else must remain on the property."

She drew a breath. "You mean the livestock?"

"Ah. You do understand. Yes. The livestock, the contents of the house, the crops. That gray horse Billings always rode. All of it."

She was pretty certain he knew she'd had almost no portable possessions when she and Shay married, the barn where she'd lived having burned. Besides the clothes she stood up in, only Molly, Ernie the work horse, her cow and some chickens. Oh. And one decrepit farm wagon.

"You do know what your Mrs. Filmore just read is not what my husband's copy of the loan says." She could see her even reply surprised him.

"Yes, well, I am aware of that. And as a personal favor to you, as long as you depart quietly, I promise not to report any of this to the sheriff. In fact, I'd hope you'd take the opportunity to leave the area. I'm sure you'd hate for Billings' reputation to be further damaged if this got around."

Pen lumbered to her feet, a rumble in her throat.

January thought she'd learned all she was going to here. For the moment, at least. Complete privacy would serve better for her next meeting with Sims.

She, too, got to her feet. Seeing no need to speak further to the man, she said, "Come, Pen," and with the dog at her side, walked out the door.

"Remember," Sims called after her, chuckling in triumph. "You have to the end of the week."

Back at her desk, Mrs. Filmore's hands crashed down on the typewriter's board, mashing keys together. Her gaze caught with January's as January passed her desk.

THEY MET IN THE BANK LOBBY, she and none other than Elvira Hammel.

So angry her vision blurred, it took Pen, pacing alongside, to nudge her leg and force January to step aside before the two women collided.

"You," a woman said in a tone of utter loathing.

January, who'd been focused on getting out of the bank before she gave way, took her deliberately blind gaze off the floor and eyed the speaker. And, to give herself credit, she did try to keep going without speaking. But Elvira stepped in front of her, dragging the girl accompanying her along by the arm.

"This is my daughter," she hissed and shook the girl's arm. Elvira had green eyes, pale as sun-faded sage, but now they snapped with fiery glints. Then louder, purposely in January's opinion, which caused bank patrons to turn and look—and listen.

"You killed her father," Elvira cried. Cried pitifully, if one wasn't face to face with her and seeing the spite in her glare and her twisted lips. "My poor little girl is an orphan now because of you, you ugly scarred creature. I'm glad your husband is dead. He deserved to die."

January hardly heard her. Had no wish to hear her since her plaint was nothing new. She'd called January an ugly scarred creature at the hearing also, and named both her daughters poor little orphans. But this girl, the younger Hammel daughter as she had brown hair instead of blonde, writhed in embarrassment. At least January thought it was embarrassment. It could've been she just wanted to speak and call January names as well, but her mother didn't provide an opening. Or maybe the girl just wanted to deny being called "little girl." Because she wasn't little. Not exactly an orphan, either, with her mother standing right beside her.

The only thing new was Elvira's glee at Shay's death.

January took a shuddering breath. "Get out of my

way," she said coolly, and she and Pen dodged around the two. She strode with long steps to the door, wanting only to escape.

Once outside, the three deep breaths January drew only partially eased the tension twisting in her innards like the uncoiling of a snake. Between Sims and the Hammel woman, she felt totally undone. But it was Sims and his trickery that upset her most.

"How could he even think I'd believe any of that ridiculous spiel—that bunch of lies?" The question appeared to be aimed at Pen, who looked up at her with sad brown eyes. "I'm glad I didn't dress up today. Wearing these duds, it's obvious he figured me for a rube who can barely read. And that," she snapped her fingers at the dog, "may just be a good thing, right about now."

Untying her horse, she led him the half-block down the street to T. T. Thurston's general store.

"Humiliating though, and tough to sit and listen to," she added as they dodged into the alley going round the back of the building. Groceries came in the back, after all, and went out the front.

Pen's tail wagged as if she understood.

Thurston, glad to get the butter, shook her hand and spoke his condolences as he loaded the roll of twine and a wood-slatted box of sundry groceries for her. The butter made a fair and even trade.

"How you doing out there?" he asked. "I heard— Well, best if I don't spread rumors, I reckon."

"Rumors?"

"Heard there was trouble over Shay's loan. Feller in the bank, he worked there before Sims bought it out, he

got fired. I heard it was because he took Shay's payment
without consulting Sims."

January froze. "Oh, now that's interesting. Is this
man around? I'd like to talk to him." Thurston had to be
talking about the man whose signature was on Shay's
papers. The one who'd notarized the deed.

But now Thurston looked guilty. "See. There I go,
shooting off my mouth. That's just something I heard,
or think I did. Kind of hard of hearing, you know. There
may not be a word of truth in it."

"But there also might." January, grateful for the information, climbed into the buckboard. Her next stop, after
parking the horse and rig out of sight on a side street
around the corner, was the sturdy old house that served
both the town marshal and the sheriff as their office. Two
small cells took up the back of the place, leaving a larger
front room partitioned to accommodate both offices.
The marshal, she was relieved to see, was out. Sheriff
Schlinger sat at his desk sifting through the day's mail,
his face puckered in a frown.

"Missus Billings." He rose to his feet. "I didn't expect
to see you here."

"I've been hoping to see you, however," she said.
"Thinking you might have news for me."

His head dipped, allowing January to spot strands of
silver hair sprouted among the brown. She didn't remember seeing them, she thought, when she talked with him
those weeks ago at Shay's funeral. But then, she hadn't
been noticing much of anything.

"No real news." He picked up a letter and waved it in
front of his face. "Until now. Today, I mean. See, a couple

weeks ago, I had me an idea."

January's breath caught. "Until now? What kind of idea?"

"I wrote to the warden down in Walla Walla," Schlinger said. "Rhodes is in prison there, ya know. I'd thought the warden might've heard about any plans or plots Rhodes might be caught up in. I know from experience our former sheriff is a man who carries a grudge. Wouldn't put it past him to hire someone to do his dirty work for him. So I figured maybe it'd be helpful to know just who, if anybody, is writing to him that he's writing return mail to. Because, knowing him, he's always working the odds."

Judging by Schlinger's expression, there must've been someone. Excitement flooded through her. "And?" Nodding, she drew the word out in anticipation.

"Turns out he does have a pen pal. Couple of them, in fact."

"One being Albert Sims," January said, as though there was no doubt.

"Yep. And you might make a guess at the other, too."

Who else had cause to hate Shay—and her? Easy answer. "Mrs. Hammel?" she said.

"Got it."

"Who I just met face on. She doesn't like me." January, though not invited, sat down across from the sheriff. "Does that put us any closer to knowing who murdered Shay?"

Schlinger, probably knowing better than to ask about Elvira Hammel, sighed like an exhausted man. "Not so's you'd notice, beyond knowing Shay's killer sure ain't Rhodes. Thought he might be in on a plot, is all, and that he might talk. All it does is show us a connection between those folk, and hell—excuse me, ma'am—we already knew that."

"Except we didn't know they were still in touch. Which, I suppose, proves nothing."

"That's about it."

She thought a moment. "Does the warden read the prisoners' mail?"

"Dunno. Spot checks only, I expect. Why?"

"I wish we knew what they've been saying to each other."

"Yeah. I asked about that." He did another of those sighs. "The warden said he don't have time to read every scrawl and that he don't remember anything in particular that caught his eye."

"But then, it probably wouldn't. Not necessarily."

"True."

January leaned back in her chair and gazed around. No one occupied the two iron-barred cells, and with the marshal out, she and Schlinger were alone. "There's something else going on, and I want you to know about it. From me." She made a pointed clarification.

Schlinger frowned. "I don't like the sound of that."

Huffing, January said, "Wait until I get to the meat of it."

"And what would that be, Missus Billings."

"I just came from the bank and a talk with Albert Sims."

Schlinger's mouth twisted. "That probably wasn't too pleasant. He's a slimy little cuss."

"Slimy is the least of it. He's also a thief. Or a would-be thief."

The sheriff stiffened, his back erect. "What do you mean?"

"I mean he's trying to steal Shay's ranch out from under me. He's falsified the paperwork and denied Shay paid the final payment on the loan on the day he . . . died. He's fired the clerk who worked the transaction and signed over the notarized deed. All of which I'm certain means Sims is tied to Shay's death."

Schlinger's mouth dropped open "Mrs. Billings, that's a serious charge. What makes you think so?"

Managing a strangled sort of chuckle, January scooted her chair forward. "Because he told me so. No beating around the bush."

"He said he's stealing the ranch?"

"He said he's taking it and for me to get out."

"He did?"

"He did."

"And did he say he fired Jim Dennis? I heard he quit and left town."

January's eyes narrowed. "That's not what T.T. told me. But either way, the man is gone. Here's hoping he just left town and that he hasn't been murdered, like Shay."

"Missus Billings, do you seriously think Sims murdered Shay for the ranch? Can you prove any of these accusations?" He looked worried now. "Sims may be a piece of slime, but he is an important man in these parts. Especially now that—"

"Now that Hammel is dead." January finished the sentence.

"Well, yeah." His fingers tapped on the desk. "I've gotta say it makes some kind of sense. Especially with Elvira Hammel hounding him. I even seen the oldest Hammel girl going into the bank the other day, and coming out hanging on Sims' arm." He seemed to push the vision away and met her eyes. "Proof, ma'am. I gotta have proof, something to go on. No going off half-cocked."

"Half-cocked? I can agree with that. But I'm telling you right now, sheriff, I won't stand for anyone trying to take everything Shay worked for away from him. He may not be here anymore to defend his property, but I am."

Nodding once, Schlinger chewed on the end of his mustache. "You sure about those papers, Mrs. Billings? You sure Shay's copies were correct and in order?"

"Oh yes. You asked for proof? Well, Sims doesn't know it, but I can prove it."

The sheriff tilted his chair back and steepled his fingers. "Tell me how, ma'am."

"You know I found the pay-off paperwork and the deed in Shay's vest pocket when we . . .when Doc . . . when—"

Schlinger, shaking his head sorrowfully, held up a forefinger to stop the stutter. "I know when," he said.

"Yes, well, today Sims made a point of extracting what should've been the duplicate set of papers from a file in his office and called in a clerk to read them to me." She huffed in disgust. "Implying I don't know how to read, the fool, but also, I imagine, so I couldn't get my hands on them to see for myself. Imagine my surprise when instead of the two-page document in Shay's possession, Sims' contains three pages."

"Three?"

"Three. He's added a bunch of nonsense that is not in Shay's copy. Nonsense added after the fact that puts Shay—and now me—in violation of terms, payment or no payment." Her face felt hot. "The ink isn't even the same color as the original. He told me he's repossessing the place and that I must vacate the property by the end of the week. Oh, and I am to take nothing with me but what I had when Shay and I married."

Schlinger's eyes seemed in danger of popping right out of their sockets. "So," he said after a moment of thought, "it'll be your word against Sims'. With Shay dead, Sims figures it'll be easy."

"But it won't be as easy as he may think. I'm not about to vacate." The scarred side of January's face seemed to flex as she set her jaw. "Plus," she went on, "the clerk, a Mrs. Filmore, had a very strange look on her face as she read from the documents. And Mr. Thurston at the store, he told me the man who signed off had worked at the bank when the papers were first drawn up. As long as he's still alive, he'd be able to testify as to which is the true copy. I think they both could." It all came out in a rush.

"Mrs. Filmore may not help you."

January frowned. "Under oath? Why not?"

"She's a widow lady with two children, plus she's got her old mother-in-law living with her. They depend on Jane's job at the bank to support them all. She wouldn't want to lie for Sims, but she'll do whatever she has to do to take care of her family."

"Including perjury, eh? In that case, I do have another trick up my sleeve."

Schlinger sat forward. "You do? A trick?"

"I do." It struck January that she sounded as if she were taking a vow. Well, and now she thought about it, maybe she was.

As it happened, she didn't get a chance to tell Sheriff Schlinger the trick's nature as a rancher January didn't know strode into the office just then. In a bit of a tizzy, he ignored her as he reported one of his beeves had been stolen. Upon following the trail, he and his lone hand had found the butchered remains.

"I know who done it, sheriff. One of them fellers working as slave labor up at the *Sue'n El* mine. I seen those miner's kids. Damn near starving, but it ain't my responsibility to put food in their bellies. Got children of my own to feed."

"You sure it was one of the miners?" Schlinger sighed, a sort of forlorn look on his face.

"I'm sure," the rancher said. "You'd better come with me right away. If we go now we can trail him. He's got a pack horse loaded. They won't be traveling fast."

Schlinger, faced with this new emergency, begged January's pardon, saying he'd be around to see her in a day or two. As soon as he got this rustling problem cleared up. The immediate problem took precedence and January stifled her urge to argue.

Maybe it was undue caution that caused her, on her way out of town, to make another stop at T.T. Thurston's store. She'd thought of another item she might be low on. Ammunition.

CHAPTER 6

THE LETTERS CAUGHT UP WITH U.S. DEPUTY MARSHAL FORD Tervo in Butte, Montana after following him from West Virginia, to Colorado, and finally, to within three hundred or so miles of home.

Almost a round trip, he thought, eyeing the postmarks.

The reason for all this travel concerned a certain B.J. Campbell, a union agitator, who had escaped custody after being arrested for leading a strike in West Virginia coal country. Ford had been assigned the chore of recapturing him. B.J. a wily cuss proficient in assuming various disguises, including a realistic performance as a woman, had led him a merry chase.

But now, job completed, after a twelve-hour snooze on a comfortable bed and noon-dinner filling his belly, he'd wandered over to the post office on the off chance he had mail. And, although he hadn't really expected any, there they were. One an envelope with three different postmarks and a brown stain across one corner, the other with the same three postmarks, but what he was certain would prove to be a footprint on the front.

They had, he discerned, been mailed within a couple days of each other and been on the road for a while. More than two weeks. Wandering out into the sunshine, he found a seat on the bench out front and studied the envelopes. He recognized the writing on the one with the brown stain, and since it bore the oldest postmark, he opened it first.

Ford,

Something fishy is going on here. Albert Sims, the president of the local bank, has false papers regarding the loan on my land. He says I owe more money on less property. I've paid off the loan as stated in my paperwork, but I've got a bad feeling this could go south. I've got a wife to take care of now and can't let this get out of hand. I don't like to ask, but what can you find out about Sims?

Anyway, I wanted to remind you about that conversation we had last spring. Remember about the key to box number 507 and the contents? Don't forget what I told you. I haven't told January because I don't want to worry her.

PS: I saw Sims with Elvira Hammel. They'd been conferring, or maybe I mean plotting, over my loan papers.

Shay

"What the hell?" Ford read the note again. What did Shay mean, false papers? How could there be false papers on a straightforward, six-year loan? But he remembered Albert Sims, who'd sat next to the late Marvin Hammel's widow at the hearing, while ignoring his own dumpy wife. And he remembered about the key Shay'd mentioned, too, and what the key went to. For Billings to send a reminder didn't sound good.

The second envelope, although of the same cheap paperstock as the first, worried him more even discounting the shoe print. Almost as though he didn't need to cut it open to know what was inside. The handwriting, pretty and precise, carried an omen.

But after a moment, he used his pocketknife, slit the envelope and pulled out the flimsy.

Mr. Ford Tervo,

Shay is dead. Murdered on his way home from town on September 12. As Shay's friend, I thought you would want to know. The sheriff has no suspects at this point, but I do. The problem may be in proving it, which I intend to do. It's my belief some of the same people from the trouble before are involved. Please wish me good hunting.

Regards,

January Billings

A terse little note. But not a surprise. Reading Shay's note first had almost been preparation. A wave of sadness swept over Ford. His friend hadn't gotten to enjoy wedded bliss for long. And his suspicion of a situation gone south had proved prescient.

He read January's note again. She wasn't asking anything of him, the writing a simple notification of Shay's death, although in the almost too abbreviated words he somehow sensed her rage as she wrote. Shay, now, Shay *had* asked something of him, and then he was killed. Murdered.

Ford shifted on the bench, his unseeing gaze roaming over Butte's main street, a depressing view at best. The noon hour was quiet as folks settled in to eat their dinners. Considering the town, he figured more than a few men were either incarcerated, working deep within a mine, or sleeping last night's overindulgence off in a bordello.

January, that beautiful scarred lady, needed him whether she knew it or not and he didn't intend to let her down.

By four o'clock he and his roan gelding were on the train, wending their way over the mountains into north-eastern Washington.

NOT LONG AFTER NOON, January's buckboard rattled over the bridge she'd built across Kindred Creek, the small stream named for her grandfather, Kindred Schutt, that awful old man. She continued on a couple more miles to Shay's house. Her house now.

"Almost home," she told Pen as they topped the final rise. The dog, stretched tail-tip to nose across the seat with her head in January's lap, sat up and 'woofed' with eagerness. January pulled the horse to a stop and let the dog down to run the rest of the way.

From this viewpoint, she had a good line of sight to the ranch buildings and the field beyond. She spotted Rand and Johnny running the binder in the section of oats nearest the stream. The threshing machine was set up nearby where there was a lesser chance of starting a fire with the steam engine. They'd made good progress with the harvest today. Shay's team of Shires drew the machinery back and forth in straight rows. Dust and chaff rose in a cloud around them, almost obscuring both man and machinery. January knew from experience that oats were one of the worst crops to harvest. With their sharp little barbs that caught in clothes and hair, they were prone to causing an awful rash and itch as they worked a way into eyes and ears and through any gap they could find.

A still pool deep enough to wash the stickers away at day's end lay in a curve of the creek bed. The men would appreciate knowing they could make use of it. She and Shay had bathed there often during the summer.

She shivered, remembering. Shay'd had an outdoor man's tan. The lower half of his face, neck and hands tanned dark; the rest of him as pale as cream, his skin a few shades whiter even than her own. They'd laughed and compared the hues side-by-side before spreading a blanket and—

Snapping the reins, she yelled, "hyah," to the horse, urging him on to a trot.

Hurrying now, planning ahead to feed two hungry men their supper, January made short work of unhitching the horse and brushing him down. While carrying in the sundry items she'd bought in town, including the spool of twine, the ammunition, and even a few groceries, she hadn't paid much attention to anything else. But when she'd stoked the stove and gotten a ham in the oven to bake, she paused a moment to take stock of her surroundings.

Where were the dogs? As a rule she'd find them underfoot as she cooked. A glance at the water bowl showed it full. Even Pen hadn't been inside since they'd been home.

"Brin? Pen?" Feeling a sudden strange reluctance, she went to the door and looked out. No tails thumped the porch floor as the scent of baking ham began to rise. No doleful eyes begged as though the hounds hadn't been fed in days. Or maybe even weeks. January snorted and called again.

This time, a soft whine responded.

"Pen?" Heart beating fast, she stepped out onto the porch. "Penelope. Brin. Where are you?"

The whine came again, sounding as if it were right under her feet. But just the one whine.

Descending the steps to the side deliberately left open for the dogs to take shelter from sun or snow, January knelt, bending almost double to look underneath. Pen's eyes looked back at her. Only Pen's. Crouched beside Shay's old brindle hound, she looked about as woebegone as it's possible for a dog to look. Brin, January saw at a glance, neither looked nor moved. And never would again.

"Oh, no." It came out a small gasp. "No."

Pen wriggled from under the porch on her belly. As she rose from the crouch, she stirred a cluster of leaves, dried and fallen early from the bushes at the house corner and windblown to gather near the steps. The leaves fell away, revealing a puddle of vomit, still vaguely damp though a layer of foam had dried.

With Pen out of the way, enough light penetrated the hollow darkness for January to spot the answering foam around Brin's lips. And there, in the puddle, something that looked like squirrel bones, eaten and minutes later, vomited up. But not before enough poison got into the old dog's system to kill her.

The memory of the note she'd found stuck to Shay's saddle rose before her eyes.

"No!" Tears dripped down January's cheeks. Tears she didn't even know she was weeping. "Oh, no!"

"Ma'am?"

The male voice speaking from behind her jerked her to her feet like a puppet on strings.

"Missus Billings, what's going on? The house ain't on fire, is it?"

January whirled. "Who was here?"

The demand came out rough and peremptory. Rand's eyes, red from the dirt and oat chaff, open wide. "Here, ma'am?"

"Yes. Who was it?"

Rand, as if he'd been caught in a gale force wind, took a step back. "I haven't seen anybody. Johnson and me, we've been working in the meadow. The dust—" He left the rest unsaid since most folks knew whoever drove the team would be lucky to see the end of his horse's tail.

"Where is Johnson?" January snapped out.

"He's watering the horses. I come over to see if you got the binder twine in town. We're about out. But, ma'am, something is wrong. What is it? You're crying."

As if she didn't know. Angrily, she swiped away the tears and stepped away from the opening. "The dog."

"Dog?" Rand glanced at Pen, then, as January had done, bent to look under the porch. "Ah," he said after a moment. "Poor old girl. I'm right sorry about that, Mrs. Billings."

Her mouth set. "Yes. Me too. While she might've been getting up in years, that's no excuse to murder her."

"Murder?"

"Somebody poisoned her." January placed her hand on Pen's head. "If I hadn't taken Pen with me today, she'd no doubt be dead too. Somebody . . . somebody wants to hurt me by getting at my dogs." Her eyelids fluttered, blinking water. "She's succeeded."

"She? She who? Do you mean . . . Why, what kind of a woman would do a thing like this? Are you sure?"

January huffed. "I'm sure. She already told me so. In a note at my husband's funeral."

Rand still seemed uncertain. "What? Somebody said they was going to poison your dog?"

She had to explain about the note, signed with a skull and crossbones, the universal sign of poison. Rand's frown grew thunderous.

Johnson who, upon seeing the two standing there, came to see about the fuss. He took his turn peering beneath the porch before offering to retrieve the dog's body.

"You want me to bury her, Missus Billings?" he asked. "Maybe up on the hill next to Mr. Billings? I figure they'd both like that. Used to see them together out on the range all the time. Up until these last few months, anyhow, when the hound got a little old."

His speech brought January to the point of tears yet again. Getting soft, she admitted to herself. "That would be kind of you," she said, her voice thick. "It's a fine idea."

It turned out Johnny was more observant as well as more distrustful than Rand. As gently as possible, he dragged Brin from the hidey-hole, having already taken note of the foam around her mouth and the remains of the squirrel in the vomit.

"Ma'am, she's been poisoned," he announced, anger clear in his expression as he straightened up. "She didn't die natural."

"Yes," January said. "I know. I've already asked Rand and now I'm asking you, did you see anybody at the house while I was gone?" Maybe, if she hadn't had that quarrel with Elvira Hammel, or if she'd come right home after the meeting with Sims and not stopped to talk to the sheriff, Brin wouldn't have gotten poisoned. Maybe she would've been in time to stop whoever did this. With a gun, if necessary, and no regrets.

But Johnny's head drooped and he rubbed at eyes only slightly less irritated than Rand's. "I didn't see anybody, Mrs. Billings. I sure wish I had."

THEY WERE A SILENT TRIO sitting at the supper table that evening. January picked at her food while the men, though they ate like hardworking men normally did, didn't appear to enjoy it much. It took Pen, lying beside January's chair, to bring the problem to a head when she turned up her nose at a filled bowl.

Rand placed his knife and fork side-by-side on the edge of his emptied plate and sat back, coffee cup in hand. "Are you thinking there'll be more trouble tonight, Mrs. Billings?"

"I don't know, Mr. Rand. I wouldn't be surprised."

"We should keep watch during the night, take it in shifts." Johnny added his opinion, and Rand nodded agreement.

Pushing her plate aside with the food barely touched, January turned a questioning eye on the hired men. "Do you think whoever did this will be back?"

"Dunno." Rand fidgeted with his spoon. "But I don't want to take any chances with having my team poisoned. If anybody were to put something in the water or the feed, it would affect my horses the same as yours."

"Or mine," Johnson put in. "I like my Brown Boy horse just fine. He's good with cows and I don't want nothing to happen to him. I'm willing to keep watch."

"Thank you both. I expect it's a good idea." Anything to put the men's worries to rest. January thought a moment. "It'll probably do for one night but not longer. Working men need their sleep. How soon will you finish the harvest?"

"Couple days provided we don't have a machinery breakdown. Trading off my team with yours helps speed things up. It's a godsend."

"I figure I can go short on sleep for that long." Johnson had strong faith in his young man's power to deny the need for rest.

"I'll do what I have to do," Rand agreed, not to be outdone.

January could do no less. "Then that's what we'll do."

Johnny Johnson, in his eagerness, settled in that evening for first watch. At midnight, with a yawn of jaw-cracking wideness that showed perfect back molars, he knocked on January's door.

Pen, whuffing and whining, nosed January out of bed at his first tap. "I hear him," she told the dog. "Give off."

She'd slept—or at least rested—atop her bed wearing clothes. Within a few seconds, she and Pen opened the door to Johnny.

"Anything happen?" she asked, knowing full well nothing had. She'd have heard the commotion if the answer were otherwise.

"Nothing." He yawned again. "If you're too tired, ma'am, I can hold on a few more hours."

She smiled at him. "You're asleep on your feet. Go on. I'll watch until it's Rand's turn."

The night passed without incident. And the next day. Then night came again, and Johnny was not so eager for his turn at watch. In fact, almost certain he'd fallen asleep, January opened the door to him almost an hour later than the agreed upon time. But then, she couldn't really blame him. She'd yielded to weariness as well, and slept through her mental wake-up time.

"Sorry, Miss January," he whispered, having been given permission, and in fact, answering the demand that he—and Rand—call her by her first name.

Mrs. Billings had stabbed every time she heard it.

"I dozed off," Johnny admitted. "But I wasn't deep asleep, honest. I'd have heard anybody sneaking around, for sure. And I checked the horses and the corrals and such before I waked you. We're good."

"It's all right." January, carrying her carbine and with Pen at her side, stepped out into the night. The air, balmy and a little humid with a particular stillness, touched her skin with a feeling as if a storm was on the way. She sniffed, testing the smell. "I think it's coming on to rain. Hope you men can beat the storm and get the oats in tomorrow."

"We will. Rand figures to finish up by noon." Johnny put his rifle barrel over his shoulder and, stumbling with weariness, headed off to the barn and bed.

January, not exactly distrustful of Johnny's avowal of safety, but not exactly trusting it either, made her own circuit around the barn, visiting the corrals where the horses and her little Guernsey cow slept. She even stood at the edge of Shay's small orchard and listened to the night sounds. Only crickets and the occasional rustle of birds marred the quiet. All, just as Johnny had said, seemed good.

The chicken coop sat almost dead center in the ranch yard, and she'd placed a bench at the side where she sometimes sat to clean the eggs. She took up a position there to keep her watch. Pen, snuffling a little at the smell of chicken, lay beside her.

Pinching herself now and then to stay awake, an hour passed as January stared into the night. She got up and walked around for a while, until another hour inched away. Then the hour when she should have awakened Rand. She'd barely sat down again when Pen, seemingly from a dead sleep, stood up, the hackles rising on her back. Something like a low moan rose in her throat.

The carbine leaned against the chicken coop's wall. January picked it up and stood too, her movements slow and silent. "What is it?" She grabbed Pen's collar when the dog jumped from the bench and would've torn off into the dark.

"Stay, Pen." The whisper almost soundless, January loosened her grip only after she felt the dog's muscles relax. "Search."

Pen knew the command. Silent now, the dog led off, heading straight for the house. For a moment, January thought about stopping her. Why the house? Wouldn't the person who'd poisoned Brin try again for the other animals, either their water or their feed? If another attempt was even what had Pen agitated. This was new to the dog. What if she only smelled a skunk, or a raccoon come up from the stream?

Pen trotted with determination, so silent she didn't even pant.

If it were a varmint, she'd bark. January didn't pant either. Tension gripping her, she just sucked in air and held it.

From here she could see the door to the house stood open, a door she knew she'd closed before starting her watch. Left open, critters were prone to inviting themselves in. She'd learned never to let herself get careless.

Crossing the open space between the chicken coop and the house, January anticipated an ambush, but all was still. At the house, she made a hand gesture. Pen froze, her tail stuck straight out behind, hackles still raised.

Soundlessly, January stepped up onto the porch, inching toward the open door from the side. Even with the adrenaline pulsing through her veins, she felt a touch of pride. The porch she'd built held nary a squeak or a creak.

She stopped, only then giving Pen the signal to proceed.

Which the dog did. In a rush. Her bellow of pain followed.

"Pen!" January leapt forward yelling, aware of her boots crunching through something that littered the floor. "Pen, hold."

A shot rang out, then a second. For a moment she thought she must certainly have been hit, although she felt no pain.

As she dove through the doorway, someone in a tearing hurry to get out knocked her to the side. The strong blow against her shoulder staggered her, causing her to slip in whatever covered the floor. Raising her carbine, she swung it at the intruder, hoping for a knockout blow. That didn't happen, although the short barrel connected. She heard a cry of pain and the ripping of cloth. An impression of a face twisted in a grimace rose up, indistinct. Female, though, for certain. She saw a fall of light-colored hair.

Pen's cries overshadowed the assailant's.

Then the person was gone, a shadow flitting across the yard toward the orchard.

Whoever it was, January didn't even try to pursue. And she dare not shoot, for fear Rand and Johnny might already be running her way.

Pen was more important. Reaching down, she lifted the dog—Pen still howling and writhing—and bore her outside. Another shot came out of the darkness, then, scant seconds later, a horse's hoofbeats thudded on the road toward the bridge and faded quickly away.

"What's going on? What're those shots?" Rand's roar reached her as he churned across the yard from the barn wearing just his britches. His hair stood on end. "Are you hurt?"

"I'll take her." Johnny, likewise shirtless and clad in britches, beat the older man there and reached for Pen.

"Yes. Take her." Unsure how she'd managed to pick up the seventy-pound dog in the first place, January's arms trembled under the weight.

Or, to tell the truth, January trembled all over, even after Johnny reached out and took Pen from hers arms. She couldn't just blame the strain. She'd thought never to feel this kind of fear again after she'd killed Marvin Hammel. But here it was, like reliving a bad dream.

"What happened?" Rand asked again. He started into the house. "I'll get a lamp. We gotta see what's plaguing this dog. Mrs. Billings, ma'am, are you hurt too?" He'd forgotten to call her January.

Whimpering, the dog stretched her nose toward her feet.

"No." January jumped to bar the door. "No! Stop. Don't go in there. You have no shoes on."

Rand, though not as quick in his obedience training as Pen, paused, toes already over the doorsill. "Ma'am?"

"Whoever invaded us tonight put something on the floor. Something that hurt Pen. Neither of you are wearing shoes. I'll get the lamp." Stumbling a little in the dark on account of whatever was on the floor being slippery, she soon found a lamp and got it lit.

The light raised a glitter on the substance spread across the plank floor.

Rand bent to look, touched the material, then gawked up at her. "Well, I'll be gollywolloped. That's glass. Ground up glass. Johnson, don't you let that dog lick her feet. It'd cut her innards to shreds."

Johnny's face turned white. "Sonof— I'd like to feed that sneaking ... " he mumbled a word " ... some of this."

He wasn't the only one. January vowed he'd have to fight her for the honor.

"Can you sit down in one of the rockers and hold Pen still?" she asked. "I'll get a couple pails of water and some cloths. Best I think to rinse it off her feet. No rubbing. Nobody else track through the house. We want to keep any traces of the person who did this intact until I can study it. But Pen first."

Grunting, Johnny sank onto the chair. "I'll hold her." He took Pen's head in hand, holding her muzzle so she couldn't reach to bite him or to lick her feet. "Damn," he said for what may have been the twentieth time.

An hour later, after who knows how many trips around to the sink to pump fresh water, Pen's feet were so clean they squeaked. Her fur had all been bathed, to her displeasure, and the smell of wet dog permeated the kitchen where they'd finally lugged her inside through the back door. A few small trickles of blood still beaded her paws in the glass induced cuts, staining the socks January had fashioned as bandages. Along with Johnson and Rand, January deemed the dog out of danger. Pen, almost asleep after her travails, lay on an old blanket in a corner out of the way.

Both men, attired by now in their working clothes and wearing sturdy boots on their feet, were done with sleep and sat at the table awaiting breakfast. The main part of the room remained closed off, waiting for daylight to examine the area. January hadn't forgotten the rip of cloth or the way the woman had cried out.

Rand gulped a scalding swallow of coffee, though he sagged with weariness. "You going to ride in and get the sheriff out here?"

"Depends on what we find. I can't leave that mess in there for too long. Pen might find her way into it again. Some of the glass is ground to dust. We could stir it up and breath it in. We'd better rig up masks before we get too close."

Rand nodded. "Hell of a note."

"What kind of a man'd do something like this? It don't make sense. Poisoning dogs, strewing glass shards underfoot!" Even half-asleep Johnny's expression conveyed his disgust.

"It wasn't a man." January made the surprising correction. "It was a woman."

"What?"

"A woman?" Rand squawked, equally dumfounded if his bulging eyes and pursed mouth were to be believed.

"Yes." She got up from where she'd been kneeling beside Pen and crooked a finger. "I saw enough of her to know her gender, but not enough to identify her. Come and see. Tread lightly, please, and don't disturb anything. Take note of everything."

But before the men could move, a noise from outside the front door brought them all around. Even Pen, rising slowly on sore feet. Her hackles rose.

CHAPTER 7

"I LEFT MY RIFLE AT THE BARN." Johnny whispered the confession, looking like he wanted to beat himself in the head for being careless.

"Yeah, me too," Rand muttered. He reached for a butcher knife January had put on the table to slice ham. "This'll work."

Holding one finger up in a "hold there and wait a moment" sign, January picked up her carbine from beside the back door and slipped outside. She tread lightly, staying on the grass as she circled around the side of the house. The sky had lightened in the east although the air was chill. A breeze had begun to stir in the branches of Shay's apple orchard. Leaves, dry from the summer drifted down, rustling as they fell and carrying a fruity scent.

Cautiously, she poked her head around the corner of the house. A horse she didn't recognize stood at the rail, hip shot and head hanging. A man sat in one of the rockers. The end of a cigarette glowed as he took a puff, but not brightly enough for January to make out his features. He didn't appear to be threatening. Not that she put much stock in how he "appeared."

She stepped around the corner, her carbine at the ready.

"Who is that?" she said. "What do you want?"

A familiar voice answered. "You're kind of jumpy, Mrs. Billings. What's been going on around here?"

January didn't know why, but all the sudden she had a lump in her throat almost too big to swallow. "Ford? Ford Tervo? What are you doing here? I'm glad to see you. And surprised. I thought you were back east chasing anarchists."

Deputy U. S. Marshal Ford Tervo grunted as he got up. Stepping down from the porch, he dropped the cigarette and ground it under his boot, making sure no sparks remained.

"I was," he said. "Then I got your letter about Shay and thought you could use some help. January, I'm as sorry as I can be. He was a fine man. I was proud to call him my friend." He hesitated. "Schlinger caught who .. . did it yet?"

"No." Her terse answer carried a wealth of meaning. "And now—" Her voice broke.

"Now?"

"Now somebody is making war on me. Me and the dogs. Shay's old dog Brin is dead, poisoned, and Pen could've been. Instead, just now, her paws have been cut to shreds. I'm afraid this is only the start. What next? The livestock? Hoot? My poor old Ernie mule?"

Ford's face gathered in a thunderous frown. "What's happened?"

"Come in," January said, "and I'll tell you. Oh, not that door." she stopped him as he turned toward the front door. "We'll go in the back."

His frown remaining in place, Ford followed her

around the corner to the rear. She noticed how his gaze sharpened in surprise at the men he found in the kitchen, one who held a knife like he was gearing up to use it. His hand drifted toward the revolver he carried on his hip. But he recognized Johnny from his work here in the spring. He nodded at the younger man and said, "You're Johnson, aren't you? Have you quit Cobb and gone to work for Mrs. Billings? I expect the grub is better here."

January imagined having a good memory for names and faces was important to a Deputy U.S. Marshal.

Johnson cracked a smile. "Well, yeah. The grub is better. But I'm still working for Mr. Cobb. Bo loaned me out to help get Miss January's oat crop in the barn." He looked at Rand. "This is Deputy U.S. Marshal Ford Tervo, Rand. Him and Shay and Miss January . . . uh—"

"I heard about the big to-do," Rand said.

Ford bent forward and offered the other man his hand. "Pleasure."

Unhurriedly, Rand set down the knife and shook. Suspicion still showed though, when he looked at Ford.

January sighed. A lot of people didn't know what to make of Ford. His Turkish heritage made him an exotic in a land where 'exotic' might be used as a reason for a hanging, simple distrust, or even as a simple cuss word. He wore his hair down to his shoulders when it wasn't pulled back, and possessed skin the color of a dark suntan. The problem being, he retained that color all the time. His eyes were gold colored, like those of a predatory eagle. Just about as sharp, too.

Ford returned Rand's stare with one of his own before he turned to January. "I asked before. What's happened here? When I saw your light shining from down the road, I thought maybe you'd left it burning by mistake. But I see not. Unless—are you just up early?"

She shook her head.

While she searched for words, he kept talking. "To tell you the truth, I didn't expect to find you out of bed yet, which is why I was sitting on the porch. New since I was here last, ain't it? Bigger? But here you and these fellers are strung as tight as strings on a banjo. What's this about the hound and your Penelope dog?" He glanced over to the corner where Pen, worn out from the trauma of the night lay sleeping, and he scowled. The dog's feet, encased in some old socks of January's, showed white against her black fur. It had been a test, hurting though she was, to get the socks to stay on her. Even now, every once in a while her muscles would jerk and she'd make a sound. "Where is the hound, anyway?"

Johnson took it on himself to answer Ford's questions before January could get her mouth open, explaining first about Brin. "Missus Billings got that note, see, so we've been keeping watch at night and just ran somebody off. But not before she managed to booger up the dog."

"Note? Tell me about it," Ford demanded.

January did better than that. She produced the note for him to see. Turning to the kitchen sink, she pumped water and put a fresh pot of coffee on to boil.

Ford huffed out something unintelligible. "And to-night? What's this all about?"

He received three versions of the nighttime activity, all of which pretty much agreed.

"Did you meet anybody on the road on your way

here?" January put a load of hope in the question.

"Meet anybody?" Ford, himself walleyed by now with weariness, scratched his head. "No. How long ago did all this happen?"

"Couple hours," Rand said, which took January by surprise.

Had it really been that long? Only then did she realize the sun had risen, filling the room with light so that Johnny, thus reminded, leaned over and blew out the lantern. None of them had noticed the disappearing hours as they cleaned and doctored an uncooperative Pen. Which meant the intruder had a two-hour head start on them. Plenty of time for her, whoever it was, to have gotten away before Ford ever reached the bridge over Kindred Creek.

"Ma'am," Rand went on in his ponderous way, "you was going to show us something just now. Something you said proved it was a woman who throwed that glass around. Not that I disbelieve you. Glass ain't a man's weapon."

"Glass isn't anybody's weapon as a general rule," January said.

Ford agreed, then said, "You're sure it was a woman? And she brought glass with her? That's about the strangest way to attack somebody I've ever heard."

"Oh, yes. Glass shards. Crazy indeed, but it's what cut Pen's feet. Come with me." January leading the way, they all trooped behind her to where the wide plank floor gritted beneath their feet. One spot drew their particular interest. It was where the woman had stood, grinding the glass to powder as she distributed the rest and waited for January and the dog. January had moved a chair to sit above a footprint clearly defined in thin slivers of glass certain to penetrate bare feet. Or the pads of a dog paws.

Careful not to mar the print, she tipped the chair to the side. "You see," she said.

The men took their time, studying the evidence with a few side glances at January's footgear.

"Well," Ford said at last, "it sure doesn't belong to either of these two."

"Foot's a little smaller than yours, ma'am." Rand's narrowed eyes measured as he glanced back and forth between her feet and the outline in the glass dust. "And thinner."

"Something's odd about it," Johnson said, his hands showing what he meant. "Like her foot is tilted or something on a skinny little heel."

"That's because she's not wearing workaday boots." The corner of January's mouth curled up. "She's wearing dress boots, like a fancy British lady riding sidesaddle. Only I'm quite certain she'd not British and I doubt she was riding sidesaddle."

Ford caught the hint real fast. "Is there a female like that hereabouts you can put a name to?"

"There might be."

"Tell me her name. I'll go talk to her. Put the full might and weight of the U.S. Marshal's office behind the inquiry."

January let go a relieved breath. They'd all seen and identified the same oddities she had. Feeling validated, she let the chair sit back down over the print. "Do you think I should save this for Schlinger to see," she asked Ford.

He nodded. "Wouldn't hurt. As long as you can keep the dog out of it until he gets here. Maybe Johnson can ride into town and fetch him."

Rand, his jaw at a pugnacious slant, had arguments

to this plan. "I need Johnson here to help get these oats in. It's comin' on to storm and we gotta get 'em cut before the rain ruins them. I can't do it all myself. And, if it's all the same to you, I'd as soon get my job done and take my team home before something happens to them."

January, wincing at his blunt synopsis, nodded as she looked at Ford. "He's right. The work needs done now. Rand, I don't blame you for wanting to be done with us. I'll ride to town if somebody will check on Pen every so often."

"I'll ride along with you. Don't like you out on the road by your lonesome," Ford protested.

"I'm not sure I like it myself." False. She knew she didn't like the idea. "I'll ride Hoot. He's got more speed than my Mollie. And I'll go armed." It would be the first time she'd handled her dad's colt revolver since the shootout in the spring.

Bustling about her kitchen preparing breakfast for three hungry men and one woman whose stomach felt tied in knots, allowed time for Rand and Johnny to feed and harness the horses and grease the machinery. The oats needed time for the morning dew to dry before they'd cut well, anyway.

Ford paid Johnny fifty cents to water his horse and give him some hay, while he remained behind so he and January could talk.

"Tell me about this woman you suspect," he said, leaning against the wall and watching her cook. "Who is it?"

She sighed. "You were here for the hearing."

Ford nodded. He'd had to testify.

"Shay and I were exonerated, but that didn't stop Mrs. Hammel's loud and protracted outburst. You heard her.

She wept, she wailed, she vowed vengeance."

"I remember. But, January, the woman was hurting. Her son dead, her husband dead. Her and those girls of hers left to fend for themselves." He shuffled his feet, as though embarrassed at talking about the scene.

January snorted. "Fend for themselves my left foot! She and the girls got to keep their ranch. And their bank account, which folks say is pretty hefty. And she got to keep the banker, Albert Sims, dancing to her tune, which is how Shay got coerced into going to town that day. The day he died." It may have been the onions she was dicing that made tears flow.

Ford shook his head. "How would a woman like that, a mother, a rich man's wife, go about getting vengeance? It doesn't make sense she'd even know how."

The look January sent at him would've frosted a creek in far-off Hawaii. "No? What makes you think she isn't cast from the same mold as her husband? You know. Greed, dishonesty, power? Or that she wasn't partners with him? Let alone the simple fact that enough money will buy anything. Including murder." Her knife stabbed into a potato. "Not that I put it past her to do the deed herself."

"Why would it take from spring to fall to start her vendetta, then?"

He was acting devil's advocate, which didn't please January.

"Oh, I don't know." She sliced some ham and chopped it in pieces, knife blade slamming into a maple-wood cutting board as though to add slivers to the pan heating on the stove. "Maybe because it took that long to make contacts with some hired killers. After all, the ones her husband had working for him ended up either dead or in prison. For the most part, at least. Maybe it took a while to find new men willing to take a chance with her."

Ford stared at her. "You really believe that."

"You bet I do," she said.

Slowly, he nodded, eyes narrowed as if thinking. "Something to look into. And Sims. I need to take a fresh look at Sims, too."

"You do that."

Ham, potatoes, and onions all mixed up in a hash went into a heavy cast iron skillet to fry. Flapjacks baked on a griddle sported her cow's fresh butter with a syrup made out of apples from the orchard. The concoction almost qualified as dessert.

"It's ready," she soon called to the men. "Everybody take a seat. Pull up a chair, Ford." It had always been a wonder to her he remained so lean as she'd never known him to turn down food. He didn't this time, either.

Having passed the washbasin as he came in, he said, "I'll wash up," and went back out to the rear stoop.

Plates went on the table with a knife and fork at each place, each man claiming a chair. January wondered if Ford remembered when she'd fixed breakfast for him back when she lived in the barn. Between him and Shay, she'd had to feed them in shifts as she'd had only a single cup, a single fork, a single plate. Marriage to Shay had been a wonder of plenty, even in the simplest of ways. Love, companionship, acceptance—scars and all. He'd told her she was beautiful.

Her stomach clenched again and she pushed her plate away.

The screech it made skating across the tabletop drew Ford's attention. He arched an eyebrow at her, a question in the making.

Her mind had yet to stray from their earlier conversation. "I can't stop thinking about her. About Elvira Hammel."

Though Rand kept eating, Johnny looked from her to Ford. "What about her?" he asked.

Ford's face went blank. "I told you I'd look into it. It'd be best if you don't spread accusations around until we can prove they're true. Please, January, leave it to me and just eat your breakfast. You've gotten skinny as a boarding house bedbug."

She had already turned to Johnny, as if to convince him of her suspicions. "I may not have proof Mrs. Hammel murdered Shay. Or that she was the woman who poisoned Brin and spread this glass. But who else could it be? I can't think of any other woman who might have a grudge against us, against Shay, that would lead her to murder him. And be so cruel as to hurt the dogs."

"But you're positive you saw a woman?" Ford asked the question.

"Of course I'm sure. I wouldn't have said so if I weren't. Truly, there is no one else with a grudge. And only one other person with anything to gain. But I can't see that person riding out here in the middle of the night to spread glass shards on the floor of my house. He's more the embezzlement type of crook. Plus, I don't think he'd be able to move as fast as she did."

"Who are you talking about, Miss January?" Johnny got his question in around a bite of apple.

"The banker, Albert Sims."

Rand dropped his fork and shot her a dismayed look. "Ma'am! You're saying Albert Sims is a crook?"

Huffing, she said, "Are you surprised? Why? Do you do business with him?"

Rand's whiskered jowls tightened. "The bank holds paper on my land. I've got two more years."

Rising, January started clearing the table and putting scraps into a bowl, while Pen, awake again, sniffed the air. Like Ford Tervo, it took a lot to keep the dog from her food.

"There are several people around here in the same fix," January said, "I suggest you take your loan papers somewhere and have them notarized and a copy filed at the county seat. Otherwise, along about 1903, or whenever your loan is due, you're apt to have Albert Sims presenting modified papers."

"Modified papers? You mean changed? Can he do that? For real?" Rand appeared flabbergasted.

"Not legally," she said, "but legal doesn't appear to weigh on him."

Lurching from his chair, Rand headed for the door. "Get a move on, Johnny. We got a deadline for them oats. And I got a date with . . . with . . . say, ma'am, can you give me the name of a good attorney? Somebody honest? If," he added with a bitter edge, "there is such an animal roundabout here."

January sometimes asked the same question.

Ford simply shook his head.

CHAPTER 8

JANUARY WASHED THE BREAKFAST DISHES IN RECORD TIME, anxious to be underway. It seemed to her time was wasting, melting away with the sun. That if she didn't get everything done immediately, then she'd never get it done. Which meant bringing Schlinger in on what she'd learned so far as quickly as possible.

Drying her hands, she called out, "Ford, are you ready to go?" Johnny had been charged with saddling Hoot for her. It would be the first time he'd been ridden since . . . since Shay's last ride.

She didn't bother with getting pretty, or doing more than tying back her hair. This would be a quick in and out of town with one purpose only.

Ford didn't reply. She figured he must still be at the barn, but when she checked Pen a final time and admonished the dog to lie still, she went out onto the porch to find the lawman slouched in one of the rockers with his head cocked to one side. Eyes closed, he was snoring loudly enough to rival the roar of Hauser's sawmill.

She touched his shoulder. "Ford?"

He didn't move. Not even a break in the regular deep snores. She couldn't help smiling. And really, it was no wonder. He'd been up for the better part of forty-eight hours, he'd said, first delayed because of trouble on the train line, then on the road to the ranch.

She'd leave him to sleep, an act of mercy, and hope he'd keep an eye on Pen when he awakened.

Johnny had left Hoot in the barn, saddled and tied in a stall. The horse stamped and shook his head as though wondering what had taken her so long. Mounting, January cast a glance at the field where she spotted Rand driving Shay's shires around the steadily lessening field of oats. Johnny followed with the wagon, gathering the bundles and transporting them to where they'd set up the separator and thresher. Smoke rose from the stack where it was already building a head of steam. With any luck they'd be done by the time she got back.

If she got back. January couldn't help thinking someone might be waiting for her along the road. Someone with lethal intentions. She kept looking behind her, then ahead, driving herself into a tizzy searching the copses at the side of the road in case someone had taken cover there.

Really, she told herself, no sane person would hang around for hours waiting in case she or one of the men rode by.

Logic didn't help. Besides, sane might not figure into it.

She stopped Hoot at the bridge—her bridge—just short of the bushes where the Hammel kid had hidden on that day last spring when he ambushed and wounded Shay. But birds flew in and out of the foliage, undisturbed by human presence.

Even so, she studied the area for a good five minutes before urging Hoot on. His hooves made a hollow thud as he crossed the bridge. Up on the hill, the gray colored stones making up the foundation of the house she'd started gleamed silver under the morning sun.

They reached town unscathed. January headed directly to the sheriff's office, hoping to find Schlinger there. She'd been a little worried. It had been two days since he'd said he'd be out to the ranch. As soon as he attended to the rancher's stolen beef, he'd said. They'd both expected to have the situation cleared sooner than this.

As she tied Hoot to the rail outside the office, her gaze caught on a couple yahoos riding close behind her. While recalling they'd pulled in about twenty yards to her rear as she hit the outskirts of town, she'd not paid them any mind until now. She didn't recognize them, not that she expected to know everybody in the area. She'd kept herself to herself in the months she'd been here. A lot of people were strangers to her.

But something about these two bothered her.

Patting Hoot on the shoulder, she watched as they came even, and although she pulled her hat lower and pretended not to, she didn't miss the way the nearest man's eyes followed her until he went past. The other man's lips puckered as though for a kiss.

"Huh," she breathed into Hoot's warm coat.

She found the sheriff in his office, all right. But far from his usual self.

January stopped on the threshold and choked out, "Sheriff Schlinger! What happened?"

The sheriff, seated in his swivel chair, had his feet

resting on an overturned apple box with a pillow supporting his back. A black cloth sling held his bare right arm immobile. The sleeve of his shirt had been snipped away, allowing the bulky bandage around his upper arm room. Hollowed cheeks and dark circles under his eyes did nothing to enhance his manly beauty. None of which served to deter Rebecca Inman who fussed around him under the guise of making him comfortable.

January didn't think the comfort process was working, especially as Rebecca took it upon herself to answer.

"He's been shot," the woman said. "Ambushed. Just like your husband, Mrs. Billings."

Schlinger lifted his feet from the box and tossed the pillow aside. "I've got a mouth, Rebecca. I can talk for myself. And you don't need to coddle me."

"But you need coddled, Hank. You're the sheriff and we have to get you back on your feet as quickly as possible."

If she hadn't been so fretted over her own troubles, January would've laughed. She was pretty sure Rebecca Inman meant "I", not "we" when it came to coddling the sheriff. Hank. His name was Hank. She hadn't known that. She also noticed the blush spreading over sheriff's cheekbones in a big wave of color.

"Who did the shooting?" she asked, aiming the question at Schlinger. "I hope you caught him."

Rebecca did allow Schlinger to speak, this time.

"Afraid not. It happened the day you were here. Don't know who did it. I didn't see anybody. Miss Inman . . ." he blushed again as he spoke her name ". . . Rebecca, is right. Smacks of the first time Shay was shot, don't it? He said he never saw who did the shooting, either."

He spoke of the spring, when she and Shay had met. They only figured out it had been Edgar Hammel who shot him later, when January identified his horse, a distinctive medicine hat pinto.

"Come on in, Mrs. Billings." Eyes narrowing, he made a gesture toward the chair in front of his desk. "I see you're going armed. What's happened."

"You first." She shook her head. Her own news could wait until the sheriff got his story told.

Seems the rancher who'd complained about his stolen beef had been mistaken, Schlinger told her. Oh, not that the beef had been stolen. Just who did the stealing. It hadn't been a miner with children to feed who killed and butchered his cow, after all. Cutting across toward Heywood mountain, at about five miles out they'd found the meat being fought over by magpies and crows after being dumped down a canyon. Mostly certainly not the act of a man desperate to feed his starving family.

"Turned me real suspicious about then," Schlinger said. "Thought it might be a trap. Still, I had no choice but to follow the trail."

The rancher, mad as a wet hen at the waste and following the sheriff's orders, turned back at that point leaving Schlinger to go on alone. The sheriff had lost the tracks when they wound around to the well-used main road and became mixed in among all the others.

The shot that felled him came from somewhere on the wooded hillside above the road. Whoever pulled the trigger had been a good distance away and shooting between trees, which was probably what saved the sheriff's life.

"He probably couldn't find a clear shot. Twas good

enough to knock me for a loop, though," Schlinger grumbled. "I barely made it back to town before I could bleed out."

Rebecca Inman clicked her tongue and renewed her fussing, replacing the pillow and drawing the apple box footstool nearer.

Then it was January's turn. Her report on events at the ranch had the sheriff sitting up straight, wincing as he did so. "Nobody got hurt?" he said. "Sounds like you folks were lucky."

"Lucky? Nobody hurt? With a good old dog dying of poison and Pen's feet cut up, I don't call that lucky." She knew her reply came out sharp and angry, and didn't care.

"I meant people."

"I know what you meant." She didn't take it any farther.

Schlinger sighed out through his nose like a horse at the end of a long ride. "But you didn't get a good look at the shooter either." He held up his good hand. "Yeah. I hear you about the glass and the poison. I expect a feller spraying bullets around is more dangerous."

Keeping a hold on her temper, January forced calm into her reply. "Not a man. It was a woman."

Rebecca's, "A woman!" may have been an involuntary exclamation, but the sheriff took notice.

"Rebecca," he said, "I'm going to have to ask you to give Mrs. Billings and me some privacy. I got a couple things I need to discuss with her."

"I'm sure I won't stop you," Rebecca said.

"Couple of things that ain't any of your business."

"What . . ." Rebecca started, only to have the sheriff's stern expression stop a protest in the making. "Oh, all right. I'll be over at Doctor LeBret's. You're out of laudanum."

"Don't bother," Schlinger said, too late as the woman had already swept out.

January arched her brows, which made the color rise in his face again.

"She's a good woman," he said, "but she does have a tendency to want to run things. Including me and the sheriff's office while I'm laid up."

"I noticed."

"But I won't be taking any more of that medicine. Whiskey will work just as well."

Both known to cloud the mind. January shook her head. "Did you know Ford Tervo is here?"

"No. I'm glad to hear it, though. I hope he's sticking around to help figure this business out, maybe check into a thing or two. See, that's what I need to talk to you about and I didn't want Rebecca spreading the news around."

She didn't care for the way he implied they'd need help. "What news? What help?"

"Well, see, it's like this." He stopped, as if thinking over those words.

January stirred impatiently. "It's like what?"

Schlinger settled himself. "I had a visitor this morning. Before Rebecca got here, which is good, otherwise the news would probably be all over town—hell, all over the country—by now."

"What are you talking about?"

"Well, see—"

But she didn't see anything at all, since the sheriff stopped there and didn't go on. He was having a hard time meeting her eyes.

"Spit it out," she said. She already had an inkling of

what he had to say. Truth was, she'd been expecting it. Or something of the sort. Even so, some imp kept her from making it easy on him.

The sheriff huffed out a sigh that even from across the desk stirred January's brown hair. "Sims paid me a visit bright and early this morning. He had paperwork, duly signed by Judge Keane."

He seemed to be waiting for her to question him, but she didn't speak.

"It's an eviction notice." The clarification clearly pained him.

"And?" Her question wasn't really a question.

"I tried to argue with him. He ended up taking the papers with him. Said he'd hire somebody else to serve them seeing that I'm laid up." A frown drew those woolly eyebrows together.

"Did you actually read the papers?"

"Caught a glimpse, even though he jerked them outta my hand pretty fast when I said I couldn't do it. From what I saw they looked legal." He shook his head. "Better get yourself a lawyer, Mrs. Billings. A good one, and soon."

"One that isn't sewed up with Albert Sims, you mean." January thought she had her anger quite well hidden, except for the uneasy, sort of sideways glances Schlinger kept throwing at her. "And I'll demand the judge recuses himself, although I'm sure he won't do it willingly. We all know Keane is under Sims' thumb, too. Otherwise, he wouldn't have signed those papers. They're probably thinking I'm too overwhelmed to fight them." She smiled suddenly. "But I'm not."

"Gunplay?" His gaze taking note of her holstered pistol, the sheriff shifted in his chair. "I won't have it. Not this time."

January leveled a stiff look on him. "Only if necessary. I won't stand by and let them, Mrs. Hammel or Albert Sims, or anyone else for that matter, take over the ranch or kill every animal on the place. After first poisoning Shay's old dog, then last night successfully getting through our defenses and managing to hurt Pen, I'm doubly on my guard. I won't balk at defending myself or what's mine. They're playing with me, so to speak, trying to hurt me. I'm sure to be the next target. Just as I'm sure you were shot to keep you from . . .interfering."

The sheriff gave a little jolt. "You think these things are connected?"

"O course, don't you? Get rid of the law and they figure to do whatever they want."

"But Sims . . . he has those papers," Schlinger said. "Why would he need to shoot me and harass you?"

"I doubt if he shot you himself, but given his acquaintance with Marvin Hammel, I expect a hired gun is easy enough to find if you know where to look. Hammel certainly managed to hire enough of them, and I expect his wife knew all about it."

"The violence, that don't sound like Albert Sims' style," Schlinger protested, even as he nodded.

Shrugging, January snorted. "No. I'd guess somebody else is behind that part. Somebody out for blood. I'm sure you know who I mean. As for Sims, well, he has papers he knows won't stand up in an impartial court. I have notarized papers saying the loan was paid in full and on time. Before time. He says the papers don't match.

That Shay altered his paperwork, but if my witness can be persuaded to testify, she can say Sims is the one with falsified papers. I've got another surprise up my sleeve, one I'm not talking about right now. Just in case these walls have ears."

Schlinger, gazing around his office, gave a start just as Rebecca came back in bearing a small vial of medicine. "You folks get done with your discussion? Because if so, Hank here needs to rest. He's not supposed to get too excited."

Smiling, January stood, and if the smile looked more like a grimace, Rebecca was too busy fussing over Schlinger to pay attention. "I think we're done." She turned back to the sheriff as the pillow got stuffed behind him again. "I wanted you to come out and check the evidence regarding the glass shards littering my floor, but I understand that's not possible now. It's probably all right. Deputy Marshal Tervo saw the evidence firsthand, and so did the two men hired to get in Shay's oat crop. Just know, Sheriff, if these people are going to push, I'm going to push back."

Rebecca's mouth dropped open. "Aren't you afraid out there by yourself?"

"Afraid? I don't let myself think of that," January told her coolly. "Maybe because I'm too angry. But I don't intend on making it easy for whoever murdered Shay. I expect justice."

"Justice?" Schlinger and Rebecca said together.

"One way or another."

"There's lines it's best not to cross," Schlinger said. "You be careful."

"Count on it." With that, January spun on her heel

and walked out to where Hoot stood patiently waiting. A flash of movement from behind the now defunct Millie's Millenary shop caught her eye. She pretended not to notice as she mounted.

She made one more stop on the way out of town. At the telegraph office she created a carefully worded note, then stood by as the operator sent it. She waited another fifteen minutes for the one-word reply. 'Done' is all it said.

CHAPTER 9

TWO MILES OUT OF TOWN, an itch, like worms beneath her skin, warned January of trouble. The sensation matched a feeling in the air that preceded the approaching storm. Rand had been right with his weather prediction. Was she correct in acknowledging the itch? As though to emphasize the comparison, within moments the sky above them turned an ominous deep purple. Lightning flashed overhead, followed by a loud peal of thunder.

But she couldn't blame the rapidly oncoming storm for her itch. Her discomfort came from being watched.

She didn't want to let them know she was aware. Turning and gawking seemed the worst thing to do. Stretching an arm as though to scratch her back, she peeked beneath her raised elbow. She caught a brief glimpse of someone following a hundred yards back.

When she reached forward again, she loosened the latch on her side holster. She hadn't needed Schlinger's warning to be careful, but it had made her more alert.

All of which did nothing to reassure her. Knowing someone hovered just out of sight at her back combined with the way Hoot pricked his ears as he looked ahead, also served as warning. Once he nickered softly, so that she lifted the reins and said, "Hush, now."

So. Two someones? A pincher movement. Being fore-warned might not prove all that advantageous, crossfire being hard to dodge.

She'd told Rebecca she didn't let herself think of fear. A lie.

"Whoa," she murmured to Hoot.

He stopped.

"What should we do, Hoot? Shall we turn around and race back to face whoever is behind us? Gun drawn, of course. I'm not taking any chances."

Hoot flicked his tail.

"Yeah. I'm not sure I like that idea, either. He'd hear us coming for sure. There'd be plenty of time for him to have his gun cocked and ready to shoot us down. No surprise there."

She thought a moment. "Or we could run on ahead and see who's in front of us. Trouble is, the same scene is waiting. He'll hear us coming and be prepared. Unless he thinks it's his partner and holds fire. But we can't be sure what he'll do."

Hoot shook his head. Up and down, not sideways. Apparently he agreed with her.

"I'd really like to ask one of those men some ques-tions. Not sure I feel up to taking two of them on at once though." January thought some more. "Best thing is to avoid them altogether. If we can get another hundred yards without them starting a war, we can turn onto the Inman sisters' land and cut across until we hit the bridge.

It's just you and me. We don't need to stay on the road."

Of his own accord, Hoot stepped forward and January gave him his head.

The gap in the trees where she intended turn off and travel across country was barely visible under the steadily darkening sky as, following the river, they swung around a curve in the road.

The man in front was waiting for them, his form barely visible among the trees because of a lightning bolt that hit the ground with a blinding flash.

Hoot's ears flicked forward again. The rider wasn't quite as well hidden as he apparently thought because January caught the gleam of metal and recognized what it meant.

Hard on the heels of the flash, thunder cracked like exploding munitions. Hoot flinched under her, but obeyed her heels in his flanks and leaped forward.

Meanwhile, the man in the trees, who'd maybe been concentrating on watching her and not his horse's increasing agitation, bellowed as the animal shied violently and tried to run. A lone shot hit the road in front of Hoot and ricocheted, *pinging* off somewhere.

January's vision, gone momentarily blurry due to the blaze of light, returned as the riderless horse ran past her heading toward town. She couldn't spot the man, but from close behind—too close—she heard another yell.

Fool. You walked right into it.

Disgusted with her ineptitude, she leaned low over Hoot's neck and urged him on. Speed was their best chance at escaping this ambush now. The pressure of her knee sent Hoot toward the right, into the gap she'd marked out. At maybe six yards in, she spotted a figure sprawled face up on the ground, a rifle still in his hand. He didn't move. Slowing Hoot, she urged him closer. A gash on the man's forehead bathed his face with blood and ran unimpeded into his open eyes but the kink in his neck told the story. That and a tell-tale broken branch of a pine tree hanging by a strip of bark just above him.

She drew Hoot to a stop.

Much as she wanted to get down and examine the man's body, January knew she didn't have the time. The other rider was pounding up the road behind her, howling like an idiot. But she took a few seconds to study the face. The clothes. Even the fancy six-shooter that had fallen from his holster and lay on the ground a few feet away.

"Matt," the other man was yelling. "Matt. Where the hell are you? Did you get her?"

Rain began falling in big, cold, splattering drops. Slow at first, then heavier, and as noisy as a waterfall as they hit the earth.

January clicked her tongue and guided Hoot farther into the trees, watching around for low-hanging limbs as they kept going. She didn't hurry so much now.

January had plenty of time to think on the ride across country towards home. Thoughts that helped take her mind off of being cold, wet, and, most of all, angry. While relieved the ambush had gone awry, in retrospect, she wished she'd handled things differently.

A man was dead and truly, nobody would find her

shedding tears over him. She wasn't sorry in the least. He'd been planning to kill her and as far as she was concerned, that said it all. In fact, gruesome as it might sound, she couldn't help thinking the story would sound better if she actually had put a bullet in him. Whoever had egged him on would know then she wasn't going to stand for this. A man dead by gunshot made him more of an object lesson than one killed by getting his neck broken when a spooked horse ran his rider into a tree limb.

She wished she'd taken the time to searched the man's body in case there'd been something to say who'd hired him. Yes, even with that other man close on her heels. With another one of those "in retrospect" thoughts, she wished she'd hung around and spied on the other man. She'd had good cover in the stand of trees and knew the terrain. And she knew the dead man had been one of the pair who'd followed her in town. The one who'd puckered his lips at her to be precise.

Shay murdered—she got that awful tight feeling in her chest again—his old dog poisoned, threats made. Somebody wanted to destroy everything of Shay and January Billings.

They weren't going to, but one thing remained. *Whose hand was behind this?* Sims? And yet, these ambushes didn't have the feel of Albert Sims's slippery mind. They were not, she thought wryly, sneaky enough. That left only one other choice.

At home, even through the steadily falling rain January saw the oats had been cut, although the steam thresher still stood in the field. Rand's team and his wagon were gone. A relief, really. It made one less soul for her to worry

about. Or maybe five souls if you counted his horses. He
certainly did.

She rode Hoot on into the barn, discovering Johnny's
Brown Boy horse occupying the stall next to Molly. A
smile touched her lips. So, he'd stayed to help her out.
Surprising to her, Ford's horse was gone.

With Hoot unsaddled, she brushed the worst of
the rain from him and placed a measure of grain in
his manger. Leaving him crunching contentedly, she
tromped through the muddy yard to the house and entered through the back door. A couple of her bedraggled
chickens clucked at her from their holding pen as she
passed, though most had been smart enough to take
shelter inside the coop.

She found Johnny sitting on the floor alongside Pen,
tilted sideways with his back against the wall. His head
sagged almost to his chest. Pen's eyes opened as January
closed the door softly behind her. Johnny didn't move.

Was he dead, too? January stood frozen in the doorway as the paralyzing thought flashed through her mind.

Pen moved then, struggling to stand up. Beside her,
Johnny spoke, his eyes still closed. "Not again, you silly
dog. How many time you got to pee, anyways?"

January's indrawn breath caused Johnny's eyes to
blink open as he righted himself and pressed against the
wall. He seemed to be fumbling for his gun, which she
spotted lying close by.

"It's all right, Johnny," she said hastily. "It's me, January, back from town."

"I . . . I, well, shoot, I guess I fell to sleep. Sorry, Miss
January."

"No, it's fine. All is well. I know you're tired. You've been working hard and staying awake half the night." A smile ghosted across her lips. "I take it Pen has been keeping you busy?"

Johnny flushed as he scrambled to his feet. "Had to carry her outside a couple times. Poor old gal's feet are hurting her pretty bad."

"Yes, I expect so. Thanks for taking such good care of her, Johnny. I appreciate it more than I can say. And I'm sure she does too." He was a kind-hearted young man, especially when it came to animals. She'd already known that. But praise discomfited him, as she could tell by his reddening cheeks and embarrassed fidgeting. She could relate. Shay had freed her from those wide-brimmed sunbonnets she used to wear in a pathetic attempt to hide her scarred face from the world. He'd told her she was beautiful, and somehow, she'd believed him.

But the fact remained she still preferred to go about unnoticed. Talking pity on Johnny, she knelt beside the dog and changed the subject. Or Johnny did, as he spoke first.

"Don't know if you could see through the rain, but me'n Rand finished up the oats. Got'em sacked and in the barn with a tarp throwed over 'em. Rand took his horses and wagon home, though. Said he didn't want the bays poisoned or something worse. Can't blame him."

January hadn't even noticed the stored grain but then, she had other things on her mind. Like somebody trying to kill her.

"I don't blame him." She scratched behind Pen's ears which seemed to reassure her old dog. Well sure, it soothed her, too. "I did notice the field and that the thresher is still out there. It's fortunate you and Rand got the oats under cover before the storm. Thank you." Hesitating, she said, "Are you ready to head out too?" She hoped not. Some company would be a comfort.

Johnny sort of hemmed and hawed. "Bo told me to stay as long as you needed me." He met her eyes. "Looks to me that means until whoever killed Mr. Billings and played these dirty tricks is caught."

Reluctant to speak of the near ambush and the dead man, January got up and went to the stove, poked up the fire and put the leftover morning coffee over the plate to reheat. She needed something to warm her innards. A nip from the bottle of Old Crow Shay'd stashed on a shelf behind the flour sounded good about now. Mixed with some butter, brown sugar, hot water and cinnamon, she'd be fixed right up.

But maybe not in front of Johnny.

"Did Deputy Tervo say where he was going?" she asked Johnny.

"No, ma'am. Said he'd be back later on, though."

"Tonight?"

"Dunno, but I reckon." Johnny glanced outside where the rain was sheeting down again. "Unless the weather keeps him away."

Dark came early with no sign of Ford.

January and the young wrangler passed the evening playing checkers. Around nine o'clock the rain stopped and the clouds rolled off toward the east. Giving up on Tervo's return, after carrying Pen outside one more time, Johnny went to lay out his bedroll in the barn. January didn't feel too sorry for him. Shay had fixed up a stall with a cot for when he'd had a mare foaling that he wanted to keep close. With an added cot, Rand and Johnny had already been using the stall for the past few days without protest.

She went to bed fully dressed except for her boots, even though she didn't think company would call on this night. Not when considering the foul weather and the fact last night's attack meant the perpetrator had been up most the previous night, too.

As it happened, she judged correctly.

But the next morning brought visitors. Three of them riding up the road to the house as if they owned it.

Mouth set, January walked out onto the porch to meet them. She carried a shotgun in the crook of her arm.

CHAPTER 10

THE THREE MEN DREW REIN AT THE HITCH RAIL IN FRONT OF THE porch where January stood. She recognized one of the men as Sheriff Schlinger's part-time deputy. The second man she'd never seen before and, judging by his toothy smile and cheap suit, had no wish to meet now. *Sleazy*, was the impression that came to mind.

Her mouth went dry. The last of the trio was the dead man's partner whom she'd last seen through an almost obscuring curtain of rain. He'd been bending over 'Matt's' body.

She waited for one of them to speak. The onus, or maybe she meant the opening salvo, belonged to them.

The deputy, she believed his name was Dabney, either first or last she'd never heard, stepped from his horse and removed his hat. "Ma'am," he said, his eyes cast down. "I reckon you know why we . . . why I'm here."

"No," she said. "I don't."

Another of the three, the one wearing the suit, also removed his hat and, though he didn't dismount, bent in the parody of a bow. "Madam. Top of the morning to you. Craig Sweeney, attorney-at-law, at your service. I'm here to make certain all the loose ends of this transaction are tied up. I expect you'll be relieved when the business is finished."

Transaction? Is that what they were calling outright attempted theft these days? January snorted. She hardly thought so.

The last of them had nothing to say. He seemed too busy, his squinty eyes darting here, darting there, as though judging how much the place was worth. In fact, his gaze paused on Shay's favorite mare and the silver-dappled foal running at her side. Hoot's mama and little brother, in fact. They'd trotted up to the fence, curious about the new horses. If January was any kind of judge, the outlaw's avid gaze indicated he meant to claim them as his pay for murder and theft.

She moved her shotgun into a more readily accessible position.

Eyeing her, the lawyer replaced his hat and spoke to Dabney. "Get on with it, man. I'm already tired of this bucolic atmosphere."

The outlaw made as if to dismount, possibly with the idea of taking a closer look at the horses, but the quick motion of January's shotgun and the shake of her head dissuaded him.

The corner of her mouth quirked. She knew and he knew about the dead man out on the road, about how close they'd come to meeting over his body, but neither mentioned it now. Neither did Dabney. She'd have liked to know if the body had simply disappeared or if it had become a mystery to be solved. Or not solved. Unless . . . had that to do with this "visit?"

Apparently not because Dabney reached to the inside

pocket of his jacket and pulled out a thin sheaf of papers. "I'm instructed to give these to you, Mrs. Billings. Sorry." He held them out to her.

January ignored the proffer, sending them a silent look of disgust.

"You've got to take them," he said when she made no motion to do so.

They seemed to be at a stalemate.

"Set'em on the porch," the outlaw advised. "We got three witnesses here to say she got'em."

"Good thinking." Sweeney seemed to view this solution with approval.

Dabney didn't like it. She could see that much. Possibly because it didn't satisfy the core of his mission, or maybe for other reasons. But he did as the other two said, even weighing the papers down with a fist-sized stone so the breeze didn't catch and blow them away.

Finished, Sweeney nodded, saying with a smirk, "Madam, you've been served. We'll expect you to vacate by this evening. If not, we'll be back and help you leave."

"You know what that means?" the outlaw asked. "Tell'er, sheriff."

"I ain't the sheriff," Dabney said.

"Tell'er."

Dabney shook his head sadly. "Them are eviction papers, ma'am. They say you gotta vacate these premises by tonight. The bank in town foreclosed and now owns this place."

"And?" Sweeney prodded the deputy on.

"We're to use all due force needed to comply."

The outlaw and the attorney shared a smug look.

"All due force needed to comply means you may be removed by any means necessary." Sweeney helpfully expanded on the premise.

"A few stubborn folks've even been shot. Seemed needed." The outlaw laughed. "And one way or another, in the end, they got booted. Feet first or head first, makes no difference to me. We find you standing in the way, you'll get mowed down same as they did."

"Watch it. There'll be none of that, Clemson," Dabney said sharply, and then to January, "Ma'am, you should look at these papers. Maybe there's something you can do."

"There's nothing." The lawyer almost growled his disdain. "I tied them up tight and Judge Keane signed them. That's it. She's out. We can do what we want with the place. Burn it down with everything in it, if we want. Get rid of the stock, dam the stream, dump salt on the ground. Anything."

January thought she heard an emphasis on *stock*. Did that mean Sims and his bevy of disgusting characters intended on killing and torturing her livestock? Shay's precious horses and cattle? But who would actually do such an awful thing? Only someone completely out of their shriveled mind and, much as she hated to admit it, that didn't sound like Albert Sims. A shady thief, yes, and in on the scheme up to his eyeballs. But probably not one for destroying valuable property where he stood to make a profit on another man's work.

So who, exactly, was running this show?

The lawyer's words had gotten Dabney's attention. "What are you talking about? There ain't gonna be any burning or salting or anything else."

"No?" Sweeney sneered. "You've served the papers. The rest is none of your business. Might be best if you left now."

At the edge of her vision, January spotted Johnny standing just inside the barn, his rifle just shy of aimed as though choosing which man to shoot first. He probably hadn't heard all of the muck they were talking, or the threats, but most likely enough to grasp their intent.

So far, she hadn't said a word, but she did now. "It would be best if you all left now. You see, I'm just about to lose my temper. This bogus claim you're making? It won't stand up in court. You people have murdered my husband, killed his dog, tried to steal his land, and have made threats against me."

"No proof," Sweeney shouted. "That's slander."

"Oh, we all know better than that." January's lip curled. "And Deputy Dabney can attest to the threats. If he will."

She waited for the slight tilt of Dabney's head before going on. "You may have heard a little something about what happens to people who set out to destroy me. I urge you to keep that in mind because the first man who rides in here with his gun out and the intention of harming me, the livestock, or the structures will find more than passive resistance. I will defend what's mine. You've been warned." She raised the shotgun.

They milled around for a bit. It was Johnny who ended it. He stepped from the barn and, having correctly judged the least experienced rider, fired a shot a few feet in front of Sweeney's horse. The noise, along with bits of gravel flying up in its face, had the salutatory result of causing the horse to pitch.

"Here, none of that," Dabney shouted as he swung into the saddle. "There'll be no shooting."

January noticed he moved faster now than previously.

Inside the house, Pen came awake and began baying, adding her voice to the shouts and whinnying of horses.

"Git out of here. All of you." Johnny's eyes snapped with anger. "Dabney, you green-assed cow turd, I'm reporting this to the sheriff. He'll have something to say about you letting these bone-gnawers talk to Missus Billings like they did."

"You'd best keep your mouth shut, sonny," Dabney sputtered. "This ain't anything to do with you."

"The hell it ain't," Johnny roared back. "You attack my friends and you've attacked me."

Sweeney's face was red with the effort of staying in the saddle as his horse kicked out at Clemson's sorrel. Meanwhile, the outlaw bellowed something about teaching her a lesson. Bellowed it twice, actually, in case she didn't hear him the first time.

But she had and the leveling of her shotgun proved to be enough.

In a rush, the three got themselves and their horses straightened out and galloped away, only stopping when they reached the top of the hill where Shay's road met with the main one. They appeared to confer for a bit before Dabney and Sweeney rode off toward town. The outlaw stayed, a distant threat.

January and Johnny, to avoid making themselves a target, backed into the shadows formed by the house wall.

"We can see him from here. Doubt he can see much of us," Johnny said.

"Yes." January looked out at the sky where clouds were gathering. "I hope another storm rolls in soon. I've got a hunch Clemson would take himself back to town rather that stand out in the rain."

Johnny laughed. "Gone soft."

"And too sure of himself. I wonder why."

"Ma'am?" Johnny'd evidently forgotten he should call her by name.

"I wonder why he's so confident. We ran him off too easily. A gunman like him? He could've handled us, I think. And Dabney, if necessary."

"Yeah. Him. Hard tellin' whose side that cow-brained deputy'd come down on. I think maybe for whoever sent them out here."

"Yes. Although I don't think he's a bad man. Just a weak one." January looked back up the hill where Clemson had found a pile of boulders thrown in heap when Shay cleared that patch of land for the road. He perched on the pile and let his horse graze as he watched them.

"So why's he out there watching us?" Johnny asked the question filling her mind. "He must know we ain't going anywhere."

January's lips twisted. "He might think he'll spook us into running for it, sitting up there like he is. And having us leave is easier than shooting us. For the moment. A man like that prefers a crowd to back him up. I expect that's what he's waiting for. Back up."

Johnny snorted. "I got half a mind to—"

"No you don't." Her correction came sharply. "You'll leave him strictly alone."

"But, ma'am. Miss January, I mean . . . I figure I could

sneak up there and take him prisoner. Wind's coming up again. The way it roars over that hill will cover any sounds I make comin' up the other side."

"Johnny . . ." she said. A warning.

"I don't mean to shoot him. Not unless he tries to shoot me. Just sneak in and give 'em a tap on the head. Tie him up or something. Keep him out of our way."

How Johnny thought to pull off any such stunt safely escaped her. Regretfully, she discarded the idea even as another came to her. Backing over to the door, she opened it, beckoned Johnny inside, and closed it again. Almost immediately a bullet banged into the house siding, luckily without the velocity to knock its way through.

Eyes widening, she stared at Johnny. He stared back.

"Go . . . Gol-durn," he said. "We're under siege."

He was right. Pinned down waiting for a bigger attack. Or so someone thought.

"All right," she said soft-voiced, "so this is officially a war. That means we have to come up with a plan to defend ourselves. Come on over to the table, Johnny. We can eat and plan at the same time."

While January put together a noontime meal of cold chicken, bread and apple pie left from the night before, Johnny got Pen up and took her out the back door to pee. Pen, January was glad to see, managed to hobble her own way back inside, and then to sit in front of the stove while January dodged around her. The dog had given up on fighting the socks.

Since it took more than a dust-up with a deputy, a shyster lawyer and an outlaw to put Johnny off his food, he ate while January made a pencil and paper list.

"First thing we have to do is get the livestock moved." January wrote it down and gnawed a bite off a chicken leg, not forgetting Pen needed a taste, too.

Johnny gawked at her. "Move the livestock? How we gonna do that? That feller sitting up on the hill is apt to shoot us—or the critters."

"That's why he needs a distraction."

"Distraction?"

"I was thinking of running off his horse." She made a note on her paper.

Johnny was already shaking his head. "Nah. First place, I don't know how you'd do that short of shooting it, and I don't like the idea of that. In the second place, he'd just come barreling down here and steal one of yours."

"Try, Johnny. Try is the important word. But yes. Having come down here is what I'm counting on."

"Huh?"

"We don't want him up on the hill where he has a clear field of fire. That means we have to root him out of his position, but without risking ourselves. Once we take care of him, we can move the livestock."

Frowning, Johnny took the last piece of pie and poured a dollop of her Guernsey's rich cream over it. The frown cleared at the first forkful. "How're we gonna do that?"

She shrugged. "How are you with a slingshot?"

"Slingshot? I ain't used one of them since I was a boy."

She judged him to be around seventeen, hardly more than a boy now.

However, he chuckled at a memory like the elderly occupant of a front-porch rocking chair. "But I did all right then."

"Good, because I'm counting on you encouraging that horse to run away."

Placing his fork and knife neatly on the empty plate, Johnny finally asked the main question.

"Miz January, just why do we have to move the livestock? And where are we gonna put them if we get the chance?"

Silent for a moment, she chose her words. "You heard that lawyer, didn't you? What he said about, salting and burning and destroying?"

Johnny nodded. "Some of it."

"Well, think. Some one of these people murdered Shay. They poisoned Brin and managed to cut Pen's feet. What makes you think they'll stop at killing all the horses, the cows, even the chickens? And us."

His face lost a little of its color. He choked a little and said, "Where you thinking of moving the stock?"

She had the place all picked out. They just had to rid themselves of Clemson first, by any means short of murder.

Unfortunately, a slingshot proved not to be the answer. Slipping out the back, Johnny went off into the orchard to practice with one Shay'd had around for chasing critters away from the hen house. On the fourth practice stone, the bands broke and neither of them were sure what to use as replacements.

Not, she thought ruefully, that it mattered all that much. Johnny had proved a sadly out-of-practice shot with the slingshot. They had to do something, though, and soon, because she expected when Sweeney's threatened time was up, there'd be a crowd of Sims' or Hammel's—since she didn't discount Elvira—hired guns show up at her gates intent on taking possession. If she'd had gates, anyway.

"You're sure Mr. Tervo didn't say when he'd be back?" she asked Johnny again. They were back in the house after the slingshot fiasco.

He shook his head.

Ford is who they needed. If only he'd come riding in and discover that outlaw waiting for them to show their noses. Ford would soon put the run on Clemson. Could be he'd even have a warrant for him, and wouldn't that be a fine thing?

But Ford didn't show up and time flew by. End of the day and the lawyer's threat drew ever closer.

Speaking of flying, that's what they needed. A silent assault from the air. A trained bird. A glider. A winged horse. A...a... "A kite!" she yelled, which made Johnny jump and reach for his rifle, and set Pen to barking.

"What?" Johnny, his head turning like an owl's gazed wide-eyed in all directions.

January jumped from her chair, knocking it over. Her pencil fell to the floor and without thinking, she stepped on it. She ignored both mishaps. "A kite. That's what we need."

CHAPTER 11

"MISS JANUARY?" Johnny stuck a finger in his ear, stirring it around as though to help her words penetrate. "Did you say kite? Why would we need a kite?"

"Kite is exactly what I said. As to why . . ." January, already on her way to the bedroom, felt as though her chest were filling with too much air. During the summer, when the evenings were long and he'd looked forward to fall, Shay had whiled away a few spare hours building a kite. A big one. He constructed it of thin strips of wood he'd begged from her store of suitable furniture lumber, newspaper he painted with some kind of glue to make it stronger, and a tail made of string and scraps of fabric tied in the middle to make them look like bows. The endeavor had stemmed from a talk they'd had, when January told him she'd never had conventional toys.

"Never?"

"Well, once. My father bought me a doll." She'd been sitting by the fire, working on constructing a smoking stand to place beside Shay's chair where he could rest his cup or his glass and an ashtray for his rare cigar.

She looked up from her final sanding of the maple-wood stand and shrugged. "Then he got word that a man and his daughter were being sought for questioning regarding an old murder here in Stevens county. It sounded like us."

He already knew the circumstances of their flight from the ranch at Kindred Crossing, back when she'd been a child. About how her dad had killed his own father after the old man had carved an S, for Schutt, in her cheek.

"Was it you?" Shay had asked.

"I don't know. He may never have found out either. But he had me wear britches, cut my hair short and we moved from Coeur d'Alene the very next night. I believe we went to Pendleton, Oregon, that time, and stayed a few months. But I had to pretend to be a boy, and he insisted I leave the doll behind. So I did."

Shay had shaken his head. "Did you cry?"

"No." She'd straightened, stretching her back. "Well, maybe a little, but only where he couldn't see me. Dad began teaching me how to build things when we got to Oregon—" She indicated the stand, complete with a copper-lined, dovetailed drawer, she'd constructed, and eyed it with satisfaction, "—things like this, and I forgot about the doll."

Shay didn't like it though, even as he admired and was grateful for the smoking stand.

A smoking stand. And what was she to do with it now? Take it apart and use the pieces for kindling? And there was his kite.

The box-shaped object hung from the ceiling in their bedroom, still unfinished as far as he'd been concerned. The last step in the kite's construction had been to paint it red, making it more easily visible against the sky. Right now, the paper parts were still mostly gray, the newspaper ink mottled from the glue. Not visible, but *invisible*.

Just right to hide in the sky as it floated overhead. Right up until it proved a great enough distraction for her and Johnny to dispose, one way or another, of the outlaw.

"Come here and help me get this down," she called to Johnny.

Johnny edged to the bedroom door. "Ma'am? Miss January?" He'd gotten real formal of a sudden.

January barely noticed his hesitancy as she pulled a stool to stand beneath the flyer. Johnny was several inches taller than she but he'd still need a lift.

"I can't reach the ceiling," she said. "You can. Careful you don't drop it. It's a little fragile."

"A kite!" He gaped up at the thing, seeming awed. "A big one."

"Yes. Shay made it for me. He meant for me to have fun, like with a toy, but I think it'll save my life. And yours." Her lips trembled until she pressed them together.

Johnny climbed onto the stool and began releasing the knotted twine that held the kite overhead. "How's a kite gonna do that?"

"By crashing." Shay's gift. She could hardly bear the thought of destroying it. But Shay, he'd be satisfied.

"Crashing? What do you mean?"

"I mean for it to come down on top of either Clemson or the horse. We needed a distraction, and now we'll have one."

Johnny nodded grimly as the final bit of twine came loose. "You got string?"

"You bet."

Once they had the kite down and the huge ball of

string Shay'd collected attached, at the first break in the rain they made their way out the back of the house again, cutting through the orchard and climbing the hill to come up behind the outlaw's position.

They carried the kite between them, fighting to keep it from fluttering when the rising breeze caught at it. They made their way up a draw which eventually brought them in behind the outlaw.

This is where Johnny saw the plentitude of string would come in handy. Although they stood in a sort of drop-off, beyond that lay a final area of open ground between them and Clemson. They would never be able to cross it without him detecting them. Meanwhile he remained well out of sight. Every once in a while they'd catch a glimpse of his rifle barrel, or spot the top of his hat. Neither felt up to aiming a gun at either target.

His horse stood within view. Tied to some brush, he switched his tail at pesky flies and ducked his head to pull at some sparse grass.

"How are we going to do this?" Johnny asked. Now they were here, he'd turned fidgety, nervous and uncertain.

January watched the tops of trees and the bend of the brush where Clemson's horse had thrown up his head, ears pricked and pointed toward the house. Every once in a while the breeze would die away and, like the horse, they could hear Pen down below baying her loneliness.

"Hope she's all right," Johnny said. "Wonder if she needs out again."

January couldn't think of that now. "She'll be fine. I just hope her racket doesn't warn Clemson something is wrong."

As though to put her words to the lie, Clemson fired toward the house. The barking stopped, then continued unimpaired. The outlaw shouted, a rude word that made Johnny blush and the horse stamp his feet and pull on the reins.

The wind rose again and Pen's wail died away. "Start playing out the string, Johnny. See if you can't get the kite aimed over the horse. He appears nervous already. Let's see if we can't get him to stampede."

On their first try, the kite banged into the dirt embankment sheltering them from view. They had to make a switch on who did what, after that. January took the ball of string, putting herself in charge of guiding the kite, while Johnny stood on tiptoes and held the box high enough for the wind to pick it up and cast it into the sky. Successful at last, it almost immediately became lost in the cloudy background, except for the bows on the tail.

Surprised at the strength of the tug, January set her feet. Presently, the kite responded to the wind, bucking and kicking, dipping down and then up.

"No, no," she moaned once as the box came all the way down and grazed the earth. But then it rebounded, bouncing upward and flying free again.

She let out more string. Johnny tried to instruct her regarding guidance, not that he knew a thing more than she did. As it rose over their heads, she heard the paper rattling, with the little surprise she had in store adding to the din.

Slowly, then faster, the kite, bowing before the wind, flew toward the horse and Clemson.

"Now?" Johnny whispered, his eyes flashing.

Clemson looked up, aware of something disturbing his horse who'd taken to switching his hindquarters and shaking his head. "Settle down," they heard him snarl. "Damn fool critter."

January figured it was a good thing the horse couldn't talk—and that Clemson didn't seem all that finely attuned to the cues the animal presented.

"Now? Now?" Johnny asked again.

Setting her feet as the kite pulled on the taut string, she said, her breath coming hard, "Not . . . quite . . . yet. Got your rifle?" She knew he did, having watched him snug the sling strap over his shoulder before they set out. But giving the boy something to do besides fidget helped calm him.

"Yes," he said.

She paid out string. All they had. It had to be the horse they attacked, she realized now. All they had distance for.

"Now," she said and gave the line her strongest jerk, first to one side, then to the other, and then a quick yank down. The paper wrapped wooden sticks lost lift, plunging downward and swooping from side to side as it fell. Straight above Clemson's horse.

Dislodged by the action, the little surprise January had rigged broke apart, raining the shot from a few shells down on the hapless animal's head and back before the kite broke apart on top of him. Terrified, he jerked with all his might. The reins holding him to the tuft of brush, already loosened by his nervous stamping, broke off away. Free now, he bucked mightily for a few seconds, which caused the saddle on his back to shake loose and turn under his belly.

Maddened, he spun away, then charged ahead. The saddle's stirrups thumping on the ground urged him on, straight down the road toward Kindred Crossing.

Her plan had worked! January wanted to laugh her glee aloud.

"What the—" With a whoop, Clemson jumped from the boulder's cover. Dropping his rifle, he chased behind the horse losing ground with every awkward stride. His bellow of, "Whoa, whoa," did nothing to soothe the frantic animal. Rather, it was enough to spur the horse's efforts to further speed.

A chortling Johnny broke cover and ran over to capture the outlaw's rifle as well as take his place amongst the boulders. Abandoning the precious kite where it had come down, January joined him. They managed to take cover as, dejection all over Clemson's bearded face, he sent a last look after his runaway horse and headed back toward the rocks.

"We got him now," Johnny said, voice low, his face lighting with excitement.

"Shh. Wait." Settling herself behind a too small rock, January hoped Johnny didn't get over-confident. Clemson was an outlaw, a hired killer. And he still had his revolver. He wasn't disarmed and helpless, not by a long shot.

She'd never know what set him off, but something caught his attention, perhaps a kind of sixth sense. That, or maybe either she or Johnny moved and he saw it. Whatever, something keyed him to the fact the fortress he'd chosen to occupy was no longer his to command.

The outlaw, snake fast, had his revolver in hand in the space of a single blink. He fired off two shots before dodging into the ditch running alongside the road. A wooden culvert ran beneath the road right there, she remembered, a ditch that would take him to the exact route she and Johnny had used to get in behind him. From there he could make his way toward the house and yard. Out of sight, just as they'd been out of his.

But for now, his rear-end showed every now and then above the ditch's edge as he crawled. For the next thirty yards or so. If only they could—

"Shoot him, Johnny," she said, her voice hard.

"Shoot him? I can't even see him." Johnny raised his head and peered around. "Just his. . ." Another shot blew the hat off his head. He yelped and ducked.

She couldn't blame him.

"Throw me his rifle." She should've brought her carbine, January thought. She had a little pocket pistol, but it wasn't good enough for the distance.

Johnny, shaken by the near miss, obeyed her command but his toss wasn't a good one. He must've been hoping for a soft landing, because the rifle ended up halfway between the two of them.

Now what?

"Fire a couple shots in his direction, Johnny, but don't waste ammunition. You don't have to hit him. Just keep his head down." Holding her breath, she got ready to dash after the rifle, needing time for a swift grab. *A very swift grab.* It meant working up her nerve beforehand.

"You sure?" Johnny looked pale. "He can see over to here."

"I know. Got no choice. Shoot!" She broke for the rifle as Johnny fired in Clemson's general direction. The bullet raised dust a half dozen feet behind him.

January had the rifle in her hand as she dove for cover.

Clemson had earned his reputation. Before Johnny could aim and fire again, the gunman jumped up and returned fire then ran like a rabbit with a hound on its tail.

Only one shot.

One too many, as it turned out.

Staggered, January lifted the rifle and pointed it in the desired direction. Only waist high, that being all she could manage. Of its own accord, her forefinger pulled the trigger, the recoil and bark of the weapon surprising in its strength.

"You got him," Johnny yelped. "Miss January, you got him. He's down." Darting from cover, he ran toward the writhing outlaw and set a heavy foot in the middle of Clemson's back.

One problem.

Clemson wasn't the only one on the ground, which, in January's pained opinion, sort of spoiled the scene.

CHAPTER 12

JANUARY DIDN'T WRITHE LIKE THE OUTLAW. Clemson, she could see through wide-open eyes, was doing his best to fight Johnny and wriggling like a caterpillar crossing grass.

Johnny pinned the outlaw down with a well-placed knee to the spine, then pulled a length of left-over binder twine from a pocket and wrapped it around Clemson's hands. When done, he jerked the outlaw upright. Every bit as smartly as Sheriff Schlinger could've done, too. She was willing to bet on it.

Meanwhile, she lay curled like a newborn babe and did her best not to move. A hot rush of blood leaked from the hole in her side. Her ears roared with her thundering heartbeat, going fast as a racing horse. Maybe two racing horses. It felt like somebody had seared the hole through her with a red-hot poker.

Was this the last sort of thing Shay had felt? She wanted to cry. For him. For her. But she didn't.

"Miss January! January, are you shot? Don't be shot."

The admonition came from Johnny and hardly made sense. *Too late, anyway.*

Her eyelids closed, a shutter to block out the gray sky. Those odd hoof-heartbeats became louder, then stopped. Saddle leather creaked, soft and familiar.

Did I die?

A new voice, harsh with concern, answered her question. "What in all of hell's fire is happening here?"

Ah. Hell, then. She'd hoped for different outcome when the time came.

Johnny's voice, closer to her now, sounded as if he stood right next to her. "Miss January's been shot."

"I can see that. How bad is she?"

She was aware of someone kneeling beside her, of them removing the rifle from where it lay across her hand as if pinning her to the earth.

"Don't know," Johnny said, sounding as miserable as if he'd been the one shot. "Pretty bad, I think. "

"That feller you got hogtied do it?" Anger. Ford Tervo as she'd never heard him before. Was he dead, too? And Johnny? No. That didn't seem right.

Hands, warm hands, touched her and her eyes blinked open, meeting with Ford Tervo's odd, amber-colored orbs. Since she saw his head set in the same background of cloudy gray sky she'd seen before the shooting started, she thought maybe she was alive. Anyway, she hurt too badly to be dead.

"Ooh," she moaned, trying the sound to see what happened. "Ow."

Ford's face, looking down at her, blurred. "We've got to get you to the house, January. I'm going to lift you onto the horse. Can you hang on long enough to get home?"

Could she? "Yes," she said between gritted teeth. "Have to."

He huffed. "Right."

Beyond him, she saw Clemson's horse, the saddle turned right side up again, standing alongside Ford's roan.

"You found his horse," she whispered. "Good."

Ford didn't appear any too happy about it. "A man finds a horse running loose with a saddle flopping under his belly, it kind of rouses his curiosity," he said, his voice arid. "Besides, I heard shots and figured where he came from." And then, over his shoulder, "Johnson, get that feller on his feet and walk him down the hill. From what I can see, I doubt he wants to sit a horse. Just see that he doesn't get around you."

"Miss January shot him in the ass-end," Johnny said. "He ain't goin' nowhere but where I say he is. And he ain't gonna have fun doin' it."

She heard a chuckle. Oh, Ford thought it was funny, did he?

The ordeal of mounting a horse—even though Ford did most of the work—drained away all of January's remaining energy. Then, with every stride the horse took, the hole in her side felt as though it were being ripped wider. The red stain on her trousers trailed longer, flowing down her leg. If it hadn't been for Ford, mounted behind her with his arms on either side holding her in a loose cage, she would've fallen beneath the horse's hooves long before they got to the house.

When they did get there, and Ford got down first, she toppled off the side into his arms like a rag doll. She knew how Schlinger must've felt, making his way back to town after being ambushed.

The worst ride of his life, he'd said, and she believed him. And she'd only endured a quarter mile or so.

Ford carried her into the house, where a badly limping Pen, smelling blood and with her tail dragging, came to meet them. Taking January through to the bedroom, Ford placed her on the bed and started undoing her shirt buttons.

"What are you doing?" she whispered, aghast, lifting a hand to ward him off.

"Just what I have to do, which is get this bleeding stopped." He leaned back. "And I can't see the wound through a blood-soaked shirt. It's no more than you did for Shay when you first met him."

January's mind drifted. It was true.

By the time Johnny arrived, poking his cursing prisoner along, Ford had removed her boots, shirt, and chemise, tied a pad over the hole in her side, and tucked her securely in bed with the blankets pulled to her neck. No lack of modesty there.

Hours passed then in a slow drag as Johnny, lifting his Brown Boy horse into a lope, dashed off to town to fetch Doctor LeBret and the sheriff.

The room grew dark before Doc arrived. Pain rose in waves as LeBret poked, cleaned, stitched, and bandaged.

Once she heard voices raised in argument, and Ford saying, "Hightail it before I arrest the lot of you. Or shoot. Your choice." And then blessed quiet until birds chittering from her rooftop awakened her at dawn the next day.

THE SMALLEST SHIFT of position instantly reminded January of events from the day before. As if she could forget, no matter how much she wanted to. The pain made her gasp, but not loudly enough to awaken Ford Tervo. He sat slouched in the household's second-best chair, one with a padded seat, sides and back, with his head leaned back and pressed into a corner. He'd moved the chair in from the other room sometime last night with the intention of watching over her. She remembered seeing him confer with Doc.

Her head felt a little dizzy, her brain a little foggy. Doctor LeBret had made her guzzle some laudanum yesterday, both before and after the messy ordeal of sewing her up, and this must've been the aftereffects. A dry mouth and bleary eyes added to her discomfort. Plus, she needed the privy.

"Argh-hum." Even clearing her throat made her side hurt, she discovered. Worse, Ford didn't stir, a repeat of yesterday's observation. When Ford Tervo slept, it was as if he'd been moved onto a world of his own, one very far from this one. The very idea almost made her laugh.

Cautiously, she pushed back the covers and, propping herself on an elbow, waited for a jolt of fiery pain to subside. In increments, she managed to sit on the edge of the mattress, and then to gain her feet. She still wore her britches from yesterday, she discovered, along with a nightdress on top.

An odd-looking sight for certain, caught reflected in the cheval glass mirror as she lurched out of the room, ghosted through the kitchen and thence out the back door.

Behind her, Ford's breath continued in an unbroken rhythm.

She caught a glimpse of Johnny as she passed down the path to the privy. Wielding a pitchfork, he was tossing manure into a wheelbarrow to be transported to a pile behind the barn. Her eyes narrowed as she noticed he seemed to be talking to somebody. Then she saw Pen lying just outside the door, keeping the boy company. From the looks of things, he'd put all the horses, along with her cow, in the barn overnight for safekeeping, and was now paying the price of their safety.

Bo Cobb couldn't have sent her a more willing helper. January's gratitude swelled, a catch in her throat.

Back at the house, she found Ford awake and busy pumping water into the coffee pot. He scowled at her when, ready to sob from the effort, she made it through the door.

"Should've used the chamber pot," he said, his eyes bleary as if he hadn't gotten enough sleep. In truth, he hadn't appeared comfortable, sprawled in the chair.

She blushed. "I managed."

"Well, I guess you did. Doesn't mean it was smart, traipsing out there on your own. What if you'd fainted?"

"I don't faint."

He may have been right, though. Wobbly as a child's top, she stumbled to the table and almost fell into a chair. "If you're volunteering to wait on me, I could use some of that water. My mouth is so dry I can barely talk."

"Doc said you'd need water. And milk, if you'll drink it. He said it'd help rebuild your blood supply." He pumped a pitcher full of water and set it on the table along with a cup. "Drink up. I'll wait for the coffee."

The cold water made January shiver.

Seeing it, Ford found her shawl and wrapped it around her shoulders. "Chills. They're a sign you've lost too much blood," he said.

"I remember, with Shay. He was thirsty too, and cold when he woke up from his fever."

January had been avoiding his eyes, but as she warmed, some of her strength came back. "Where were you? I thought you must have abandoned Johnny and me."

"Abandoned? No, ma'am. You oughta know me better than that. But I figured a trip into Spokane might be more productive than talking to the sheriff. I knew you could handle him on your own."

He looked hurt at her accusation, although she didn't really buy into it. Ford Tervo was too confident for such details to cause him bother.

"Of course," he added, "I didn't know then that he'd been shot. Otherwise I might've thought otherwise about leaving just then. But it looks like you made it safe there and back and the trouble didn't start 'til the next day." He eyed her sharply as he spoke.

"I guess that's about right." She would've shrugged to show just how right it had all been if her side hadn't hurt so much. The trouble is, Ford wasn't much fooled by her playacting.

He caught the coffee before it boiled over, and when the bubbling stopped and the grounds settled, he poured them both a cup. Sitting down, he said, "Is it?"

She'd forgotten the drift of the conversation.

"Is that when the trouble started? Or was it before, maybe during the storm?"

She should never, January reminded herself, forget that Ford was a U.S. Deputy Marshal and that his job was to catch criminals. He wasn't just a friend. Anyway, he'd been Shay's friend, not hers. He had no special bond with her. All innocence, she drew the shawl more tightly around her. "Why are you asking?"

"So you don't know anything about the body a wrangler found in the woods yesterday?" His question might've seemed off-hand, but she knew it wasn't.

She didn't have to fake a gasp. She'd figured Clemson to have taken care of that. Unless— "What body? What woods?"

"There's a little cluster of timber halfway between town and this ranch. The body'd been there about a day. The feller's neck was broken."

She shook her head and kept her eyelids from fluttering. What a good thing she hadn't given in to her first inclination, which had been to put a bullet into the man even though he was already dead. Otherwise, Ford would probably be arresting her about now.

"Do they know who he is?" she asked. "Is it anyone local?"

"Sheriff says he's a stranger that rode into town with Clemson. Clemson says they split up when they left town the other afternoon. He said he thinks you probably killed him?"

"Me? Why on earth would I do that?"

"Just what I asked him. He didn't have a good answer. Anyways, the feller wasn't shot or knifed or beat up any. Schlinger looked around and says it appears to him to be an accident. There was a bad storm that day. Lots of thunder and lightning. The sheriff figures the man's horse spooked and he got bucked off. I figure he was right, only nobody knows what the dumb bas...fool was doing in the woods during a thunderstorm. Worst place in the world to take shelter."

This time, she did manage a one-shoulder shrug. "I'm sure I couldn't tell you." Only she didn't mean couldn't.

She meant wouldn't.

To her relief, Ford let the matter drop. He, it turned out, had a different matter of discussion, the reason he'd gone to Spokane. But first he went to the door to check on Johnny's whereabouts. The kid, he reported, was still hard at work in the barn. Refilling their coffee cups, he sat down again.

"Last spring, Shay and I had us some good palavers." He stirred a spoonful of sugar into his coffee in an absent-minded way, reminding January she'd never seen him take sugar before.

In the spring. How January longed to turn the time back, even if it meant reliving those harrowing events. "Palavers about what?"

Ford studied her for the moment it took to still the tremble of her lips and the wobble of her chin. "Shay told me that when he got the loan to buy this property, he'd already heard things about the way Albert Sims did . . . does . . . business. So he took an extra precaution. He had his paperwork copied and notarized and stored the copy in a lock box at the Spokane and Eastern Trust Co. bank in Spokane. Dunno if you know this, but banks have to keep records of who goes in and out of the vault where the lock boxes are kept. To get in, you've got to have identification, a key, and a bank official with another key to open it up. "

January's eyes widened in surprise. "He told me about copies filed at the courthouse, but not about this."

"Yeah, well, I expect he forgot after things quieted down. He told me because he thought he might be killed and he wanted somebody to know." He looked away. "It's one of the reasons I'm here. I wanted to be sure the papers were still there and that you knew about them."

Reaching to her injured side, January winced. "Had Shay given you a key?"

"No. His key was here. In the barn in an old tobacco tin that mostly held some nuts and bolts. He'd told me where to find it, in the spring. I wasn't sure it'd still be there. But it was, so I went to Spokane and checked with the bank."

She swallowed around a lump in her throat. Hadn't Shay trusted her? After a moment, she found her voice. "And are the documents in the deposit box?"

"Yes. You won't have to worry about losing this place to Albert Sims anymore. And, according to the bank records, no one has opened the vault since it was rented, with the rent paid on time every year."

All good, she supposed. But not, January thought, running light fingers over the bandage on her side, that a sheaf of papers would do her any good if she were dead. Because somehow, unlike what Ford appeared to think, for all Shay's precautions with the property, she didn't believe this was over. With Brin poisoned, Pen hurt, and the attacks on herself, the situation smacked more of revenge than simple greed. And since they hadn't succeeded in killing her—yet—they had no reason to quit.

To FORD'S MIND, the way to put a stop to a situation that threatened to become a war was to prove the ownership of Shay's property once and for all. Place the paperwork in the hands of a good lawyer and let him take care of it. Once completed, Sims, the Hammel widow, or anyone else would play hell making any sort of claim. There'd be no justification for persecuting January, and if they tried, they'd be arrested. Simple as that, to his lawman's instincts.

When he woke from his nap and found January gone to town without rousing him, he went out to the barn and had a look around. He found the tobacco tin Shay had pointed out on a shelf and opened it. Dumping out the contents, he found the small brass key mixed in with the nuts and bolts, just like Shay had said.

He almost waited for January to return and make the trip to Spokane with him. Then he thought, no, she wouldn't want to leave the ranch unattended for that long. Judging this an affair where time counted, within minutes he swung onto the roan and made tracks for the railway station. The train to Spokane left at noon.

He didn't regret the decision, as by the time he reached his destination and wrangled his way in to a certain Mr. Llewelyn, a lawyer the marshal service had previously employed, into accompanying him to the bank, closing time had come and gone.

"The morning will do as well," Llewelyn said cheerily. "In the meantime, how about a drink? I have some fine brandy, here, and man, you look like you could use it. A tonic, if you will."

What could Ford do but agree? And the brandy was fine, no arguing that. And if he thought once or twice about January as he lay on a lumpy bed and listened to the big city commotion going on in the town streets, if she'd been in the next room, well— Yeah. Better she remained at home.

The next morning promptly at 9 a.m., he and Llewelyn

met outside the Spokane and Eastern Trust Co. and walked through the door into the quiet, serene lobby, all marble and carved oak. Ford wasn't much surprised to learn they knew Llewelyn here. To retrieve the papers took only moments. Affidavits and copies made to verify custody of the documents took more minutes, but when settled, Llewelyn was ready to present the articles to the judge.

"Don't worry." He patted Ford on the back. "Your widow lady is good as gold. I'll let you know before the week is out."

All very well, Ford thought wryly, as long as somebody didn't kill her meanwhile.

A prophecy that almost came true. He didn't think he'd ever felt such rage as when he found her lying in a puddle of her own blood.

CHAPTER 13

EVERY SMALL MOVEMENT PULLED AT JANUARY'S STITCHES. And when they pulled, they hurt like . . . well, to be blunt, like Hades. Even so, within a couple days, she moved more assuredly, that is to say, without letting on how much it cost her. She didn't think she'd try heaving a saddle onto Hoot's back any time soon, or even onto the smaller Molly. Wisely, she left it up to Ford to take a break from nursing her and to ride into town, talk with the sheriff, and seek out the latest news.

Sometimes she wondered if Albert Sims would even get his hands slapped. Probably not if, as she suspected, Judge Keane was in on Sims' loan swindle.

As for Pen, the dog only limped now when somebody looked at her. Who'd ever thought the old girl could be such a canine actress. There didn't seem to be a thing wrong with her other senses and she stayed close to January. In protective mode, January thought, scratching her friend behind the ears.

That's why, on the third night after Clemson's failed attempt to kill her, not an hour after she'd gone to bed, Pen's cold wet nose in January's ear served as an alert. At first, upon hearing the soft footfall of someone moving in the outer room, she thought it must be Ford, returning late from town.

Pen didn't agree. The old dog lumbered to her feet, a low growl menacing in the dark room.

"Shh." January, ignoring the twinge in her side and moving slowly so the bed wouldn't creak, swung her legs over the side. Given Pen's reaction, someone had entered the house. Someone *not* a familiar friend.

As always in this last month since Shay's murder, her dad's .38 Colt revolver sat on a bedside table. She picked it up and stood, one hand on Pen's head.

The dog quivered.

"Shh," January breathed again.

Outside her bedroom, she heard the telltale sound of someone brushing against the chair that come bedtime, she'd scooted over to block the way into the room.

It could still, she tried to assure herself, be Ford coming in from a late-lasting spree. But she didn't think so. Neither did Pen.

Looking around the room for a place to conceal herself, she noticed that when she'd gotten up, she'd flung the blankets in a heap. A pillow lay in the bed, looking much like the body of a person.

An idea formed. "Hah, a ruse." Leading Pen by the scruff of her neck, they moved to the door, taking a position where they'd be behind it if ... when ... it opened.

Footsteps, light and slow, but sure, as if not worried about noise, came ever nearer, stopping just outside. Most certainly not a tread belonging to a man. The chair got set aside.

Then silence. Time passed with a silent listener, one on each side of the wall.

A full minute before the door creaked and began inching open. Under January's stilling hand, Pen's muscles tensed. So did January's.

At the edge of the door, metal gleamed. The barrel of a small pistol pointed into the depths of the room. Clutched in a pale hand, the pistol barrel aimed toward the bed, where it appeared someone lay sleeping.

Come on. One more step.

January willed the person act on the ruse, to take that one more step. She'd slam the door, then, knocking the gun from the hand holding it, and capture whoever this turned out to be. She had a gun, she had Pen. They could do it.

The plan almost worked.

Would've, if an over-eager Pen hadn't gotten in the way. The dog's lunge got in the way of January from slamming the door. It slammed into Pen instead, which caused a gawdawful squeal.

Instead of the hand holding the gun, the door glanced off the pistol barrel. The shooter's aim got shoved off kilter of the intended trajectory. As a result, instead of hitting the bed, the bullet went up and plowed a hole in the bedroom ceiling. And there was no sound of the gun hitting the floor afterward, but just a muffled shriek, a gasp, and the click of the revolver chambering a fresh cartridge.

Pen leapt for the person, the wolf-like sounds issuing from her throat enough to strike fear in January's heart, let alone the person attacked.

A louder shriek echoed in the room. Pen's full weight slammed into the person—the woman—January knew that much for certain, at about thigh-high. The woman went down on one knee with the dog's teeth clamped on a black-clad arm. Pen shook the arm like a dead rat until the gun fell to the floor and slid across the room.

"Hold, Pen," January cried as, recovering from the spasm of pain her lunge against the door had caused, she stepped forward to take control of the situation.

But the girl, January could see enough of the intruder to get a sense of youth, caught Pen in the chest with the toe of her boot. The dog, willing, though still sore from the glass episode, cried out and eased her grip on the girl's arm. In instantaneous reaction, the girl flung the dog off and took to her heels, as lithe and swift as a big cat, knocking January aside as she ran.

She'd left the front door open when she sneaked in. Dashing through it she ran, oddly enough, straight toward the barn.

January shaking with reaction, worried again for her dog, tried to run after her but found herself hurting and so weak she could barely move. Even so, seeing the person silhouetted against the night, she fired a shot into the ground behind those flying feet.

The girl shrieked again, pitched high as a hunting hawk.

The barn door slammed open and Johnny Johnson burst through. He wore pale colored long-johns, a gleam of white against the dark, and bore a shotgun in his hand. The runner, looking back toward January as though checking for pursuit, didn't see him until it was too late. They crashed together, Johnny, knocked to the side and grunting, and the girl stumbling and uttering that ear-aching cry again.

"Hey!" Johnny sputtered, jerking his shotgun, which the girl had grabbed onto as they collided, out of her grasp. He wasn't real gentle about it, either.

While he stood gobsmacked, she fled on, dashing out of sight around the corner of the barn and disappearing into the orchard. Johnny ran after her, three steps, four, then stopped.

"Miss January?" Johnny called, twisting sideways to her and starting to back off. "You all right? You ain't shot again, are you?"

"No, I'm fine." A lie. "But what about you?"

"Take more than her to do me damage," he said. His actions spoke otherwise. In fact, his odd behavior puzzled her, until she figured out his attire, or lack thereof, and bare feet must've been the reason.

She took pity. "Get dressed. We need to make sure she's gone."

Johnny waved the shotgun over his head and went back to the barn, relief in every step.

A quarter hour later, with the house lit up and Johnny safely clad in his rather grubby working clothes, they met in the kitchen. January had flung a robe over her nightdress, although she'd pulled on her boots, leery of more ground glass, to check the floors before turning Pen loose.

The dog, with the action safely over, lay on her rug, gnawing on the ham bone January had been saving for the bean pot. A well-earned reward for valor.

"I checked around the barn and into the orchard. Saw where she'd tied her horse. She's gone." Johnny slumped onto a chair, his blue eyes reddened as though he'd fought back tears.

"Good." January stared at him. "Johnny, what's wrong? Are you hurt? The animals are all right, aren't they? Your Brown Boy? She didn't get to them? Put out poison where they could get at it?"

He shook his head, the picture of dejection. "Not that I know of."

"Then what's the matter?" She pondered, then her eyes narrowed. "Ah. You saw her clearly when she ran into you, right? You know who she is. And you don't want to say."

A dip of his head, one that stopped short of a nod, and the way he avoided her eyes, indicated she'd guessed right. "Johnny, I don't think that's anything you can keep to yourself. Shall I make guess?"

He looked up at her.

"It was one of the Hammel girls, wasn't it? I don't know their names."

Straightening his slumped shoulders, he sighed. "Melissa. I went to school with her, up until a couple years ago." He shrugged. "She was always pretty proud."

January frowned. "Proud of what?"

"Of being Melissa Hammel."

"Huh." January snorted forcefully enough to make her stitches pull. "Well, your old friend tried to kill me tonight. And I suspect she murdered my husband. Her or her mother."

"You killed her father. I reckon she's trying to get even."

Was he defending her? January wondered, her anger sparking. "Her father was doing his best to kill me at the time. That's after her brother tried several times to kill Shay, and almost succeeded then. So don't expect me to feel real sympathetic toward her. I don't."

"No, ma'am, I don't expect you do. I don't either. It's just that . . . she's someone I know. Used to know, I mean. It's hard to think someone like that, a girl, is a killer. But don't think she was ever my friend. I ain't good enough for the likes of her."

"She's not good enough for you, John Johnson, and don't you forget it." She hesitated. "Well, I've got her gun, although I suppose she can get another in a matter of minutes. And there's a bullet in my ceiling that I hope the sheriff can match to the one that killed Shay. I hope she goes to prison and stays there until she's a hundred years old."

Johnny cast a startled, sideways look at her. "Ma'am?"

Her voice grew louder, if more tremulous. "And where the devil is Ford Tervo? He should've been back from town by now. Who knows but what he's lying dead out there along the road somewhere, ambushed like Shay." She paced a quick, if limping turn around the kitchen before stopping at the sink and pumping an overflowing glass of water. "Get some rest, Johnny. First thing in the morning, you saddle up and head into town. If you don't find Ford's body, that's good, but we'd best inform the sheriff about what happened here tonight."

Johnny got up from the table. "Yes, ma'am. Don't figure to sleep much, though."

"No. Neither do I." She forced a smile at him.

He did seem weary. Tired of her troubles, January thought, and probably wishing he could get back to his steady, if unexciting job with Bo Cobb. She couldn't bring herself to blame him.

But the night wasn't done with her.

Sometime during the hours between the Hammel girl's attack and morning, January startled out a restless sleep. If she hadn't known better, she would've thought someone had fired up the threshing machine, still sitting out in the field where the oats had been. Certainly, what she heard sounded like a machine.

Turning her head toward the window, open a little for the fresh, if cool night air, she listened harder.

No, not the thresher, but definitely the *phfutt, phfutt* of a gasoline engine.

She sat up, wincing at the pain. Who could that be? She'd never seen, or even heard of a motorized vehicle driven out so far from town. Not at night, at least. Breakdowns with the few automobiles were too common for most folks to risk being stuck on roads more suited to horse and buggy.

Muscles tense, she waited, expecting something to happen. But the motor came no nearer, idling in that one place for a good five minutes. No shots were fired. No cattle bawled or horses whinnied. On the rug beside the bed, Pen slept soundly.

After a while, January drifted off again, and when she jerked herself out of near sleep a few minutes later, the night was still, the vehicle gone.

In the morning, her first thought was that it had been a dream. The vehicle, she meant, not the visit from Melissa Hammel. If she needed a reminder, the bullet hole in her ceiling, revealed the moment she opened her eyes, served quite well. As did the ivory-handled .32 revolver sitting on the table when she got to the kitchen.

Johnny, as it turned out when he came in for breakfast, may have thought he wouldn't sleep, but evidently he had. Soundly, too.

"No, ma'am, I didn't hear a motor running." He dropped an oversize smear of blackberry jam onto a rewarmed biscuit. "Are you sure that's what it was? Maybe it was the creek. It could've come up during the night, what with all the rain."

One of January's fine feathery eyebrows lifted. "I know the sound of a creek when I hear one, Johnny. Whether it's a trickle or a flood."

Johnny subsided. "Yes, ma'am. I suppose so." A frown wrinkled his brow. "Who do you know has an auto? And why would one be way out here, where there ain't a road fit for it? In the middle of the night, no less?"

Oh, she knew of a few, all right—heard of them anyway—but she didn't want to name the suspect first. Either of the suspects. "T.T. Thurston has a truck," she said. "And that lawyer from Colville. There are several in Spokane from what I hear."

From the look Johnny gave her, he knew she was avoiding the issue. "I know Hammel had one. A fancy Pierce-Stanhope. But I ain't seen it since he . . . died. Could be his widow sold it."

She nodded. "Albert Sims has one too, or so I hear."

"I wonder," Johnny said, a faraway look in his eyes, "if you can track one of them like you can a horse. Find it's home barn."

January's pulse made a little jump. "What a good idea!" She took a quick turn around the kitchen, waving a spatula. Pen, having smelled the food and anticipating the bites Johnny was prone to sneak to her, sat at his knee and turned her head to follow the motion. "If only I weren't so . . . oh, shoot, Johnny. Maybe you'd better see if you can trail the car instead of reporting to Schlinger.

Saddle Molly for me and I'll get to town."

"Doc said you wasn't to exert yourself. It's only been three days."

"Really, I'm fine and dandy. Good enough not to bleed. Unless somebody shoots me again, but I doubt they'd expect to see me riding to town."

"You better stay to home. I'll go to town after I trail the car as far as I can."

Tickled by the way the boy took charge, January had to agree. In truth, fine and dandy didn't exactly describe her condition.

A while later she waved him off on his self-imposed task, and began her morning chores. Thankful Johnny had milked the cow and separated the cream before he left, she began the slow, admittedly onerous task of churning butter and boiling water to clean the equipment. Tending the chickens was the easy part, fussing along with the hens as she gathered eggs from their nests.

Loitering there is why she had the perfect spot from which to observe her next visitor without him knowing.

Pen had warned her, of course, with a low rumble and the bristle of hair rising on her back.

Even so, when January went to the chicken coop's low doorway and peered out, she was hoping—no—expecting to see Ford Tervo. Or maybe Bo Cobb, come to check whether Rand and Johnny had gotten the harvest taken care of before the rain. She would even have been glad to see Sheriff Schlinger, come to think of it.

She didn't recognize the person riding a medicine hat pinto down the trail from the road. But she did recognize the horse.

She spun back into the building. "Rat scat." Getting a hand on Pen a blink before the dog rushed out to meet the stranger, she hauled the dog back inside. Heaving on the seventy-pound dog hurt like thunder, a grim reminder that she was in no condition to tangle with yet another gunslinger.

"Hush, Pen. Stay." She swung the door half closed, aware of the acrid odor of chicken manure and feathers hovering about.

The dog didn't like being closed up in the coop. January didn't either, but she couldn't leave the building now. Not with the hard-faced stranger riding up to her door and stopping no more than seventy-five feet away.

The pause gave him time to look around, inspecting the place as though deciding if he wanted to buy.

January's heart pumped hard in her chest. She pulled the .38 from under her apron, all too aware of its shortcomings.

The horse was what spooked her, she realized. More than the hard-faced man, and the way his gaze, judging by the tilt of his head, darted about the place. Looking for her? Looking for someone to shoot? Maybe, considering the low-slung gun on his hip. More even than the way he urged the horse forward until it almost had to climb onto the porch, or the way he dismounted and stalked through the front door of her house without bothering about an invitation.

Yes, the horse. The same horse young Edgar Hammel had ridden when he came to kill Shay. A prettily marked black-and-white pinto with black ears over a white face, and a black, heart-shaped spot on his chest. Under different circumstances January would've admired the markings.

The horse had a new rider today. But did he have a new owner?

CHAPTER 14

WHAT IS THAT MAN DOING IN MY HOUSE? The question burned in January's mind. She truly hoped he was a thief. Just a thief.

Regretfully, events from the past spring were still too recent to be dimmed in her memory. The fire that destroyed the barn on her place at Kindred Crossing had been meant to burn her and Shay alive. It would be easy for this man to set the house on fire.

Or he could steal the folding money Shay had tucked in a pigeon-hole of his rolltop desk. Or the money she earned from her cow's butter and the chicken's eggs. Money she hid in the bottom drawer of the coffee grinder. Neither would take that much of a search to find.

Likewise, he could simply go on a round of destroying everything. Rip and tear and vandalize until all the things Shay'd had from his parents, and everything they'd collected in their time together were beyond repair.

She couldn't let it happen. And she couldn't bear to wait, hidden and afraid. Even so, she dithered. Was she strong enough to do this?

"Heel, Pen," she said, using the dim light to check the
.38 Colt and make certain of a cartridge in the chamber
before stepping from the hen house.

Silent as wraiths, the two of them scurried across the
yard to the porch, pausing briefly as they went past the
pinto and then, footsteps almost soundless, climbed the
steps. They reached the doorway where January stopped,
nerving herself to enter.

From inside, she heard a snort, a chuckle, and the
thump as something heavy hit the floor, then the distinctive sound of fabric ripping. Next came the smack
of the desk's tambour slamming down and the crash of
glass breaking. What was it? The elegant glass ashtray
Shay'd picked up one day in Spokane? Or perhaps the
recently filled inkwell, part of the desk set? No time to
worry about any of that now.

Footsteps, the thud of boot-heels against plank floor
firm and loud, signaled the man's approach. Even they
sounded angry, as though perhaps he hadn't found what
he'd been looking for.

Pulling Pen with her, January pressed her back against
the side of the house. The man, medium tall and thin
for his height, had his head down counting the wad of
money in his hand as he left the house. The gun barrel
shoved hard against his spine, along with a large black
dog snarling at him with sharp white teeth exposed,
came as a distinct surprise.

"What the hell?" His hands shot up, the bills still
clutched in his fist.

A pistol rode his right hip, the grip turned outward.
Which meant, unless he practiced contortionism, his gun

hand was already occupied...with money stolen from her.

Seeing the extra pistol shoved in his belt at his back, January smiled grimly. The same pistol that the girl had dropped the other night. Could it be the reason he was here, to make sure the damning proof didn't get into the sheriff's hands? Likely the money he held was just an extra piece of luck.

Luck for her. She hoped. She ripped the pistol from his belt, letting it fall to the porch floor.

"Drop the money." Her voice low and firm, she felt him tense when he realized her sex. "Don't think I won't shoot you. I'm looking forward to it."

He thought to spin and take her down. She sensed it through the barrel of her gun. Ramming it hard into his spine, she said, "Keep your hands up. Just drop the money."

He breathed in hard, snuffling through his nose. Angry, she bet. And best of all, concentrating on the money. Regretting, no doubt, the loss of his prize.

But slowly, his fingers opened. Bills fluttered down.

She thought later she'd never moved so fast in her life as she did when she snatched his pistol out of the holster and tossed it spinning off the edge of the porch. Then, as his hands automatically started to fall, she jabbed him again.

He howled like a wolf as he turned, batting at the pistol in her hand. But he hadn't counted on Pen.

If he meant his yell to scare off the dog's attack, he thought wrong. The noise infuriated Pen. She snarled and grabbing the descending hand, bit down hard with powerful jaws. The yell turned into a scream as he tried to pull away. A sorry reaction that resulted in Pen's teeth digging in all the deeper.

Pen had him thoroughly stirred up facing her. The man scrambled frantically, kicking at the dog and shredding his hand in the attempt to get loose. January grabbed up the rope she'd taken from the pinto's saddle and snared the loop around his free hand as it swung around. Yanking the loop tight, she jerked his arm backward.

"Drop it, Pen," she said, and as the dog obeyed, grabbed that hand too, blood and all, and corralled it with the other. The whole episode happened so fast even she marveled at the efficiency of it all. But she saved the thinking for later, when she had time.

For now, she kicked the would-be thief in the back of his knee. When he went down, she said, "Move," and yanked on the rope.

He didn't like giving in. Not one bit, but the pressure on his roped hands as she jerked got him moving. Looping the rope over the porch rail she used for leverage, she managed to drag him, fighting as he crawled, close to the post where she tethered him. Not for the first time, she thanked strength acquired from building bridges, erecting stone foundations, and an everyday life of work.

Not once did he stop his yelling, his cursing, not even after he got taken off his feet. Combined with Pen's snarling, barking and lunging around the man, January had no chance to notice the rider who came down the hill, his horse at a flat-out run.

It took the sound of applause reaching over her own heavy panting to bring her out a daze. Sweat dripped into her eyes as she looked up. Where had she dropped her little pocket gun? She couldn't even remember.

But it was just Ford Tervo sitting aboard his horse and

grinning at her. "By damn, Mrs. Billings, I didn't know women could be as strong as you."

"Didn't you?" Straightening, January thought she might faint. The pain in her side, forgotten—or maybe just ignored—while under duress, now made itself known with a vengeance.

"You took that feller down as smooth as if he'd been an eight-week old calf."

Smooth? It hadn't felt smooth. January stroked Pen, who wagged her tail. Her hands, she noticed, were shaking. "I had help."

"That you did. Every lady ought to have a dog as good as your Pen." Ford grinned again as he glanced around, not quite able to hide his worry behind the amiability. "Where's Johnson? Shouldn't he be around somewhere? He hasn't been leaving you alone, has he?"

Backing away from her prisoner, January let herself down into one of the porch rockers. Sitting helped conceal her quivering legs. She didn't think they'd hold her upright for much longer.

"No. Nothing is wrong with Johnny." She thought it over and added, "At least, I don't think so. There's been a whole lot of excitement around here while you've been gone."

If that was an invitation to say where he'd been, it failed to reach its mark. Ford cocked his head. "What kind of excitement?"

"We had another midnight visitor. One who aimed to kill me."

Ford stepped from his horse, all trace of levity gone. "Him?"

"No." Scowling, she glanced at her prisoner. "Not him. Although he probably thinks he missed his chance. This one is just a hired gun who takes orders and pay from a higher-up."

As if that were a signal, the man began straining at his ropes. "You're gonna be sorry about this, woman. I ain't the only one who works for . . . the boss."

January snorted. "The boss." She glared up at Ford. "He means the Hammels. Collectively or just one of the girls I'm not sure yet, but it's probably the whole kit and caboodle of them. Plus Albert Sims."

Ford frowned. "Maybe we should talk where this galoot can't listen in."

Could be he was right, January thought.

"You don't let me go, you'll be sorry," the galoot said.

January didn't bother to answer.

"At least get me to a doctor. That damn dog probably has hydrophobia, tearing into me the way he done. I'm gonna have 'im put down. People can't keep rabid dogs around."

Though exhausted, January heaved herself to her feet. "Oh, shut up. I'm sick of your ignorant voice. Quit while you still can. Any more of your caterwauling and I'll knock you in the head." She meant it too.

His face serious, Ford helped her pick up the money the thief had dropped, him being more able to bend than she. The first time she tried nearly caused a black out, upon which he urged her to sit down. Ignoring the advice, she gathered up the guns. The one she'd taken from the outlaw, a long-barreled Walker Colt, and the smaller one with ivory grips Pen had shaken loose of Melissa Hammel's hand the night before. Finally, after a short search, she found her own pocket revolver sitting on the windowsill nearest the porch door. She didn't even remember putting it there as she hog-tied the man.

Ford started into the house in front of her. He hesitated at the door, blocking the way and barring her entry. "Have you been in here yet?"

She shook her head. "Is it bad?"

"Maybe you'd best not look." His expression told her it was. "I'll clean the place up as soon as I take care of this yahoo."

"Clean it up?" She shuddered. "The inkwell? It was the inkwell, wasn't it? I'm sure I heard it hit the wall."

"Afraid so."

"What else?" Not wanting to look, but unable to stop herself, January pushed him aside. "Oh," she said. "Oh."

Beyond that, she couldn't force words past numb lips. Yes, she'd heard the crash and tinkle of breaking glass, the thud of dropped objects onto the floor, guessed there'd be damage done, but somehow she hadn't expected *this* . . . *this* shambles.

The man had smashed the inkwell, all right. He'd flung it against the wall where blue ink streamed down the wallpaper she and Shay had put up one day. They'd been laughing, she remembered, getting almost as much paste on themselves as on the wallpaper. The effect had turned out pretty anyway, turning their ranch home into something more personal. Something finer. But now Shay's overstuffed armchair had been ripped open by one of his own kitchen knives, the felted horsehair spilling out and mixing with ink that'd pooled on the floor. The cigar stand was overturned and the desk's tambour askew. Glass once again littered the floor, but instead of the powdery stuff spread by the previous visitor, the pieces all came from her broken possessions.

The kitchen area was even worse. The man had gone on a rampage of wanton destruction, emptying containers of food and shelves of dishes. How on earth, she wondered, had he caused all this damage in so little time? Why had he? She walked away, outside, unable to look anymore.

If she hadn't been so angry, January might've cried. Not that crying could ever make one single thing whole again.

"Want me to shoot him for you?" Ford asked, his expression leaving her in no doubt as to whether he meant what he said.

She gave a shiver. "I wish you would. Only you're the law. I don't suppose shooting him would be ethical."

Ford appeared to be thinking. "Only if he tried to escape. Maybe we can arrange it."

Unsure if he was joking, she finally shook her head. "He should be made to say who sent him here for starters. Tell us who his boss is. Not that there's any doubt, considering the horse he's riding."

"The horse?" Ford turned to look at the pinto.

"Don't you remember? It used to be Edgar Hammel's," January explained. "But just for the record, if this fellow is reluctant to talk, perhaps he could be encouraged."

A wicked looking grin broke over Ford's face. "Encouraged how?"

"Fists?" January suggested. "Whips? I've got a quirt in the barn. Or a pistol-whipping might not come amiss. That's if he doesn't listen to reason and tell us what he knows."

The outlaw broke out cursing, foul enough to make a bordello bouncer quake. They pretended not to hear.

"You think that stuff, fists and whips and all will make him talk?" Ford asked over the man's noise.

"One way to find out."

"Although it might be best to make him shut up first and start from scratch. I'm tired of him yowling like a cat with a stepped-on tail." Ford spun on his boot heel. His fist slammed into the outlaw's soft gut.

The outlaw broke off in mid-curse, gasping. He kicked out, aiming for Ford's nether region and Ford hit him again and then again. The outlaw fell back against the ropes tying him to the porch on legs gone rubbery.

"Ordinarily," Ford said to him, panting a little, "I don't hold with beating on a man who can't fight back." His teeth bared. "But with you I'm plenty happy to make an exception."

January, after a first widening of the eyes, steeled her expression. Tried. She had to look away first. Inwardly, her heart beat hard, shocked at Ford's explosive violence. She may have instigated his actions, but hadn't really thought he'd carry through. Or not like this.

A fourth punch had the outlaw fighting for air, bent double and breath rasping in his throat. Ford slapped his face then. Slapped it hard, so that blood dribbled down his chin from smashed and broken lips.

Ford backed away after the last blow.

January eyed him. Self-loathing. That's what she saw in a quick glance, but when he faced the outlaw again he hid it well.

"Enough," she said. "That's enough."

* * *

To Ford's disgust, the outlaw, most likely inured to violence from his stint in prison, never did break. Loosened up some, is all, while Ford surreptitiously held his sore hand behind his back and tried to flex the fingers. He didn't want them stiffening up.

While plenty vocal in berating Pen and January about his dog bit hand, their prisoner had less to say about anything else, including his own name. Ford had to go at that sideways. A simple search of the prisoner's pocket helped with the discovery.

"Orin Miller." Ford held up an envelope, surveying the hired gunman's reaction. "That must be you."

The gunman didn't answer, but the way his eyes shifted said enough. He sat with his back against the porch pillar now, sagging to one side.

"Yeah, must be. Otherwise you wouldn't be carrying this letter around." Ford waved the envelope in front of Miller's face. "See here? Plain as day. Your name and an address in Walla Walla."

Miller grunted.

Ford quirked a half-grin toward January. One she didn't reciprocate. He couldn't blame her. Even though his tactics had gotten some answers, they didn't set well with him anymore than they did with her. "You want to take a guess at what that address is, Mrs. Billings?"

January may have had a hunch, but she left it to Ford to say.

"Walla Walla State Prison. What position do you think he held there? Guard or prisoner?"

"I could guess," she said, finally playing the game, "but maybe the letter will say,"

"That's private." Miller glared. "You got no right to read my mail."

"You had no right to enter my house, destroy my things, and steal my money." January glared right back. "Please do read the letter, Marshal Tervo."

Addressing Ford by his title had the gunman shift like he had an itch. "Marshal?"

"U.S. Deputy Marshal Ford Tervo." Ford gave a waggish bow of his head. He opened the letter and read. The missive being short, it only took a minute or so. "Well, I'll be." He glanced up at January. "It's a job offer. Some well-meaning person wants to give this feller a chance to do right and earn some money. Says there's work for him as soon as he can get here. Doesn't say whether it's honest work or not, but I don't suppose it matters to either of them."

January's eyes sparked, lighting their forest green depths. "Really? And does this well-meaning person have a name?"

Miller writhed against his bonds.

"Why, yes, as a matter of fact. One of your neighbors, if I'm not mistaken."

"Let me guess," she said in a wondering voice. "Not Mrs. Marvin Hammel, by any chance. She is such a do-gooder."

She acted as if she found matching his playacting fun. Maybe, his hope rose, she would get over seeing the beating he'd given Miller. Not exactly ethical, in anyone's judgement, but necessary.

"Got it in one," he said. "And guess who recommended him to her."

"Um, let me see. Not his fellow prisoner, Elroy Rhodes,

by any chance?"

Ford laughed. "Pretty dang smart, aren't you?"

The prisoner rumbled something in his throat, like a volcano getting ready to blow.

He'd have been better off to keep quiet as Ford's expression changed as he turned to Miller. "Watch your mouth. Mrs. Billings doesn't appreciate your foul language, neither do I. All I want to hear is you saying what your job here entailed. Besides destroying this nice house and stealing money from a widow, that is."

Miller stopped his blather then, although January spoke up. "I think his main job was to recover the revolver Melissa Hammel dropped here the other night when she tried to kill me."

Ford's neck crackled as he swung around to gawk at her. "What? She—" He stopped. His brow furrowed. "Isn't the Hammel woman's name Elvira?"

"The apple doesn't fall far from the tree," January said. "Melissa is Marvin and Elvira Hammel's oldest daughter."

"Holy . . . " Ford stopped himself just in time. "You're sure about this?"

"Oh, yes. Johnny and Melissa bumped into each other as she was running away. They went to school together. No mistake."

"Well then, here's all the proof we need. Eyewitnesses and handwritten messages. Mrs. Billings, I believe we've got this problem sewed up."

Shaking his head, Ford turned back to Miller. He might've been smirking a little. Might've? He knew. "You know this little set-to is going to send you back to prison, don't you?"

* * *

WHAT WITH MILLER'S spurs drumming and digging into January's new porch as he renewed his protests, Ford trying to outshout Miller, and Pen barking her displeasure at them both, January considered her options.

Weary beyond belief, she spun and entered the house, slamming the door on all three.

CHAPTER 15

LEFT ALONE AS FORD TENDED TO THE OUTLAW, January stood in the middle of the room, surveying the damage done to her home. Overwhelming her despair, her anger grew with each new discovery. If only she could go to sleep and have all this gone when she awakened.

"Shay?" She breathed his name into the emptiness. "What am I going to do?" She wanted him standing beside her so badly it was like agony. She wanted his arms around her and to hear him saying everything would be all right. That he'd take care of whatever needed done. Urging her to be strong. Smiling and saying they were partners. That they'd be together the rest of their lives.

She'd allowed herself to believe him. Needed to believe him. Thought the dream was coming true.

But it had all been a lie. He'd let himself be shot. Murdered. And left her alone, just as she'd been before she met him.

Her mouthed twisted.

I can't do this. What's the use of trying?

The thought came at her with the force of a bullet.

Ford had spoken of her strength just now, but maybe that was *her* lie. An illusion. She wasn't strong inside herself. Not at all. How she'd been able to haul Miller across the porch at the end of a rope—wounded, no less—puzzled her as much as it evidently did the men. Although physical strength had never been a problem. She'd always been able to create her way around typical female frailties. What held her down now was grief.

She was certain Miller had come for the Hammel girl's gun, stealing whatever he found as he went. But Shay's desk had been also been targeted. Other damage struck her as too methodical to be spur of the moment. Had he been looking for something else, as well?

The papers she'd hidden in the orchard, for instance? Had Sims not given up on his plan to take the Billings ranch? Shay's ranch?

Ford said that was no longer a possibility. She wished somebody would tell Elvira Hammel and Albert Sims.

What was she supposed to do, sit here and let these people come at her from all sides?

No, she decided, fear settling like a stone in the pit of her stomach. Never as long as she lived.

Behind her, a knock sounded, causing her to whip around. A moment later the door opened and Ford stepped inside, allowing a look at where Miller remained tethered to the porch. His own neckerchief had been stuffed in his mouth, finally silencing him, his spurs removed and his feet bound together. Pen lay watching him from a few feet away, her body poised to tear into him at a second's notice.

Miller watched Pen right back.

"How many of them do you think there are?" January asked before Ford could speak.

"How many who?"

"Other men like Miller who've received letters offering gun-for-hire jobs. Did the letter say what she's paying?"

Ford hesitated. "One gunman is too many. Some of their kind balk at killing a woman. The thing is, you being a woman, others might think you'd be easy money. The letter mentions pay of a hundred a month with five hundred dollars for whoever successfully completes the job. The job isn't exactly spelled out in black and white. I expect the applicants were told their mark upon employment. Probably didn't want anything in writing."

January managed a weak chuckle. "Leaves the field wide open, doesn't it?"

"Dunno." Ford eyed her, then grinned. "Three are already taken out. Might narrow down the job hunters down some when they learn their odds aren't as good as they thought."

"That's probably why the Hammel girl has taken on the task herself." January's eyes narrowed, the scar on her cheek suddenly burning red. "But if she thinks to best me, she'd better think again. I am not losing this place. Not to anybody." She thought a moment. "Especially anybody named Hammel."

"Good thinking."

True to his word, Ford pitched in to help January with the clean-up. What could be saved she cleaned and put back in place. What Miller had destroyed had the pieces gathered and disposed of. A few things, she set aside for repair; for instance, Shay's chair, the cigar stand she'd made for him, and the rolltop desk.

Ford even brought Miller in and at gunpoint, forced him to scrub the floors and cupboards with strong lye soap. Miller complained of the way it got in the dog bites and burned his hands.

"It'll take more than lye soap to get your hands clean," January replied, her lip curling.

But nothing, they found, could save the ink stained wallpaper. It would need ripped down, and the floor beneath sanded. Even then, January thought there'd always be a splotch of discoloration to remind her of the invasion.

Angry twice over, she had Ford drag a protesting Miller outside and tie him to the porch rail again, leaving the door open so they could keep an eye on him.

"You should rest, January." Ford caught hold of her elbow, stopping her as she tried to move the heavy desk by herself. "You look like death warmed over."

The banal old phrase failed to settle her. "I *feel* like death warmed over," she said, jerking her arm from his grasp.

Later, Ford's reassurances having failed to soothe her, January's worry over Johnny's long absence grew. She'd nearly paced a hole in the floor before he finally showed up. He rode directly into the barn, tending to Brown Boy before presenting himself at the house.

Giving Miller a goggle-eyed stare and a wide berth, Johnny patted the pinto as he passed. He stepped onto the porch, hailing January while still outside. "Is it safe to come in?" he called.

"Of course." Her short reply sounded testy, and got no better-tempered as her questions tumbled over each other, "Where have you been? We've been waiting *hours* for you. Did you lose the trail?"

"Lose the trail? Me? 'Course not." Johnny doffed his hat and slapped it against his knee. Looking over his shoulder at Miller, he cocked a thumb. "Who is that and why's he tied up?" An observant fellow, the condition of the room soon registered on his brain. He eyed the ruined wallpaper and askew desk tambour with disgust. "Did he do all this?"

"Well, it wasn't a whirlwind."

Casting another sideways look at Miller, Johnny nodded. "Ain't surprised. That's the pinto Eddie Hammel used to ride, ya know. Means this feller came here from the Hammel place."

Her forefinger, held like she wished it were a gun, pointed at Miller. "You hear that? Everybody knows. It's prison again for you, buster."

Miller glared over the top of his gag.

"But why'd he do it?" Johnny asked.

"He came for Melissa's gun," January said. "And whatever else he could find."

"Huh." Johnny took another careful look at the man. "What happened to his hand?"

"Pen happened." Ford answered

Johnny snickered. "Serves him right. She's a good old girl."

Anxious to hear Johnny's news, January brushed their nonsense aside. "Never mind Pen's adventures. What did you find out? Where the motorcar go when it left here? Who does it belong to?"

Johnny, helping himself to coffee and eyeing the cracked and empty cookie jar disconsolately, settled himself for storytelling. "Like I figured, trailing a car is some easier than tracking a horse or a cow. For one thing, you ain't hardly ever gonna see tracks from more than one at a time. Not on this road, anyways. So there ain't no way to mix them up."

January waved for him to continue.

"So me and Brown Boy just followed along easy as pie." Johnny looked toward the kitchen. "Speaking of pie, that feller didn't ruin *all* the food did he? I'm hungry."

"Talk first, then eat," Ford said, sternly enough Johnny didn't argue.

"I don't suppose you've ever been to the Hammel place?" he started.

She shook her head, although Ford nodded.

That's right, she thought. Ford was well acquainted with the Hammel ranch having taken a job as a gunman for Hammel last spring, hiding in plain sight. It'd been part of his work to bring Hammel to justice.

"Well," Johnny said, "the main house sits in a little bowl where it's sheltered on three sides. The fourth side faces the river. I followed them tracks right up to the front of the house where I seen the motorcar sitting."

January gave a start. "Did anybody see you?"

"Nah, not right then. If anybody asked, I figured to tell 'em I was looking for a job."

"Good thinking," Ford said, "since Mrs. Hammel is advertising to hire a certain kind of man. Always best to go in with a plausible story."

"But I'd just crossed over the hill towards home when I met up with Jerry Arnault, one of Hammel's ranch hands from way back. He asked me what I was doing there, so I told him about looking for work."

"What did he say?" January wondered suddenly if all

the Hammel hands were in on Elvira's plans. She soon had an answer.

"He said I shouldn't ought to do that. He said everything's gone to hell these last few months and that he's figuring to quit and try for a job somewhere else. Most of the hands have already left. Jerry says there's been some shady looking characters riding up to the house lately and getting hired, but they're not doing ranch work. He knows bad stuff is going on, and he wants no part of it." His mouth twisted. "I thought to ask him who owned the motor car. Just to be sure, ya know."

Ford sat up. "Yeah? So who does?"

"Mrs. Hammel, that's who."

"She knows how to drive?" Certain she could soon learn if someone would teach her, January felt more than a little envious. She thought she'd like having all that power at her command.

Johnny grinned a little. "Not her. Melissa. She's the one who knows how to drive."

"Ah." January pondered a moment. "I suppose she wanted to come collect her gun last night. I wonder what changed her mind."

"Jerry said her and her sister were both out in the car last night." Brow furrowing, Johnny added, "I don't remember much about Allie. She's younger and from what I remember, nicer." He paused. "But not as pretty. Or as highfalutin."

"Highfalutin?" Ford said.

"Full of herself. Proud. I'll bet it's Allie who talked Melissa out of sneakin' into the house again."

"If so, she apparently didn't stop Melissa, or her mother, from sending Miller this morning." January wasn't ready to credit the second girl yet.

"Well, no. I guess not."

Ford grimaced, then sighed. "I wonder if talking to Mrs. Hammel would do any good. Try to make her see sense."

"Are you volunteering?" January asked.

"Not sure I'm the right one to do it. She's sure to remember me from the trial. And before that, when I supposedly worked for her husband. Schlinger, now. Seems to me this is part of his job."

Johnny's mouth turned down at the suggestion. "But Sheriff Schlinger got shot, too, just like Shay. Just didn't happen to kill him."

Wincing at his bluntness, January looked grim. "In an ambush no doubt planned at that woman's express orders. Johnny, did you see any strangers around the Hammel house?"

"Didn't see anybody but Jerry. Spotted several extra horses in the corral, though. Could've been men in the bunkhouse that I didn't see."

"Could you ask Arnault about the new hires?" Ford asked.

"You mean go back there?" Johnny appeared a little uneasy at the idea.

Ford nodded, but January drew a line here, not wishing to put her young friend in more danger than he was willing to take on. "No. I don't want Johnny put at any more risk. We need to talk to Schlinger before we decide what to do." She drew herself up, the pain in her side flaring as she moved. "Now. Before Mrs. Hammel or Melissa has time to wonder where this character has gotten to." Her thumb indicated Miller, who kept straining at his bond and getting nowhere. Ford was not exactly a novice at restraining prisoners.

Johnny got up too, his young face drawn. "Can't we eat first?"

It was slim pickings, finding food Miller hadn't succeeded in destroying. But he hadn't found the root cellar or the springhouse where January kept milk and butter and eggs, so, with Ford's surprisingly competent help, she found enough to fill the men's empty bellies. As for herself, she had no appetite—her regular state since Shay had been killed.

Over his protests, she and Ford left Johnny, along with Pen, at home to guard the place when it came time to head for town.

January rode Hoot who, with his smooth running walk stepped along fast enough Ford's horse and the pinto with Miller aboard trotted to keep up. The afternoon sun beat down, warm even though autumn drew in with its shorter days. The journey might've been pleasant if not for their destination—and the business when they arrived.

She stopped at the site of Shay's shooting, allowing Ford to draw even with her. "Did you know this is it?"

"It?"

"Where Shay was murdered?"

Hoot danced in place, tossing his head as though he remembered, too.

"Whoa. Easy, Hoot," January said softly.

Ford glanced around, his gaze searching. "Not much to distinguish this spot from any other."

"True. Except for a trail leading to a ranch in the back country. A cluster of tracks showed a buggy had been stopped here. "

"Schlinger investigated, I reckon."

"He did. The tracks indicated the horse and buggy had sat here some length of time. They—somebody—was waiting for him, Ford." Her voice broke. "Other than those tracks, nothing was left that might provide a hint of who shot him."

Reaching over to his prisoner, Ford ripped the gag from Miller's mouth. "I don't suppose you know anything about this."

Miller swallowed convulsively, trying for spit to moisten his vocal cords. "I don't know nothing about nothing."

"I believe him." The affirmation was drawn from January. "According to the postmark on his letter, it happened several days before he got here."

"Doesn't mean he hasn't heard about it."

"Well, I ain't," Miller said.

Swallowing hard, January urged Hoot into motion. Only when they reached town and drew up in front of the sheriff's office did something in her relax. She hadn't been sure they'd travel safely this far.

Ford dismounted, going over the help January whose white face had grown pinched with pain. A hail stopped him as he lifted his arms to receive her.

It came from Sheriff Schlinger, who pushed out through the open door of the Barefoot Saloon.

"Who you got there?" Schlinger, striding toward them, raised his voice to carry across the street.

"A guest for your boarding house," Ford called back.

Leaning above him, January made a huffing sound. "Fun and games," she said, but somehow, she doubted her own words.

CHAPTER 16

DODGING A KICK, Ford pulled Miller from the saddle and manhandled him into the jail, the prisoner protesting all the way. January, after a moment's thought, took the pinto around back where he'd be off the street. She had a notion the fewer people saw them, and the horses, the better off they'd be. She judged it best if Mrs. Hammel or Albert Sims didn't learn too soon their emissary had been thwarted.

Ford shoved Miller into a chair and stood behind him.

"What's this one done?" Schlinger asked, eyeing the prisoner with a dyspeptic expression.

Leaving the explanation to Ford, January claimed the other chair, sinking down and focusing on what he said and what he didn't say.

Schlinger shook his head in a befuddled sort of way. "But what was he after? Did he just wander in, looking for whatever was laying around?"

"Hardly." January took up the story for herself. "Although he did that too. Take whatever he could find, I mean. And when he didn't find everything he'd been sent for, he destroyed the rest."

The sheriff ignored the crux of the tale. "You aren't real smart, are you?" He studied Miller. "How long have you been out of prison? Three days? And here you are again, about to head right back behind bars. What got into you, tearing up this lady's house?"

Miller hung his head.

Schlinger bent over his logbook, laboriously documenting Miller's name and list of offenses for the record.

January, her side on fire and aching with weariness, wished he'd write a little faster. A whole lot faster, truth be told.

Giving her a glance, Schlinger sat back and handed her the pillow he'd used when he'd been laid up. "Getting shot ain't no fun."

"You don't have to tell me." With a short gasp, she tucked the pillow between her and the chair back. "Thanks. It helps."

"I know." The sheriff grimaced. "Not that I'm admitting it to Rebecca."

But then they went on to more serious things, starting with the first attempt on her life.

Schlinger's face grew stern, closed. He seemed to find the blank spaces on his desk of particular interest.

January had expected questions. Lots of questions. The sheriff didn't ask any of them. Not until she told of Miller breaking into her house, the destruction, and most of all, what he'd been looking for and at whose instigation.

For the most part, Miller remained silent. So did Ford who, withdrawing from the discussion, took on the role of an observer. January couldn't help being surprised at them both, frowning as she finished her report, including Johnny's news.

Shooting a quick glance at Ford, the sheriff shifted in his seat. "I'll have to talk to Johnson myself. Secondhand information don't work."

"When?" January question sounded more like a demand. "When will you be out. You need to see the damage Miller did to my house, as well."

"Yeah." Schlinger shifted in his chair. "Probably be a day or two. Got a lot on my plate right now."

She frowned. "And Mrs. Hammel?" Ford had handed over Miller's letter.

"I'll have to talk to her, I suppose. To Mrs. Hammel. This letter seems to bring her into the situation." He didn't appear overjoyed at the prospect.

"And Melissa, as well," January added. "Right now, she's your main target. She's the one who tried to kill me."

Schlinger fumbled with a pencil, rolling it back and forth on his desk with short strokes of his forefinger. He eyed her with what looked like doubt. "Are you sure? It doesn't seem likely."

"Oh, I'm sure, all right.

"But she's just a kid. What? Fifteen? Maybe sixteen at the outside?"

"A kid?" January's scar flamed, remembering herself at sixteen. *She'd* been no kid. "She's apparently old enough to drive a motorcar. She's old enough to sneak into my house and try to kill me." Her hand slammed onto the desktop, making the sheriff's pencil jump. Her voice lowered to a hiss of rage. "And she's old enough to have poisoned a gentle old dog. She most likely murdered my husband. You don't really see her as a child you need to handle with velvet gloves, do you? If so, you're badly mistaken. She's every bit as vicious as her brother was. As her father. And, most likely, her mother."

"Easy, January." Ford's words were quiet, a warning.

"Yeah. Easy, Mrs. Billings. You're talking like a crazy woman. Best you don't fly off the handle. You're making serious accusations against a young girl. What if she's innocent? You could ruin her reputation for life." Schlinger earned himself a disbelieving glare with this proclamation.

"Fly off the handle?" she repeated. "A crazy woman? Seems to me I'm entitled to my anger. I am, after all, the one she just did her best to kill. My husband is dead. And what do you mean, what if she's innocent? She's not innocent. She sneaked into my house with the intention of murdering me and I caught her before she succeeded. That there's a bullet hole in my ceiling instead of in me is thanks to my good dog. What are you going to do about it?" She quivered all over, the remembered event renewing the tension. Why was Schlinger trying to avoid placing blame on the girl? She knew what the girl had done. What did she have to do, die before the sheriff took action? If even that stirred him to respond?

A rime of sweat beaded Schlinger's forehead. "None of these accusations are proved."

Miller's sudden pained yip drew January's gaze. Ford, she saw, had his fingers digging into the man's shoulders with an eagle claw grip.

"Not proved?" Her eyes went back to Schlinger and her voice went up a full octave. "My God! I was face-to-face with her. Johnny Johnson saw her. I have her gun, taken from her very hand. How can you say it's not proved?"

Schlinger's face had turned so bright a crimson he

seemed to glow. "The thing is, Mrs. Billings, you appear to have your own axe to grind."

"My own axe, you say?" Her teeth ground together. "What do you mean?"

"Mrs. Hammel came into the office this morning, early. She tells me you've started a vendetta against her. Against her girls. Says you're making up stories—lies. And I—" Pausing, he took a breath. "And I can't take sides. I've got to listen to both of you."

January started to shoot to her feet, her action turning into something more like a stumble, but she hurled the pillow at Schlinger with good force. She wished it had been a brick.

"You know that's not true. The vendetta, if that's what you call it, is coming from her and Albert Sims. For God's sake! They just tried to steal Shay's ranch out from under him . . . from under me. You know it as well as I do. You were there. And one of those people," her voice sank to a whisper, "murdered Shay. Somebody who seems to have gotten away with it."

Schlinger flinched.

After a while, when he didn't say anything, January said, "Tell me, Sheriff Schlinger, what am I to think?"

"I got shot," the sheriff said at last.

"So what? So did I. You had weeks before that, when apparently nothing was done. I thought you were trying. But now? I'm not so sure. Your attitude is a complete turn-around from only a few days ago. I'm entitled to an explanation."

Ford abandoned his stance behind Miller to take up one behind her. "Shh," he said in her ear. "January, don't say another thing."

She shook him off, her lip curling. "I always heard you were a stand-up sort of man, Hank Schlinger. Shay told me you were. He voted for you when Rhodes got booted out. So what is it? Did that gunshot wound cause your spine to melt?"

The sheriff stood then, hands clenched on the edge of the desk. His face flamed. "Get out of here before I throw you in jail right alongside Miller. In fact," his eyes narrowed, "maybe I'll just turn him loose right now. I've only your word to say he did anything."

January seemed not to have heard him. "And meanwhile, Shay's killer goes free. I won't stand for it, Mister Schlinger, you hear me? I won't."

Her departure, Ford told her later, was dramatic as anything he'd ever seen in a theater, worthy of any high-toned stage-worthy actress. Maybe even Sarah Bernhardt.

Sarah Bernhardt? January hardly knew what to make of that.

Just as Ford, judging by his frown, didn't know what to think when January, instead of leaving the pinto hitched outside the jail, grabbed the reins and led him off behind her.

"What are you going to do with that horse?" He nudged his roan to catch up.

The corner of her mouth twitched, moving the S shaped scar with the motion. "Use him as a calling card," she said.

Eyes followed them as they rode out of town. January felt their weight, gauging, judging. Some friendly, some, perhaps not. Tongues would soon wag.

And then she'd see.

* * *

FORD WAITED UNTIL they'd left the town limits behind before he placed his hand over January's, forcing her to pull Hoot—and the pinto—to a stop. "What are you doing, January? Besides making an enemy of the sheriff."

"I told you." She jerked her hand from under his, wincing as she did so. Ford knew the pinto, unaccustomed to being led, had been tugging and trying to get away. It put a terrific strain on her wounded side.

"Anyway, what does it look like?" She sounded snappy, almost like the first time he'd met her.

"I don't mean about the horse. Not entirely. Although I wouldn't be surprised if you taking the horse could be construed as horse stealing." His mouth curled up on the corners before he could stop it.

"Could it? I, on the other hand, see the acquisition of this horse as compensation paid for damages incurred during the commission of a felony."

"There is that," he agreed, amused at her stiff, lawyer-like language. "Although I'm not sure Schlinger or Mrs. Hammel will agree."

She turned to him, her scarred cheek burning again. "Well, that's the point, isn't it? Maybe now she'll come out in the open where everyone can see what she's done. What she's doing. Her and Sims. And now I wonder about Schlinger."

"You sure this is what you want? Schlinger may be trying to remain neutral. He doesn't want to appear to take a side, something that could compromise a prosecution. Isn't that what Rhodes did? Take sides?"

January's mouth tightened. "I need to know who Schlinger is working for. Is it Elvira Hammel or Albert Sims or who, because it sure isn't me. Make it clear, one way or the other."

"He'd better be working for justice," Ford said, low and almost inaudibly.

January didn't appear to hear him as she clucked to Hoot and they started off again. "As for her, everybody knows this pinto belonged to her murderous son. I hope by claiming him she's driven into coming after me again. I'll be ready for her this time. Her or Sims or her daughter or any of those hired guns. Or Schlinger, if it comes to that."

Ford's stomach gave a kind of lurch. "Ready for her?"

January's smile chilled him. "I stocked up on ammunition the other day. Blood has been spilled, Ford. Shay's blood, my blood. Do you think I'm going to hide in my house and wait for one them to kill me? Or take Shay's ranch? Or even for someone, God knows who, to protect me? Well, I'm not. I'm not made that way and I can protect myself. They come at me, they'll meet the business end of my gun. Whatever it takes."

This was the most speechifying he'd ever heard from her. Maybe the most words in total in the time he'd known her, and he couldn't help agreeing. Within limits. Wasn't protecting her why he was here? But now, as he could clearly see, was not the time to try to dissuade her.

He'd asked for time off the marshaling job with the idea of aiding the new widow. Time off granted because of the satisfactory completion of his previous assigned job. From now on he'd have to act as a private citizen in order to help January. Maybe even go beyond the law. His hand went to the badge pinned on his coat. He'd have to take it off for a spell. Maybe forever, as he set aside the duties that came with wearing the six-pointed star.

With a little grunt, he reached over and took the pinto's reins from January. It was a measure of her misery that she let him.

JANUARY, terrified of making a fool of herself if, by chance, she got dizzy and fell off Hoot, viewed the road ahead with jaundiced eyes. Town and the Billings ranch had never seemed so far apart, the trees lining the road like an old-growth forest, as dark and foreboding as in some old fairy tale and no doubt harboring the wolves slavering at her door.

She could only be glad that after his first warning for her to have a care, Ford had said nothing more. A relief. She hadn't the strength to argue, or even to think, holding herself in the saddle by clinging to the horn like some weak city-bred tourist.

Finally they crossed the bridge over Kindred Creek, the water gurgling beneath the horses' hooves. Her bridge. Sometime later the trail to the house came into sight, blurring until everything ahead merged together. Thankfully, Hoot knew the way home. And Ford. She almost forgot him. Her head seemed to weigh like a cannonball, bending first her neck, and then her whole body until the only thing preventing her from lying against Hoot's black and silver mane was the saddle horn. At the bottom of the hill, she opened her eyes when Ford reached out to steady her and struggled to pull herself upright.

The journey ended at last. At the house, she dropped to the ground, leaning against Hoot until she stiffened her knees and got her legs going. The trip to town had exhausted her—unless the fault lay in the battle of words she shared with the sheriff. She passed through the front room barely aware of the destruction Miller had wrought. Once in the bedroom, she collapsed onto the bed. Pen, who'd greeted her with wagging tail and eager panting, trotted at her heels, whining at the uncharacteristic behavior.

January's eyes stayed closed. "I'm all right, Pen. Don't worry. Just tired."

But was she all right? What if Elvira Hammel and her plague of daughters came now, tonight?

She fell asleep before she could answer that question.

JOHNNY WAS in the barn waiting to help with the horses. He took the pinto's reins as Ford brought them all to a halt.

"What happened?" the kid asked, staring at the pinto. "Miller didn't get away, did he?"

"Not yet."

"Not yet? What does that mean?" Johnny followed as Ford settled Hoot into a stall. "How come you still got his horse? Edgar Hammel's horse. Why didn't you leave him for the sheriff?"

Ford huffed, unbuckled the cinch and removed his

roan's saddle. "You'd better ask January," he said. "Not now," he added as Johnny turned toward the house. "She's worn out. As to what happened—" He made another of those cryptic huffing sounds.

"Is Miss January all right?" Johnny's anxious question cut through Ford's hesitation. "What's doing with Miller?"

"He's in jail. For now."

"For now? He'll be sent back to prison, won't he?"

"I don't know." Ford picked up a brush and swept it over the roan's back in a long stroke. "Schlinger is acting strange. Like he's doubting January's and my word on what happened out here. He threatened to turn Miller loose."

"Schlinger'd turn that outlaw loose?" Johnny's astonishment showed in a frown so massive as to draw his eyebrows into a single line above his nose. "That don't sound like him. He's always been our friend. Bo Cobb's and Shay's and Bent Langley's. And Miss January's. Don't know what would change that all the sudden."

"Getting shot. Maybe even a bribe."

"A bribe? But—"

"And having January call him on it." Ford started brushing again, the horse's hide twitching with pleasure. "Not the wisest move she's ever made. Made him mad and they got into a standoff. She can tell you about it. But not until tomorrow, when she's rested up some."

If, he thought, she got the chance to rest. Depending on how Schlinger handled Miller's arrest, they might have visitors tonight. Unwelcome visitors. Unwelcome to him, but what about January. Stirring the Hammel woman into further action is what she'd had in mind when she brought the medicine hat pinto back to the ranch.

A teaser. A game of some strange kind of tag.

Beneath his disapproval of her actions, he understood. How could he not?

Shay had often prodded at him for taking too many chances, yammering that it was too dangerous. Like when he went to Hammel last spring and got hired into the enemy camp.

Sometimes he wondered if Shay had really known the woman he'd married. Known that January, while outwardly cool, had depths that could rise up and overwhelm like an ocean wave. As for him, he'd always sensed that in her, from the first time they met and she'd been ready to shoot him.

He smiled, remembering.

CHAPTER 17

A KNOCK ON THE DOOR AS SHE MIXED PANCAKE BATTER THE NEXT
morning startled January. Dropping the spoon she was
using to beat eggs into the bowl, she approached the door
with some trepidation. Her Colt was concealed under the
apron she wore over britches and shirt.

Ford or Johnny would come in the back, so who could
it be? Not, she supposed, that anyone bent on shooting
her would knock first.

She opened the door a crack, then wider. She didn't
recognize the man who stood there, but at first glance he
appeared harmless. "Sir?"

"Ma'am." The man, tall, burly, and with kind blue
eyes, stood twirling his hat round and round by its brim.
"I'm here for my horses."

"For your horses?" she said like a mindless echo.

"I'm DePaul from the County Engineers Corp. I've
got . . . had—" he stumbled over this part "—I made
a deal with Mr. Billings last fall for two trained heavy
work horses, for delivery this October. I am," he repeated,
"here for my horses."

She'd almost forgotten the contract Shay had signed, though he'd bragged a little about it. This then, was the agent at the county roads department, in charge of procuring horses and equipment and keeping the roads open when the snow flew or smoothing ruts created in the spring mud.

Once she learned who he was, January sensed a weight lifting off her shoulders. There'd be money coming in, and at least this fine team would be away to their new home. She hadn't stopped worrying about someone poisoning the stock, just like someone—the Hammel girl, to be precise—had poisoned Brin.

But she felt guilt, too. "My husband is dead," she said.

He nodded. "Yes, ma'am. I know, and I'm sorry as I can be. But I figure the horses are still here and our contract holds."

"Yes, of course. They are. It does. I'm sorry to be so slow. I should've delivered then to you before now. I'm afraid the team hasn't been worked since Shay's murder." She didn't flinch from the word, although DePaul did. "They're apt to be a little unruly."

"S' all right." He smiled. "I've worked with Billings trained horses before. Soon as we get to know each other, we'll be fine."

Beyond the porch, she spotted Ford and Johnny hurrying toward them. As she watched, Johnny split off to go around back, while Ford continued on toward the porch. Not sneaking, but walking softly. Just cautious, looking for a trap, most likely.

Knowing they were both still watching her back made January feel all soft inside. She hadn't realized she'd been worried until Ford came into sight. She'd been afraid after her behavior yesterday he might have left in disgust during the night.

Meeting Ford's questioning gaze, she gave a little nod, one that meant, "All is well." He nodded back.

Ford mounted the porch and it became clear that DePaul, offering his hand and name, took Ford for an employee. Ford said nothing to dissuade him.

January summoned a smile. "Come in, both of you." She held the door wider. "You had an early start this morning, Mr. DePaul. Have you had breakfast?"

His feet stirred. "Coffee and a biscuit. I could eat."

He didn't appear to have missed many meals. "Then it's settled. We'll have a bite, then fetch the horses."

She noted DePaul's start at the sight of the ink-stained wall and broken furniture on the way to the kitchen, but he asked no questions and she didn't volunteer.

The less he knew the better, she thought. Especially after what had happened yesterday with the sheriff. She'd rather put it all out of her mind.

First light had awakened her feeling ragged at the edges, her stomach aware it hadn't eaten since . . . well, she didn't quite remember when. Consequently, the breakfast invitation had more to do with her than just being neighborly. Hunger gnawed her insides, the first time in days she'd felt a desire to eat. And now she'd have Ford and Johnny to cook for, as well as DePaul. For a moment the idea seemed overwhelming.

Lacking her usual energy, she finished mixing the flapjack batter while Ford, at her direction, cut slabs off a ham and got them frying in a skillet. She greased the griddle with bacon renderings and ladled on dollops of batter. Johnny, summoned from guarding the back door, set out butter and syrup.

"Shay called the horses Ladybird and Romulus," she told DePaul as she worked. "I suppose you can change their names, if you like."

DePaul, selecting one of the chairs, sat, careful to keep his feet tucked under the table and out of her way. "Seems to me horses know who they are. Ladybird and Romulus are fine names."

They ate quickly and left the dishes in the pan.

As had become her habit in these last few days, before going out to the pasture where Ladybird and Romulus grazed, January stuffed her pistol into her boot holster and pulled her pants leg down over it. DePaul watched the precaution with questioning eyes, although he said nothing. Shrugging into her coat, as last night had turned cold and the morning was brisk, she invited the county engineer to accompany her out to the pasture.

"I'll ride out and collect the team," she said, seeing that Johnny already had Molly tacked up and ready to go. "You can study their action on the way back. I'm sure you'll be satisfied."

Grinning in anticipation, DePaul nodded.

The draft horses were accustomed to Molly grazing companionably alongside them, while Hoot always tried to give them orders. Best, January felt, to keep the horses calm for the trail. Shay had told her it was no easy task to manage one heavy horse, let alone two, at the end of a lead. Any upset would only quantify the behavior. If they were hitched to a load and being driven, it would be an altogether different matter.

January and Molly passed through the gate Johnny held open and rode toward the horses. Across the way, in the recently harvested oat field, the thresher still sat exposed to the elements. It needed put away, something January put on her mental list. The sun reflected off the machine although the grass was still wet from last night's melted frost. Loosening the rope from her saddle, January held it in hand, ready to catch the horse.

Startling in its abruptness, a flock of geese, up until now peacefully grazing in the pasture alongside the horses, rose up as one and flew overhead. There were maybe a couple hundred of them all squawking loudly, the beat of their wings a thunder in the sky.

She was looking up, trusting Molly to take her where she needed to go, when the sharp crack of a rifle split the air. At the same time, a flock of tree sparrows exploded in a cloud from the cottonwood trees near the river.

Back at the fence, DePaul yelped. She turned just in time to see him slap at his cheek. Ford yelled, "Get down," and tackled the bigger man. Johnny stood like a fence post saying, "What the . . . "

"Hyah. Hyah, git." January screamed too, digging in her heels and driving Molly straight at the draft horses. They were bound to be the next target. First her, she meant, then the horses.

No! Not if I can help it.

Slowly, too slowly for comfort, the horses broke into a ponderous run away from the screeching harridan on Molly's back and headed toward the barn.

Another shot, or maybe it was the third or fourth by now, burned past her, hitting a few feet to Molly's left.

Coming even with Ladybird, she leaned over and slapped the mare on the rump with the rope, urging her to greater speed. The three horses raced.

"Open the gate," January shouted. "Open the damn gate."

Ahead of them, she saw that Ford had snatched the rifle Johnny had taken to carrying from the kid's hands and was scanning for a target. So it was Johnny who, finally urged to action, got the gate open seconds before she and the horses got to it. They thundered through, barely avoiding trampling Johnny in the rush.

Ford opened up with the rifle then, aiming where he judged the shooter hidden.

DePaul lay prone on the ground, wisely keeping his head down. January slipped from Molly's back beside him. Ladybird and Romulus slowed and, of their own accord, disappeared into the barn.

Finally the gunfire died away. Ford because Johnny's rifle ran out of ammunition, and the shooter because—

"I'm taking a look," Ford said. "Don't think I hit him. I think he got away."

He snatched Molly's reins, mounting with a swing of his body and set off at a lope toward the creek.

January tensed hard enough to break muscles, but after a bit, when no more shots were fired, she let go, sagging a little when she stood. "Mr. DePaul, are you all right? Johnny, are you?"

"Think so," Johnny said.

"Who was that?" DePaul, plucking gingerly at his bloody cheek, got to his feet. "What's going on here?"

January's breath came fast, as if she'd been the one running instead of Molly. "Trouble," she said. "Nothing new around here. Someone wants me in the ground alongside my husband."

Shock spread over DePaul's face. "Ma'am?"

Johnny, having taken his rifle from Ford, dug in his pocket for more cartridges. He looked pale, reloading. "Do you think it was Melissa shooting at us?" he asked January.

"Do you?"

He shook his head.

"Melissa?" DePaul's eyebrows rose. "That's a female name."

Neither of them denied the fact.

DePaul's attention narrowed on Ford, following his progress toward the cottonwoods. "Mrs. Billings, if you'd kindly remove this splinter from my face, me and the horses will get on our way. Too dang dangerous around here if you ask me."

January suppressed a rising inclination to break down and bawl. Once started she might never stop. "Yes. Of course. I'm sorry." She took a breath. "Johnny, get some halters on Mr. DePaul's team, please. Mr. DePaul, come with me."

A woman in charge. She should be proud of herself instead of exhausted and, dare she admit it, scared.

Back at the house, she settled DePaul in a chair. Dawdling until her hands stopped shaking, she assembled supplies. Tweezers, a bottle of carbolic acid, from which she splattered a few drops into a bowl of water, and gauze, although she had no idea how to fix it over the man's face.

A face pale around the splinter, she noticed.

"Weren't you afraid?" He turned toward her although she pushed his head back into a position where she could see better.

"Afraid?" She stood above him, her tweezers poised. "Yes, when I think about it now. Not really at the time. Mostly mad. This isn't the first shot anyone has taken at me lately. I guess I'm getting used to it." A lie. Nobody got used to having bullets thrown at them.

DePaul went a little cross-eyed as his gaze followed her hand. "There's a rumor in town you've been shot, one reason I thought I'd better get this horse deal done before . . ." His brow wrinkled and for a moment he looked doubtful. "Sorry. That doesn't sound right."

She huffed out something between a laugh and a hiccup. "Yeah. Before I'm shot dead, like Shay. I'd as soon you got your horses, too. Makes one less thing for me to worry about."

With that, her hand darted downward, the tweezer made a tiny snapping sound, a tug pulled on his cheek, and she moved away. An inch-long splinter was clamped in the implement's teeth, the last half-inch or so showing blood.

DePaul's yip came after the fact. "Ow."

"Got it," she said, and dabbed at the wound, bleeding freely now, with a wad of cloth. "It came away clean."

His check, not one drawn on Albert Sims' bank she was glad to see, finished their business. Standing on the stoop waving DePaul off, January had one last bit of advice. "Stay alert, Mr. DePaul. And please, take good care of those horses."

He was out of sight before Ford got back from his scouting expedition.

* * *

GUIDING MOLLY around the fenced portion of the property, Ford used every bit of available cover. He kept the cluster of cottonwoods—their leaves turned a glory of gold overnight—in his line of sight and saw when the swallows came back. The birds quickly settled and perched among the branches, chittering softly. He figured it meant the shooter had fled. Fled or lay dead in the grass.

He suspected the former. The silence, though good in one way, since he'd as soon not get ambushed, might be bad in another. It would've served them well to discover what kind of opponent they were up against, whether the Hammel girl or yet another hired gun.

He put his money on the hired gun. What gently reared girl was going to lay on her belly hiding in the bushes for hours on end, on the off chance of shooting somebody? Besides, Melissa Hammel was said to be an excellent rifle shot. According to Johnny, at least. He insisted she wouldn't have missed. Not that many times.

But there was a deciding factor. Ford had marked the level where he'd seen the sun glancing off a rifle barrel, and it had been too tall for the girl. He remembered Melissa, if only vaguely, having seen her around the Hammel ranch in the spring. Unless she'd grown most of a foot taller in the last four months, which he doubted, their shooter had been someone else. Someone as tall as Ford himself.

He slowed Molly as he drew near the cottonwoods. Since he hadn't seen a horse, either coming or going, he figured the shooter must have waded the creek—low at this time of year—leaving his mount on the other side.

Dismounting a hundred yards from where the shooter had stood, Ford left Molly and went the rest of the way on foot. It took only moments for him to find the tree the shooter had stood behind. It had an errant branch running parallel to the ground at a height to make a fine rest for a rifle barrel. Footprints pressed into the fallen leaves indicated a six-footer had stood there. Brass casing gleamed in the trampled grass, sunlight glancing off the metal where the rifle's bolt action had ejected it.

No body. No blood.

The shooter had escaped. A few fresh divots in the tree bark showed Ford's returning fire had come close. Just not close enough.

Keeping a sharp eye peeled in case he was being watched, he followed the scuffed ground to the creek bank. Boot prints showed where the man had crossed the stream twice, coming and going. He'd walked on rocks where he could, splashed into the water and mud where he couldn't. It was a narrow, fast running creek, although shallow at this time of year. Once across, Ford found where the man had tethered a horse, keeping him hidden and out of range of gunshots. A pile of fresh horse turds showed he'd been there a while.

The forest started in earnest here. Ford looked around for a while, but found nothing to identify the shooter. The man had gotten away clean.

Ford spat into the brush and rode toward the house.

JANUARY SENT JOHNNY to make a foray out back of the house, checking the orchard and around the farther pasture for any sign of intruders. Shay had separated the mares and foals from the rest of the stock and kept them out there for the summer, but now, she feared they were at risk.

Johnny had protested a little. "Pretty sure Deputy Tervo meant for me to stay here and look after you." He squared his jaw. "In case your wound starts bleeding again, or somebody makes another try at you. He said I shouldn't leave you alone."

"I'll be fine. The wound is fine. Doc sewed the edges together like putting a seam in a pair of britches." Actually, as if yesterday's trip to town hadn't been bad enough, the ride to gather DePaul's horses, then the dash back to the house, had caused the wound to throb with every beat of her heart. Not that she planned on telling Johnny so. Ford, either. She checked her shotgun and sat down in one of the porch rocking chairs, more than happy to get off her feet. "I'm going to sit right here and keep watch in case there's a second attack. The rifle is just inside the door." She forced a smile. "If anybody comes in shooting, you may believe I'll take cover. Me and Pen both."

Pen, lying beside the rocker, thumped her tail on the porch floor.

When Johnny still didn't move, she said, "I'm still the boss here, young sir, regardless of what Ford Tervo may tell you. And I want you to check the back side of this place, paying special attention to the mares."

Grimacing—and was that a scowl on his face?—Johnny finally nodded. "He ain't gonna like it."

"What I do isn't up to Ford. And watch yourself, Johnny Johnson. You hear me? Don't try to fight anybody on your own. If you see anyone or anything that seems out of place, you hightail it back here and tell me. Got it?"

"Yes, ma'am. Got it."

He caught up his Brown Boy horse and went riding off with his mouth in a pout. Clearly, he didn't like it any more than Ford would.

The solitude when he'd gone was like a balm, allowing her to drop the pretense that she was fine. To catch her breath, thaw her frozen muscles, to go ahead and pucker up and cry out loud to Pen, "Ow, ow, ow," on a rising note.

The admission actually helped, like ripping off a bandage and waiting for the shock to fade. Even with Shay, she remembered, it had been difficult to admit any weakness. They'd been married two months before she'd told him the full story of her scarred cheek. Of the pain; the terror; the guilt.

"Guilt? Honey, why would you feel guilt?" Anger had made his voice go deep and catch in his throat. But the anger had not been at her. Never at her.

It was different with Ford. And as far as Johnny went—well, how could she even mention such a thing as pain and fear to a man/boy like him, let alone admit to it?

A single gunshot jerked her out of the rocker.

CHAPTER 18

WHO'D FIRED THE GUN? A rifle, given the echoing report.

Heart hammering as though to escape her chest, January stepped to the edge of the porch. Unsure from which direction the shot had sounded, her head turned toward the orchard of its own accord.

The direction Johnny had taken. *At my bidding.*

Standing on the porch let her see Ford on Molly, racing toward the gate that would let him into the orchard.

So. He was all right, but he'd heard the shot, too. And felt the same alarm.

The gate was there to divide the horse pasture and keep the critters out of the fruit trees. Finding and opening it would slow him down.

She didn't take time for the steps. The jump from the porch jarred her, but she ignored the pain. Calling to Pen, she hurried around the side of the house. They would cut through the orchard from here, shorter than the route Ford had to take on horseback.

She forced herself into a jog, then, holding the shotgun ready, ran. Pen kept pace. After what was probably only a couple minutes but seemed to take hours, she caught a glimpse of Brown Boy through an opening where one of the apple trees had died and been removed. He was trotting riderless, the reins flopping loose, putting him in danger of stumbling over them.

Slowing to a walk, she went toward him. "Whoa, Brown Boy. Good fella. Hold there. Whoa, whoa," she called softly, panting with the effort not to cry out.

Well-trained, at the sound of his name Brown Boy stopped, allowing her to catch up and grab the reins. There was blood on the saddle, splashed hot and bright red in the sunlight. Although a queer buzzing filled her ears, she tugged the horse along with her and kept going.

Don't die, Johnny, don't die. Don't be dead. Don't die. The words resounded in her head like the chorus of a mournful song. Somewhere not far away she heard a horse neigh. Someone, a man called out a word, indistinguishable in the distance. Then the sound faded.

It wasn't Ford, she knew that much. She heard him, with Molly at a dead run, running toward her from the right.

Bringing up the shotgun again, January held it out before her, knowing a moment of regret that it wasn't her carbine. The second she spotted whoever was there, she'd shoot, man, woman, or semi-child.

Hard on the thought, she heard a moan and Pen, ignoring a whispered stay command, darted ahead. A few steps more brought her to the farthest edge of the orchard, where the forest took over. That's where she found Johnny, sprawled like a doll with the stuffing pulled out amidst forest duff, fallen leaves, and dropped, winey-smelling apples. There were pear trees here too, yellow jackets heavily at work in rotting fruit.

Quelling the urge to run to Johnny, she halted, listening, looking, testing her surroundings. Aware of Ford and Molly getting close, she heard nothing now from the other side. She believed the shooter had fled.

Pen, already standing over Johnny, barked with a short, imperative sound.

Keeping a wary lookout, she hurried toward them. Crouching on her knees beside Johnny she touched the side of his neck, feeling for a pulse. Found it at last, faint but there, tripping away at a terrific rate.

He lay face up, the front of his shirt saturated with blood. It took a moment for her to find the wound. A bullet in the chest. Through a lung. She knew that much as she heard the hiss of air. His skin had turned blue and even unconscious, he was gasping.

It reminded her all too much of when Shay had been shot. The first time. The time he *didn't* die.

What should she do? What was the *correct* thing to do?

Rocking back on her heels, she tried to think. She'd heard about someone who'd gotten a piece of shrapnel in a lung. It had been when she and her father lived in Kellogg for a short while and her dad worked in one of the mines. There'd been an explosion in another shaft and he'd been on the rescue team. He'd told her what they did to help the other miner, but— Her mind stuttered. But the man had died three awful weeks later. Infection deep inside his lungs, according to the doctor.

She wouldn't let that happen to Johnny. Absolutely not.

So a bullet had gone in, but had it come out? Grasping him by the shoulders, January attempted to turn him. It didn't work. Johnny wasn't big, but she was still weak from her own wound and she was afraid of hurting him even more.

Then Ford was there, stepping from the saddle as Molly sidled uneasily at the smell of blood. Brown Boy dipped his head and whuffled at Johnny's boots.

"Is he dead?" Ford eyed her, his mouth set.

"Not yet. And he won't be if I have anything to say about it."

"What do you need me to do?"

She knew the way she looked at Ford showed panic. And rage. And determination. She set her teeth. "Turn him over. I need to see if the bullet went through."

Nodding, Ford knelt beside her, taking over the lifting job.

They found an exit wound in Johnny's back. Maybe good, maybe not.

Ford shook his head. "Through and through. We have to get him to the house. No use trying to do anything for him here."

She nodded. When she went to rise, Ford stopped her with a hand on her shoulder. "Wait. He could still be around. Did you see anyone? Hear anyone?"

"He's gone." She scoffed at herself. "As long as he doesn't go around to the other side and come at us again."

"The sooner you're under cover, the better I'll like it. You and Johnson both." He helped her up.

Suiting action to words, Ford helped her onto Brown Boy, then, grunting with the effort, lifted Johnny up in front of her. The boy roused a little at that, muttered something, then slumped again.

January clasped her arms around him.

Ford's eyes narrowed. "Can you hold him? We don't want him to fall. Don't want *you* falling off, either."

"I promise you, neither of us will fall." If she sounded a little grim, well, grim was the word. But she'd do it, hang onto Johnny and not let go.

"I believe you." Ford climbed aboard Molly and, taking Brown Boy's reins, led off. He didn't, she noticed, let up his alert stance for a moment. His head kept a constant turning, doing his best to see all ways at once.

Returning to the house proved an ordeal. January's arms trembled with fatigue as they stopped at the porch, even though it took only a few minutes.

"Can you lift his feet?" Ford stood at Brown Boy's side, taking all of Johnny's weight as the boy collapsed from the horse's back.

"Yes," January said, though not sure. Intent on the job, she stumbled on the steps, causing Johnny to moan at the jolt.

"Careful," Ford said.

"I'm trying. Take him into the bedroom." Somehow, she held on as they got him into the house. She was panting almost as badly as Johnny from the effort.

Ford, at her direction, propped Johnny on the pillows as his breathing, shallow and weak, seemed easier with him more upright. Quickly collecting her scissors from the mending basket, she cut his shirt away, careless of the blood on her blankets. Despair flooded in. How could he possibly survive? How could he have any blood left in him?

The mending basket contained an old flannel nightgown with a torn sleeve. Snipping off the sleeve, she folded it into a pad and pressed it over the wound, then did the same to the exit wound with the other.

Now what?

Swallowing hard, she looked at Ford, aware of his amber eyes on her, dark with concern. "Do you know sage?"

"Sage?"

"A plant," she said impatiently. "It's that sort of fuzzy, dull-green, smelly plant by the end of the porch. I use it in cooking."

He appeared just as bewildered as before. "Yeah?"

"Yes. If you would pick some of the freshest, largest leaves, I would appreciate it."

"What . . ."

"Just do it!" She hadn't meant to shout. "Sorry," she muttered. "Then ride into town and bring Doc. Take Hoot. He's the fastest horse here. Faster than your roan."

His reply was meek. "Yes'm."

"And be careful."

There didn't seem much else she could do except sit with Johnny and hope he knew he wasn't alone. When Ford disappeared over the crest of the hill, January stirred up the fire in the cook stove and boiled a big pot of water. She also boiled the sage leaves long enough to make them pliable and kill any bugs that might linger. After they cooled, she pressed them over the bullet holes. Instantly, Johnny's breath seemed to come a little easier. The color of his skin changed from almost blue to plain white.

She thought it might be an improvement.

* * *

FOUR HOURS, everlasting hours, crept past before Ford, with Doctor LeBret in tow, returned. Hours during which, every fifteen minutes, January renewed the sage leaves she'd used to seal Johnny's wounds in an effort to keep the pressure in his lung constant.

Ford, in an unexpected act of wisdom, called out from the top of the hill leading down from the road. An unintelligible call, as it happened.

Pen heard him first and raised her head from her paws. Getting to her feet, the dog ambled to the door and sat there.

"Is it Ford?" January heard a voice, no, voices, now as well.

The dog didn't seem alarmed. Even so, January, sitting beside Johnny and counting his breaths, picked up the rifle. She joined Pen, who scratched at the door asking to be let out. January only put her weapon down when the men were close enough she could spot Hoot's silvery shine and make out her name as Ford called again.

It was fully dark by now. In an excess of caution, January stood aside from the doorway as she let the men in.

"At last," she breathed. "I was beginning to think you were taking out somebody's appendix, Doc . Or weren't coming."

Doc patted her shoulder as he headed for the bedroom. He'd become familiar with the house's layout by now. Overly familiar, as she'd heard him say.

"Well, you do keep my life exciting, Mrs. Billings. I don't think I've been home for supper more than twice in the last week. I've seen more of you than I have of my wife. As she lets me know whenever we happen to meet up."

He already had his case open and his stethoscope stuck in his ears. "You can go, January. I'll handle this now."

His words were incredibly reassuring.

She found Ford standing by the kitchen stove, pouring

a dollop of Shay's stashed whiskey into a cup of sweet-
ened coffee.

He sighed when he saw her. "Want one?" He held the
cup aloft.

She started to shake her head, then reconsidered. "Please."

When he'd made the drink, they sat at the kitchen
table, fragrant steam rising from the hot liquid.

January breathed the steam, then took a sip. Almost
instantly a burning sensation hit bottom in her stomach.
It felt good. Strange, but good.

"I talked to Sheriff Schlinger," he said, watching for
her reaction. "Reported the shooting. Reported both
shootings. The one from this morning, too. Probably a
good thing. DePaul had been in and told him about it."

She paused in the act of holding the cup to her lips. "And?"

Ford's jaw clamped. "He said he'd be out in the morning to
check on Johnson and look around where the kid was shot."

After a second, or maybe ten, January said, "That's
all? He'd be out sometime tomorrow and take a look?"

"He said it'd be dark before he could get here. Not
much to see in the dark."

January took a big swallow of her toddy. Coughed.
Ford made strong drinks. "But he knew about the shots
around DePaul earlier. And he didn't come then. He's
been bought off, Ford."

Ford, staring thoughtfully into the diminished
contents of his cup, finished it off and got up to make
another round. "We don't know that. We do know this
isn't what he bargained for when he took the job. Some
cattle rustling, some petty theft, quarrels over grass and
water. That's his kind of crime. Straightforward. Little

men doing little dirty deeds."

Doc's voice came from behind them. "Don't blame Hank too much, January. He's still recovering from that gunshot wound himself. From a deliberate ambush, just like Shay. Doubt he figured on pitting himself against murderers. He's a good enough man, just not a brave one."

"If he's afraid, or not up to doing the job, maybe he ought to step down." Not mincing words, January didn't even try to stop how cold she sounded.

Doc responded with something between a chuff and a laugh. "Seems to me that's pretty much what he's done. He just hasn't made it official." Doc looked over at Ford as he pulled up another chair. "I could use one of what you're having."

Ford, as the self-proclaimed bartender, got up to fix Doc's toddy. "Schlinger doesn't have a deputy, does he? Somebody who can take over?" He put whiskey at the bottom of a cup, sprinkled on some sugar, and filled the cup with coffee. He set the cup and a spoon in front of Le Bret.

"There's a part-time older feller," Doc began, only to be stopped by January's scoff.

"Yeah. Name of Dabney. Not any better at the job than Hank, I'm afraid. Pretty much useless." Doc stirred to dissolve the sugar. "Schlinger was the deputy under our now incarcerated LeRoy Rhodes. See, when Rhodes started deputizing whichever of Hammel's men was handy, Schlinger quit. Couldn't stomach Rhodes doing Hammel's dirty work for him. Schlinger just hasn't settled on anybody to fill in for him since the election."

January made a sound deep in her throat and drained her cup. "Hogwash," she said. "We need somebody who'll actually do the job and we need him now."

"How about you taking over, Tervo?" Doc said. "You're already a U.S. Deputy Marshal. You've got the experience."

Grimacing, Ford shook his head. "What you need is a local lawman. This is beyond my jurisdiction here. And I don't want it."

"Nobody wants it." Doc tilted his cup and took a swallow.

"I just want it all over and done with," January said. "I want Shay's murderer caught and punished right alongside whoever shot Johnny. How is he? I should've asked first thing."

Doc's shoulders hunched. "He's lost a lot of blood. I put in a tube to keep pressure in the lung. All we can do is wait and see. Try to keep the wound from infection." He patted January's hand. "You did well, January. The sage leaves were a good idea."

January didn't find his report overwhelmingly reassuring. "Maybe he saw who shot him. An identification might stir Schlinger to action. Meanwhile, I've got the gun I suspect was used to shoot Shay. I've got the horse from the man who tried to kill me. I've got an eyewitness to yet another attempt on my life." Her head turned toward the bedroom and her lips turned down. "As long as he lives to talk about it. I also have proof of a plot to steal this ranch out from under Shay, and there's someone else, a completely impartial witness to yet another shooting. DePaul," she added to Doc, "in case you wondered. I'm not just inventing these things. The evidence is collected. Now somebody needs to go after the criminals."

Unaware, excitement had cut through her weariness. Her voice had risen. Bleary-eyed, she met Ford's amused gaze, and Doc's wondering one.

"What?" she said.

CHAPTER 19

SHERIFF HANK SCHLINGER SHOWED UP AT THE BILLINGS RANCH several hours past the time he'd been expected. To be precise, about the same time January began wondering, worrying over really, if he'd been ambushed along the road.

Not the case, as it turned out. He'd managed to hitch a ride in the Inman sisters' pretty little red-painted buggy. Schlinger rode passenger as Rebecca Inman tooled along at the reins of a brown Morgan gelding. The pair of them were as cheerful as if they were on a pleasure outing.

The cheer struck January as offensive when considering Johnny's present condition. She most certainly didn't see it as the act of a lawman hunting for a killer. Not by a long shot. In her opinion, a buggy ride with his lady friend was far from the proper behavior of a lawman bent on conducting a serious investigation.

On the other hand, she was familiar with Rebecca's tactics when it came to men. Schlinger may not have had much choice.

But if she wasn't impressed with Schlinger's methods, the sheriff seemed equally displeased to see the group gathered on January's porch. His cheer faded at her opening salvo.

"I'm surprised to see you. I thought you must've decided what's happened here beneath your notice." Her expression grim, January gripped the porch post, her knuckles white.

The sheriff flushed a mottled shade of dark pink as he alit.

More angry than embarrassed, she thought, which did not bode well. Beyond caring, she stiffened her spine.

Bent Langley, come to check on his neighbors and staying to hear the latest news, openly listened, his eyes snapping with interest. Ford, alongside Art, Langley's son, perched on the porch rail, while Bo Cobb and Doc, tarrying while making his rounds, occupied the rockers. To a man, their ears perked like a pointy-eared terrier dog.

Ignoring Rebecca after a first hello, January went down the steps and met with Schlinger beside the buggy. A discussion began that grew in volume as she pressed the sheriff regarding what he planned to do about the shooting. Not only Johnny's, but her's, DePaul's close call, and even his own. Every now and then Rebecca made some interjection, which the other two ignored. The sheriff had an excuse for everything.

"I'm short on help," he shouted at last. "I'm doing what I can."

"Then get help," January shouted back.

"Well, I will, when I can find somebody willing to go up against the Hammel money and influence."

So. He finally admitted he knew where the blame fell. The time, she knew, had come.

January's distress at Johnny almost being killed while working for her ran deep. What started out as a neighbor helping the new widow get in a crop had turned into something a whole lot more serious. Intolerable, in fact. And while it may have been unfair, she blamed herself. Other people, she felt certain, would blame her too. Johnny had been shot on her property, in her defense, doing her bidding. Which, as she remembered all too well, he hadn't wanted to do.

She didn't want to take her next step either, but with her neighbors looking on, it appeared, just like Doc and Ford had said last night, she had no choice. A deep breath filled her lungs, but she still felt dizzy.

"All right," she said to Schlinger, holding up a quelling hand. "Enough. You won't take action, so I will. But I want real authority."

"What?" The sheriff stopped his round of excuses and stared at her. *Glared*, rather. "Authority? Authority for what? What are you talking about?"

"I'll be your deputy. I'll take care of these crooks myself."

His mouth dropped open. Shut on silence. Then, "Woman, are you out of your mind?"

"Probably," she said.

Rebecca's eyes grew wide and round. The men on the porch wore matching smirks. Pen padded down the steps to stand beside January and whine.

"No." Sheriff Schlinger looked down at her and shook his head. "Oh, hell no. I won't do it. I'd be laughed out of the county—the whole state—if I did." His face had turned from an odd dusky pink to as red as one the apples hanging on a tree in Shay's orchard. A Wealthy, one of

the most colorful. Shay had told her even its flesh sometimes carried a red tinge, just like Schlinger's did now.

Ignoring the men on the porch who hung on every
word, January struggled to keep her voice even. "I
didn't—I don't—much like the idea either. But more than
what I like and what I don't, I care about keeping this
county safe and preserving this ranch. If you aren't up
to it, I am. When it was Shay and me together, and U.S.
Deputy Marshal Tervo," she made a gesture behind her
at Ford, "we took care of a pack of criminals running
rampant. But, as we're discovering, we missed some
and those have bided their time. Apparently we didn't
cut off the snake's head, only its tail. They succeeded in
murdering my husband and are out to get me, too. They
almost succeeded with Johnny. So now what? Who do
you suppose will be next?"

She stepped back from the Morgan's head. "Well, I
won't stand for it. You shouldn't either."

Five pairs of eyes swiveled toward Schlinger, but Rebecca got in first. "I'm surprised at you, January Billings.
You know Hank is doing the best he can. You aren't the
only one. Hank has been shot, you know."

"I do know. The good Lord knows he repeats it often
enough. He's made it an excuse for sitting on his backside
and doing nothing." January flashed her an aggravated
look. "Which is my point. So has Johnny Johnson been
shot. So has my husband, in case you've forgotten." The
last part came out too loud for a calm woman. "Believe
me, I haven't forgotten. So deputize me and I'll take care
of the problem. I'd rather be legally empowered and have
your backing. If you don't, I'll take care of it anyway, but

I'll make sure everybody in the county knows it's because you won't move on these people."

Schlinger slammed his palm against the buggy, causing it to lurch and the horse to start. He grabbed the Morgan's bridle. "That's a threat."

"Not a threat. The truth, and you know it."

The sheriff looked to the men on the porch for support, but found none.

Bo Cobb spoke up. "Mrs. Billings has the right of it, Schlinger. She has my vote, too. The latest victim in all this works for me. He's a fine young feller who don't deserve getting shot by a killer what's been allowed to run loose. I'm for anybody willing to go after him whoever he is. Or she. Man or woman. Old or young."

Rebecca had her opinion. "Yes, Mr. Cobb, but everybody knows Mrs. Billings has made her mind up on who to blame. What if she's wrong? What if she goes after the wrong person?"

"She's not wrong." The answer resounded like the chorus of a song issuing from five—no—make that six throats.

Because even Schlinger, looking hangdog and unhappy, joined in. He nodded to Rebecca and repeated, "She's not wrong, Rebecca. Mrs. Hammel is the chief instigator, even if she isn't doing this with her own hands. Proving it is something else."

January was seething. "How many times do I have to say it. I have proof. I have a gun, I have a horse, an eyewitness, a note and a letter. What else do you need? Writing on a stone tablet?"

Rebecca, frowning in what January considered a rather unattractive way, said, "I don't understand, Hank. If Elvira is the culprit, why haven't you done something about it?"

"I've been shot." Schlinger pulled the sympathy card out of the deck yet again.

"Oh, pish posh," Rebecca said and effectively slid the card back in.

The deputizing ceremony didn't take long. The oath January took to uphold the law of the county and the state of Washington reminded her in an eerie sort of fashion of the vows she and Shay had taken a few months earlier when they wed. She had a notion the marriage rite was what Schlinger based this one on.

At any rate, she held up her right hand and said "Yes" instead of "I do," and it was done. She became the county's newest and rawest deputy. With five grinning witnesses. Grins that faded all too soon. The situation and the danger, were too real to be taken lightly.

With the I's all dotted and the T's all crossed, Doctor LeBret gave final instructions as to Johnny's care, said he'd see them tomorrow, and followed Rebecca Inman's buggy down the road to town.

"What," young Art Langley asked in the following silence as the billowing dust settled to the ground, "are you going to do first, Mrs. Billings?" Bright-eyed and bushy-tailed, it appeared he was counting on immediate action.

"Arthur," Bent said on a note of warning, but clearly, he, too, wanted to know. Going by his vigorous nod, so did Bo. Only Ford hung back.

January wished she could trade some of the pain and weariness weighing her down for Art's eagerness. She wrapped her arms around her body and pressed her hand against her wounded side as though to hold back the ache. To tell the truth, her stunned mind was having a hard time catching up to what had just happened.

"I've preparations to make today. Tomorrow, first thing—" she thought a moment. "First thing, I'm going to return Edgar Hammel's horse to his mother."

Ford, his already dark face darkening even more, stood up like he'd been poked in the behind. "January!"

"What did you say?" Bo Cobb shouted, although she knew he'd heard.

Art's eyes got big. "You're going over to the Hammel place? By yourself?"

She swallowed. "Yes. By myself."

"You got bal...guts...little lady." Bo removed his hat and bowed his head. "I salute you." The hat went back on. "Think you might be a little crazy though."

Bent wriggled like he had some kind of itch. "You sure about this, Mrs. Billings?"

She nodded. *No.*

"I don't know what Pinky's gonna say." Bent fidgeted more. "Yes, I do. She's gonna say I shoulda stopped you."

"Oh?"

"How you figure to do that, Pa?" Art asked.

Bent narrowed his eyes at her. "Good question, kid," he said after a brief study. "And the answer is, I probably ain't."

Ford chuckled, although it was hard to judge whether the sound was amused or merely an acknowledgement.

Her neighbor was right, January thought. Although an even better question might've been, "How do you figure to get away alive?" The very words going round and around in her head right now. Absently, she polished the badge Schlinger had given her with her shirt sleeve. Most probably she'd learn the answer tomorrow.

✳ ✳ ✳

FORD, although unaccustomed to nursemaid duties, found himself not only tending to Johnny's needs, but also performing the kid's chores. Which included graining Shay's nursing mares, cleaning the barn—especially since they were keeping the saddle horses inside safe and handy—and, as now, chopping wood for the cookstove.

Ruefully, he examined a burst blister on the palm of his hand. He hadn't done labor like this for a long time. He'd grown soft.

Soft like January's skin. The thought spun in from nowhere, and not for the first time.

Inwardly, he gave himself a rap on the noggin. Best he not think of her in that way—as if he could stop himself. He'd thought it as he changed her wound's dressing this morning, silently bemoaning the scar she'd have while she'd sat frozen as a lady-shaped icicle. As if she didn't even feel his hands on her. But she had. He'd felt her skin quiver.

He knew she wouldn't like the scar, raw and puckered. Look how she felt about the one on her face. Oddly enough, he never really saw it anymore. Or didn't pay any attention, anyhow. Shay, he remembered, said it had taken about an hour for him.

That had been when he'd asked Shay about the slightly raised, shiny white S branded into her cheek. Shay told him January had lived through a family tragedy but if he wanted to know more he should ask her himself. It wasn't his, Shay's, story to tell. "But I wouldn't, if I was you," he'd added.

Ford thought he'd take Shay's advice. Little Mrs. January Billings could be plenty scary, with a stare as cold as her name.

His ax slammed into a tough chunk of tamarack with a crack like a rifle shot when it split. A piece flew off, banging into his knee.

Cursing, he straightened and rubbed the smarting appendage. Stupid to let his mind drift. Next thing he knew he'd be chopping off his own foot.

Anyway, Johnson needed more help than January could supply at present, so that left only him. It wouldn't be right, her being so recently widowed, having to help the young hired hand to the toilet. He was pretty sure their easy friendship would suffer under the mortification. On both sides.

He raised the ax for another blow.

"Ford?"

Taken unaware, he missed his aim point, ending up by driving the ax deep into the chopping block.

"You're supposed to be resting." He straightened. "So you'll be strong for tomorrow. You'll need all the strength you can muster."

"I know."

"And alert. You've gotta stay alert. If Mrs. Hammel has hired many hands on Rhodes' advisement, you're apt to need eyes in the back of your head. Mrs. Deputy."

January shrugged. He could tell she'd caught the nuances of his "Mrs. Deputy" comment, even though he hadn't added a thing to it.

"Best choice is to go in wearing a badge, I suppose, but I'd go whether Schlinger had handed it to me or not," she said.

Or whether he liked it or not. Which he didn't, even though it had been his suggestion in the first place. He'd had the night to dwell on the notion and wished he kept his mouth shut. What had he and Doc been thinking?

"Yeah. Schlinger knew that. He might think the badge lends a bit of protection." Ford's brow puckered into a frown strong enough to cause a headache behind his eyes. "Don't you believe it. A badge doesn't do much of anything except pin a target on you. Most particularly around the men Mrs. Hammel will have hired. Each one will have a grudge against the law."

"I figured. But ... " she hesitated.

After a while, when she didn't continue, he said, "But?"

"Is going there, taking the pinto back and speaking to Elvira Hammel smart or stupid?" She was obviously having second thoughts.

"It's brave," Ford replied after a moment. "Or foolhardy. Depending on what happens. Might be both. I'm not sure what you'll gain, except maybe an escalation of animosity."

She made a little sound in her throat. "At least I won't have to feed the horse."

He didn't try to stop his smile, twisted or not. "Truth there."

"Do you think she—or her men—will try to gun me down?"

This is what had him coiled in knots. What made him determined to ride along with her with his own five-pointed badge pinned bright and shiny on the left side of his chest. A target.

"Yes," he said, his heart beating hard.

But whether in the open, where they stood a chance of defending themselves, or from ambush, well, he just didn't know.

* * *

JANUARY'S PLAN, if one could even call what she intended to do 'a plan,' depended on showing up at the Hammel ranch early and catching Elvira Hammel by surprise. Preferably before the hired men Ford warned against were stirring.

Also, judging by what she'd seen of Melissa—mostly at the wrong end of a gun—at a time when the girl was apt to still be abed. Given her penchant for attacking in the middle of the night, it seemed a reasonable premise. If possible, she'd rather avoid Melissa and take on just one Hammel female at a time. Melissa would come second.

Which is why she sat at the kitchen table an hour before daybreak, wrapping a thicker than usual bandage around the wound in her side. The stitches Doc had set looked fine, not inflamed at all. Washing them every day with lots of soap and warm water had, she was convinced, kept infection at bay. Not that the wound didn't still hurt. It did. The thick bandage was to provide some extra cushioning.

A frown twitched across her face. Melissa still worried her. Ford insisted on accompanying her, which meant Johnny, too weak to lift a pistol, would be on his own while they were gone.

He'd have Pen to keep him company, but what good would she be if a girl with a poisoned heart and a gun decided to show up?

Last night, when January announced her plan to call on Mrs. Hammel early, Ford didn't argue, just set his mouth and kept it shut. She could feel tension simmering within him, although anyone else might not have noticed. And there was something in those eagle-sharp eyes of his. Something she couldn't quite place. Anger? Yes. And determination.

The same tension boiled in her, bubbling ever more fiercely. Finished with the bandage, she tucked in her shirt, and stepped into her boots, then went to check on Johnny.

She found him awake. More or less. Drifting in and out, most likely.

"You going?" His voice sounded like a frog's dry croak.

"Yes. As soon as Ford brings the horses. How's the pain?"

"Uh."

Not exactly an answer. Wishing she could give him more laudanum, January wanted him alert enough to protect himself—if it came to that. She tucked her little boot pistol, a short-barreled hammerless revolver, under his pillows. "Just in case."

Johnny's head moved in a nod. ". . . careful."

"Always." Starting to leave, Pen disconsolately following at her heels, she turned back. "Take care of Pen for me? If anything happens, I mean?"

"J . . .Janua—"

But January ignored his beginning protest. "Stay," she told Pen and closed the door on the pair of them.

From outside she heard the clank of bits and bridle and the clomp of hooves.

Ford, there with the horses.

Pulling on her coat, she blew out the single lamp she'd lit and went out, her Colt in a side-holster and carrying a shotgun.

Astride his roan, Ford led Hoot and the pinto up to the porch.

"Thanks." January stuck the shotgun into her saddle scabbard. "I wasn't sure you'd show up."

"Don't know why I did. I don't like this. It's a good way to get killed." Though still too dark to see his face, his voice rumbled displeasure.

"Then stay here," she said. "Look after Johnny and the place."

She lost most of what he muttered under his breath, except it included the word "idiot."

Hard to tell if he meant himself or her. Likely both.

It was an hour's ride to the Hammel ranch. She'd never been there, but Ford knew the way and led off at a trot.

"You all right? Want to turn back?" He sounded hopeful as they reached the top of the hill and the pile of boulders where the remains of Shay's kite lay smashed. They stopped for a moment and looked back at the ranch buildings, dark and silent in the hour before dawn.

"No turning back. I'm perfectly fine." Shivering, she fought the urge to slump. Frost coated the grass lining the road, turning it silver in the dim light. The horses' breath gusted out in clouds. She blamed her chill on the temperature, turned cold overnight, and knew it for a lie. She was scared, plain and simple.

"Yeah, fine," he said and looked straight ahead.

 She cast him a wary glance, sure he had plans of his own even if he refused to tell her what they were. They didn't speak as they followed the river west. Its gurgle and rush made an excuse not to talk. Holding the horses to a fast walk, they passed beneath trees and crossed rocky patches barren of vegetation. Once, a parcel of five deer rushed out in front of them, causing the roan and the pinto to shy in startlement. Hoot paid the deer no particular mind.

After a while, they passed the narrow opening to a gully almost deep enough to be called a canyon. Ford pointed it out as where he and Shay had hidden when, in the spring, the Hammel bunch had set out to attack Shay and then her.

They didn't talk after that. Not until they rounded a bend in the river and spotted a grouping of buildings about a quarter mile away. A single light shone in what she thought might be a cook shack. The house loomed, big and stately and almost evil.

CHAPTER 20

STANDING IN HER STIRRUPS, January leaned over Hoot's neck and eased herself erect, sucking in air as her stitches tugged. She pretended not to see the look Ford shot at her.

"Looks like we're right on time," he said, wisely not mentioning her momentary weakness.

"Yes. The prime hour." She studied the area, her sharp gaze going from barns, to bunkhouse, and finally, the ranch headquarters, a house splendid enough to qualify as a mansion. Hammel had definitely planned to be the big man in this part of the country. As important as Clark or Glover or Campbell, over in Spokane, with his house as fine as any of theirs.

Although, as far as January knew, those men were rumored to be a whole lot more honest and ethical in their dealings than Hammel ever thought of being.

"What do you want to do?" Ford asked when she said nothing more. "We could turn around and go back. You don't have to confront her, you know. Present your evidence and let the courts take over. After yesterday, you can count on Schlinger doing his job. With Cobb and

Langley speaking up, he'll have to."

"Maybe, but I'm not going to wait months, or even years, for the courts to take action. I'm going to end this now." The bite in her words came across sharp as a knife's edge. "Shay deserves justice."

"I know that. And revenge?"

"Yes, revenge, too."

She jogged Hoot's reins, but Ford leaned over and stopped the horse.

"Will you listen to a bit of advice?" he asked. "I came with you today for one more look at this place. Really look, January."

She did. "So? What do you want me to see?"

"The big house. The space between barn, bunkhouse, the open ground."

"I see it."

"Do you? Do you see there's plenty of shelter for them, but no place for you, for us, to hide when we ride down off this hill?"

A light came on at the back of the big house and she shivered. "I see," she repeated.

Ford shook his head. "I don't think you do. I'm your friend, January. I was Shay's friend. I'm also a U.S. Deputy Marshal with years of experience. When I say the defender is always going to have an advantage when it comes to a fair fight, you'd best believe it. I mean not only under the law, but from the logistical view. Courts are more likely to think the aggressor is on the wrong side. Your case will be made better if she comes after you."

"I can't wait on her to make the decision."

He grinned with a wicked glint. "And that's why I'm

saying go ahead and give her the horse. Just be prepared for the result. It's apt to stir her fighting blood. But it will also serve notice. She'll know you're ready for a fight. Then one of two things will happen."

He seemed to be waiting for January to say "what," so she did.

"She'll either step down, or she'll be out for blood. If she chooses the latter, you're sure to have a battle on your hands—a regular old-fashioned firefight. Just don't pull your gun first."

She looked at him, her expression sour.

"The winner, if there is a winner, will be who can last the longest," he said. "But if you choose the battleground, the advantage is yours."

Silent, absorbing his advice, she watched as daylight rose over the eastern hills and forced away the shadows. There wasn't much time left to surprise the early riser, and Ford, she concluded, was right. Beyond this slight rise, the land around the house was not only flat, but cleared of boulders, trees, and even of smaller vegetation. Anyone riding up was like a single green tree in the desert, a beacon for death-dealing lightning strikes.

Sighing, January held out her hand. "Pass me the pinto's rope. I'll go alone from here."

"Alone?" Ford, already in the act of handing her the pinto's lead, flinched back. "No."

"Yes." Grabbing the lead, she nudged Hoot, then stopped again. "Please, Ford. I'm not completely out of my mind, you know. Believe me, I don't feel easy about riding up to the Hammel house with Edgar Hammel's horse in tow. Still, as long as she doesn't shoot me out of the saddle, I think I can handle Elvira. One on one, for sure, maybe her and Melissa together, as well. But when the time comes, if Hoot has to run for it, I'd like to know I have someone at my back looking out for me."

His jaw clamped, ridges of muscle making a bulge. "Listen to yourself, woman. Doesn't sound like much of a plan."

"It's the best I can do. With you on this rise with a clear field of vision, if someone—anyone—takes aim at me, I hope you'll be ready to stop him. Or her."

"And if no one tries anything?

"Then I'll meet you back here in a few minutes and we'll go home. For now."

He poked at his ear as if he wasn't hearing right. "Then what?"

"Then we'll get busy with the next part of the plan."

She could tell by the look on his face he hadn't known there was a *next* part. Funny. She hadn't either.

* * *

GRIT AND THE ODD STONE turning beneath Hoot's and the pinto's hooves grated loudly as January guided the horses into the Hammel dooryard. So did the rush of her own uneven breaths, sometimes held, sometimes expended as if blowing out a flame. She guided the horses around to the back, to where she'd seen the light.

Out of Ford's sight, not a comfortable thought.

Stopping at a large rear stoop, she took another of those shaken breaths. Time to roll the dice.

"Hello the house," she called, not very loud. There was only one set of ears she wanted to reach. It seemed strange to her not to be greeted by a dog, although a tabby cat sat washing its face where the door stood slightly ajar.

Through the window, she saw the woman poking wood into the stove had halted all movement. Blonde hair, a tangled mass, flowed nearly to her waist. Elvira Hammel, up and starting her day.

Turning at January's hail, Mrs. Hammel stepped forward. Backlit by a lantern standing on a long table, January saw she wore a flannel robe in a dark-colored plaid. She pushed it aside as she nudged the cat out of the way with a slipper-clad foot. Also, she held a long butcher's knife in one hand.

January hated knives.

"Who is that?" Elvira Hammel demanded, peering through the narrow door opening. Then her gaze focused on the pinto and caught. She gasped and swung the opening wider. "Helmet!"

At first, January couldn't imagine what that single word meant, then it dawned on her. The pinto's name. Helmet. An appropriate moniker for a medicine hat. At the thought, her tension loosened. She was ready for this, knife or no knife.

"Miller, where have you—" Elvira stiffened. Her eyes shifted back to January and squinted. "You!" she said on a tone of utter loathing.

"Yes. Me. Mrs. Shay Billings." January's tone was no more friendly than Elvira's. "I'm returning your horse to you. In case you haven't heard, his rider's mission failed." She made herself sound every bit as arrogant and confident as any of the Hammel clan.

"Why aren't you dead?" Elvira whispered. "You're supposed to be dead. You should be."

January was relieved the woman avoided subterfuge. What would be the point between the two of them? "But I'm not," she said,. "You've failed to kill me, your daughter failed, your hired guns have failed. Give it up, Mrs. Hammel. You will not succeed."

She touched the star pinned to her coat lapel and saw Elvira's astonished glance lock onto it. "Before you ask, yes, this is real. As a deputy sheriff of this county, I am duly sworn to uphold the law. I'm giving you fair warning. The next time I come to you it will be to arrest you. The next time you or yours comes after me, I will be shooting back. And I won't shoot to wound. I *will* shoot to kill. Risk your daughter as you please. But remember. I warned you."

She felt sure the other woman would read her speech as an invitation to escalate. Exactly the reason she'd wanted Ford to stay beyond earshot. He probably expected her to conciliate, to try for a less violent solution, but that had never been in her plan. A straightforward woman, the only thing she could see to end this was to have everything in the open. One of them would win when the other was dead. Only then would it be done. Shay would have his justice and she her revenge.

Or she, as Elvira intended, would be the one dead.

A faint smile curled her lips as she faced Elvira Hammel's furious glare.

They understood one another now.

"The horse?" she said.

"Take him or leave him. I don't care. It's only a horse."

She'd leave it, of course. January gathered Hoot's slack

reins but didn't move when another voice spoke. A girl's voice.

Elvira stiffened.

"Mother?" A girl wearing an ankle-length pink night-gown stepped into sight and pushed past her mother onto the back steps. "What is she talking about? What's she doing with Eddie's horse?"

"Yes, Mrs. Hammel, why don't you explain to your daughter why I have Eddie's horse?" Smirking, January tossed the lead shank toward the girl, relieved it was Allie and not Melissa. Twisting awkwardly, Allie caught the rope.

Ignoring January, Elvira snapped at her daughter. "Leave the horse, Allie. I'll speak to you later. When *she* is gone."

January caught Allie's eye. "Don't believe everything you hear, kid," she said, knowing it would infuriate Elvira.

"Pardon me?" the girl asked, but January wasn't inclined to repeat herself. She'd been here too long already.

Besides, Elvira was coming toward her, pushing her daughter aside with the knife she held pointed as if to stab January if only she were within reach. Or Hoot. Hoot *was* near enough.

"I'm going to kill you," Elvira screamed.

Spinning the horse, she lifted him into a gallop, back the way they'd come.

Behind her, Elvira shrieked something indecipherable but furious. Allie cried out. As January glanced back, she saw curtains move in an upstairs window. A moment later, a man clad in long-johns ran from the bunkhouse holding a rifle.

From the rise where Ford waited, she spotted him casually raise his rifle and heard the report as he fired. Looking over her shoulder, she saw a puff of dust fly up in front of the man at the bunkhouse. He darted back inside.

Then she and Hoot reached the ridge and with Ford's roan racing alongside, they headed for the ranch.

THEY'D GONE A FULL MILE down the road before Ford pulled up. January stopped too. Or Hoot did, of his own accord. January, drawn inward, seemed not to notice. Ford saw her shiver once, then again. Short bursts, her skin pale and the scar on her cheek stark white. The morning was chilly, even though clear, with the sun only slowly warming.

But it wasn't cold enough to cause a person to shiver.

"You going to tell me what happened back there?" he asked.

She gave a sigh. "Nothing much happened. I thought there'd be more."

"Nothing much? Excuse me for saying so, but you left in a hurry."

January had no ready reply. He was right, after all.

He huffed a laugh. "You weren't gone long. Probably didn't have time for either one of you to really get going."

"Were you thinking there'd be a cat fight?" One fine eyebrow lifted and her mouth twitched. "We almost reached that point. She made threats, I made threats." She stopped.

Ford pulled the dun's head away from a clump of dry grass as the horse tried to snatch a mouthful. "Then what?"

"Then her daughter turned up. Not Melissa," she hastened to say. "The younger one."

Was that disappointment? She fell silent again but Ford, certain there was more to the story, said, "And?"

"And nothing." Her hazel eyes cut toward him, dark and shadowed. "Elvira had a knife. A carving knife. So I left."

A carving knife. The vision flashed through his head. January had every reason to dread carving knives. Shay had told him about old Kindred Schutt, her grandfather. He'd had a propensity for carving knives too, and marking his property with them. Somehow, he'd thought January his property.

But January shrugged, clicking her tongue to start Hoot moving again. They went on a few strides before she added, "But she'll be coming after me. Today or tonight. Maybe tomorrow. She won't want to wait long. Not after I teased her."

Teased? *Or provoked?* "No. Probably not." He hesitated. "I don't suppose she mentioned what she has planned."

"No. Just that she wants me dead," she said so offhand he'd have thought it didn't matter.

They'd known Mrs. Hammel's desire. It was the reason he'd wanted to be with her. He'd have liked to found out how many gunmen Mrs. Hammel had hired. How many they'd be up against. If angry enough, she might've named names, revealed timing, destination, plans.

January had the heart of a lioness and a temper with a smoldering flashpoint. He hadn't quite realized her inner fire until now, as generally she covered it up quite well. Let free, it might become something that didn't play well in a game that needed strategy.

Ford couldn't help wondering where all this was going to end up.

* * *

THEY WERE almost home when they passed January's bridge over the creek.

January reined Hoot in and sat a moment, looking over the site. She never passed it without wondering if she should do something with the burned barn. For instance, haul off the charred, half-burned timbers and dump them in a gully out of sight. The area offended her eyes. At least the hidden springhouse remained in good repair, its trick trapdoor, the place she'd captured the former sheriff, showing only a few inches above the rumbling creek. You'd never see it if you didn't know where to look. The water was low now, until the fall rains began in earnest.

A couple rock piles dotted the pasture where she'd planned to build stone fences. On the rise above the burned-out barn, a pyramid of stones meant for the house foundation sat where she'd abandoned them on the day of Shay's murder. The cellar, she noticed, first absently, then not so absently, was invisible from the road, waiting for walls to a house that most probably would never be built.

January sighed as tears filled her eyes. Tears of regret for a life that would never be. Tears for a man whose life ended too soon. Her chest felt stuffed with pain.

AT THE RANCH, they found Bent Langley and his son Art waiting for them. Bent, having seen them coming, walked out on the porch to meet them.

"I brung Art over to do chores while Johnson's laid up," he said, his eyes on Ford who quickly dismounted and stepped over to aid January. "And I brung my daughter Evie to help with Johnson. My wife thought you wasn't ready to take on all you're trying to do, January, you hardly being out of your own bed. Be a deputy, run a ranch, fight a war."

He flung out the last part like it was something he'd memorized, and January thought maybe he had, word for word. It sounded like something Pinky might say.

January dismounted into Ford's waiting arms, her legs unsteady and barely able to hold her. It felt good, even for those few seconds, to rest in a man's strong arms.

Oh, Shay.

After a moment she straightened and shrugged apart from Ford. "I won't say she's not welcome, Bent. But I don't know as it's safe for her to be here. Elvira Hammel has made Johnny a target right alongside me and I don't want to put your girl in danger. The same goes for your son."

Bent's face screwed into a grimace. "Don't figure Art would agree with you, January. He makes up his own mind. Besides, Johnson is his friend."

A girl's face, pretty and pert, peeped out from behind her dad. "I can handle a gun, too, Dad. You know I can."

Bent shrugged and nodded. "She can," he said to January.

The statement didn't make her feel one iota better.

She'd seen the girl, Evie, before, helping her mother when once she and Shay had Sunday supper with the

Langleys. And at Shay's funeral, Evie had set up tables, cleared dishes, and broken up a fight between a couple of ten-year-old boys before they got too rambunctious. January had no doubt the capable girl could handle a gun. What's more, at an age with Johnny, she may not have been terribly fond of the Hammel girls and their assumed superiority. Still, this was neither her fight, nor a rift between children.

Ford, reaching to gather Hoot's reins, grinned at her. "Don't look a gift horse in the mouth, January. We need all the help we can get. Matter of fact, I wish we had time to get Johnny over to Bent's place."

Bent nodded, but January shook her head. "A good idea, but he can't be moved. Maybe tomorrow if we're still alive."

She hobbled up the steps and plopped into one of the rockers. "But I'll tell you what. We can."

Brows drawing together, Ford flipped the reins over the hitch rail. "We can what?"

"Move."

"What do you mean?" Bent frowned too. "Move what?"

"Us. I know just how we can stop them before the Hammel gang can get this far."

"How?" Bent sounded both hopeful and disbelieving at the same time.

"You know what stands between this place and them, don't you?"

Ford's head lifted as realization struck.

Bent was slower. "Whaddya mean?"

"Kindred Crossing. The bridge." She said the words like a prayer. "And maybe a bag of tricks." She looked at Ford. "It worked before. Why not again?"

CHAPTER 21

January's first order of business was to check on Johnny. She crept into the bedroom where he lay motionless under a brightly colored quilt. The room was cool, dim, and quiet, except for the gasping sound of his breathing. She could hear the slow in-and-out of it through the narrow tube Doc had inserted through his chest into the lung.

Johnny lay on his back, of course, propped a few degrees upright by a folded blanket and her two pillows. His face, though still pale, showed a trace of color. Pink color, she noted thankfully. Not blue and not white.

As she approached, his eyes opened. "Hey," he said.

Evie had brought in the kitchen stool to sit on and keep watch over him. January sat down and took his hand. "You were right about not going into the orchard. I'm so awfully sorry."

"I shoulda been watching closer." His voice, barely louder than a whisper, sounded cracked and dry. "Shoulda paid attention to Brown Boy. He told . . ." His eyes drifted closed again.

She leaned forward. "Did you see who shot you? Johnny?"

"Shot me?" His words slurred.

"Was it Melissa?"

He seemed to be fading out of consciousness.

"Johnny? Was it Melissa?" she asked again.

His eyelids, marked by long dark lashes like a child's, fluttered but didn't open. "Melissa? I'm . . ." He sank into sleep without finishing and she had no choice but to leave him to his rest.

In the kitchen, a pot of soup—January thought it might be potato smelling of bacon and onions—simmered at the back of the cookstove. Evie stood, face flushed from the heat, cutting slabs of roast beef and placing them between slices of bread, both of which she'd managed to bake in the time since she'd arrived.

January had a hunch the girl was showing off her homemaker skills and conceded she had a handle on them. Except, just who was the show for, anyway? Her dad? Doubtful, and certainly not for her brother. For Johnny, even if he was too weak and out of it right now to know? Or Ford, who smiled at the girl and winked, making her blush?

The men sat around the table, drinking coffee as if they had nothing better to do. But then Pen, outside running her own form of patrol, bayed a warning, and Ford leapt toward the door. He grabbed up the rifle propped against the casing as he took a gander outside.

Bent, standing far enough behind him not to shake his shooting arm, prodded him in the back with a forefinger. "Who is it?"

Opening the door wider, Ford sat the rifle back in place. "It's Bo and a few of his men." More loudly, he called out to the men filing into the yard. "Come on in. We're just about to have a planning session."

To January's astonishment, considering the hurry he'd been in to leave the moment the oats were cut, one of the men was Rand. He didn't appear all that happy to be there. Just determined. "How's the boy?" he asked, which endeared himself in some small way to her.

"Weak," she replied. "But he'll make it." She almost swore she saw a tear well up in Bo Cobb's faded-sky eyes at the news. He seemed to be steeling himself to go in to see Johnny.

"You been there yet?" Bo asked. "Over to the Hammel place? I'll ride along with you if you ain't took that pinto back yet."

"Taken care of. Been there and back."

"And got out alive." He seemed vaguely surprised. "I'll be damned."

"Don't forget," she told Bo, holding back a smile, "I am Sheriff Schlinger's deputy. Deputy Billings. It has a fine ring."

He gave her a wry look. Maybe, she conceded, not impressed by her bravado. Not that she blamed him for his doubts. She had plenty of her own.

January found new strength with her neighbors standing with her, helping make a feasible plan. Better yet, it took no time at all to bring them round to her way of thinking. The most worrisome part, she discovered, involved timing. Ford had warned her and he brought the problem up again. When would the other woman strike? How long would their group be waiting?

Some of Bo's men had questions. How were they to stay warm? How were they to remain alert and ready, sitting outside and remaining silent if it lasted into the night? January and Rand already knew a little something about the staying alert and ready part.

"Don't just sit," Rand said. "Get up and move around."

"Will we have coffee?" Bo asked.

"I'm afraid not. We won't want to start any fires. Not even for smokes." January's negative reply caused some grumbling but didn't have any of them backing out.

"Hope it don't take 'em all night," another man said. "Don't want to miss my supper."

He was young, January noticed. Not much older than Johnny. Johnny didn't like to miss meals, either. The realization had her ushering the men to seats around the table and sitting everyone down to a bowl of Evie's good potato soup and some soda crackers. Bo's wranglers who lacked chairs hunkered against the wall and held their bowls in their hands.

She put the best face on the situation she knew how when somebody asked about Elvira's reaction to her early morning visitor.

"Mrs. Hammel was upset," she told them. "Enraged, I might say. And not especially impressed by my deputy's badge. I wouldn't be surprised to see them on their way by now."

Bent choked, which set Art to patting him on the back and made the others, even Rand, grin.

"Well, jumping jimimetty," Bent said when he could breathe again, "what are we doing here? Sit around like a bunch of garden slugs and we'll be too late to catch 'em by surprise. Let's get moving. I'm ready." He turned to his daughter. "Evie, wrap up them sandwiches. We'll take 'em with us."

* * *

Bo Cobb had come prepared for more than a visit with Johnny. He did step into the bedroom for a moment to emerge wearing a sober expression and shaking his head. As everyone trooped out to mount their horses, January discovered he'd brought along a pack horse laden with a couple rifles, three extra pistols, boxes of ammunition, and a few lengths of rope.

Spying the rope, she drew Ford aside. "Do you suppose Bo intends on hanging somebody?"

Ford, tightening the cinch on his dun's saddle, glanced sideways at Bo. "I wouldn't put it past him. We'd best not let him do that, you know."

"I do know." January agreed wholeheartedly with Ford. While prepared to defend herself and her home with guns, a hanging was far out of her realm. No vigilante, she just wanted Shay's murder solved, the attack on Johnny avenged, and the killer put away. Or dead, she had no problem with that as a solution. Only then could she grieve in peace.

Ford boosted her onto Hoot, a relief as she'd wondered if she had enough strength left to climb into the saddle. Within seconds, everyone had mounted, leaving Evie and Bo's cook, an older man, to watch the house, prevent an agitated Pen from following them, and keep Johnny safe.

Pen's protesting barks formed a background as Evie waved them off from the porch steps. She held a large revolver close to her side in her free hand and wore a determined look on her pretty young face. Not that January planned to let the Hammel gang to get far enough the girl would need to use it. Not even close.

Her nerves jumping like grasshoppers on a bed of hot rocks, January led the few miles to the bridge. Scanning the area one more time, she became aware of Ford watching her, his golden eyes lit from within.

"What?" she snapped out. On the verge of issuing the first of her orders, she wondered if he planned on countermanding them. Better not. She knew what needed done.

But he shook his head, smiling a little. "Where do you want me, Deputy Billings?"

She didn't have to stop to think. She pointed toward some bushes, their leaves not yet fallen, on the riverbank maybe fifty feet downstream from her bridge. There was just room to conceal a horse and his rider from the main road there. She knew. It's where Edgar Hammel hid that day in the spring when he shot Shay.

"Let them pass," she said. "We'll box them in. All of them. I don't want a single one getting away. If they start shooting, they'll be in a crossfire."

He nodded. "I'll see to it."

When he'd moved into position, his roan seemed to meld with the turning leaves and tree trunks. Ford himself became invisible.

Bent and Art Langley she placed together on what she thought of as her side of the river. The side she lived on before she married Shay. Art to lie atop the springhouse roof sheltered by the stone, and Bent concealed by the riverbank where he had a clear field of vision. They were close enough together to talk. She thought his father's voice would keep Art steady.

Rand and one of Bo's men took cover in what was supposed to be her new house's cellar, two others found spots on either side of the bridge. Just past the bridge, on Shay's side, Bo dragged a tree downed in a summer windstorm across the road to block it, then stretched the rope between a couple standing trees to further halt any travelers. He and January found spots across from each other.

January hoped the Hammels wouldn't keep them waiting long. A cold wind had picked up, moaning in the swaying tree tops.

One hour passed, then a second. Time enough for some of the men to become restless. The sandwiches had been eaten. A couple times men left their station to find a place more private to shake the dew off their lilies. January grew chill, huddling into a coat that turned out to be not quite warm enough.

From across the road, she heard Bo's soft grumble. "What's takin' 'em so dang long?"

As though his words had been a signal, she lifted her head and tilted it toward town. A moment later, the sound she'd heard became clear.

The pop and sputter of a motor car.

"They're coming," she sang out and heard the warning travel from man to man. "Stay quiet. Hold your positions."

Even then it seemed to take a long time until the gleam of a blue-painted auto, the last rays of sunshine glinting off its brass light and horn, came into view. Elvira Hammel sat in the front seat of the car, which Melissa drove. Elvira wore a red scarf tied down over a wide-brimmed hat, holding it on and keeping her hair from blowing. Melissa's lighter blonde hair fluttered out behind her head like a flag. The car came slowly, as a gaggle of riders on horseback followed amidst a cloud of dust.

They should've assigned a scout to ride ahead, out front of the motorcar, January thought, her mouth quirking. But she was relieved they hadn't.

The men on horseback rode by Ford without seeing him. As they passed the bridge, Bo's men holding silent and unseen, she saw the Hammel men bore rifles they held upright like a squad of soldiers on parade. Almost funny until it occurred to her the guns could be snapped into firing position in mere seconds.

Apparently the parade wasn't all for show.

On they came, until the log across the road stopped them. Melissa evidently spotted it late and braked only a few feet away.

Elvira got out of the motorcar and, walking up to the log, kicked it with the toe of her riding boot. She turned around as the men bunched up behind her and gestured toward one of them.

"Some of you men get over here and move this. Be quick about it. I want the Billings woman dead before dark and that piddly house burned to the ground. Kill anything that moves." She sounded deranged, her temper boiling to the surface. Also impatient, as if everyone was moving too slowly to suit her. Her intentions were repeated for everyone to hear. No ambiguity or made up excuses.

Some of her men, the ones who appeared to be regular cowhands, exchanged worried looks. Others, rough and grim, shrugged.

January need have no regrets or make any excuses for whatever happened next. She touched the badge pinned to her coat.

Gathering herself, she got to her feet and stepped into the road behind Elvira.

CHAPTER 22

A STRONG SENSE OF MISGIVING SET FORD'S BLOOD TO THRUMMING. He recognized the man keeping pace at the passenger side of the motorcar. The feller was leaning in close and talking to Mrs. Hammel. Ford saw her laugh at something he said and reply with a quip of her own. They both laughed, loudly enough he heard them from where he stood holding his hand over the roan's nose.

The girl driving the car, Melissa, Ford assumed, seemed to be concentrating on keep the vehicle's narrow tires out of the wagon ruts and going in a straight line. The girl's face looked drawn and tight. And unhappy. He wondered why. This expedition must be what she wanted. But then she looked over at her mother with an angry expression and he had the answer. The two acted altogether friendlier and better acquainted than propriety allowed. The girl sure enough seemed to think so.

Well, Howard Sweeney had always been one to have a way with the ladies. Although, Ford remembered with an inner snicker, it'd been a jealous woman who'd tattled about his whereabouts one night. Ford had arrested him on the spot, resulting in the gunman doing time in Walla Walla State Prison. The thing is, Sweeney should've still been locked up.

Cursing under his breath, Ford had to wait until the entire cavalcade of would-be invaders passed before he could fall in behind them. A few were regular cowhands who didn't look happy and he heard one say to his saddle pard, "This ain't right. I ain't shootin' nobody." He pulled his horse to the side. "You with me, Ben?"

The man, Ben, nodded. Sweating heavily, he looked relieved. "Yup. I quit this cat puke outfit, as of now."

The two fell back to the end of the gang, and another joined them. A reluctance to shoot didn't keep the three of them from following the prison hard cases, no doubt to watch the proceedings. If they'd been smarter or wiser men, Ford thought, they would've departed on the spot.

But the delay gave him time to think. Hadn't January mentioned something about a slimy lawyer named Sweeney who'd tried to serve papers to evict her from the ranch? If he remembered correctly, Howard Sweeney had a lawyer brother who'd so far escaped incarceration.

Put together, it probably meant they'd all gathered here with former Sheriff Elroy Rhodes as the connection. Sweeney's personable reputation carried beyond just women. Personable enough maybe to hoodwink the male parole board into issuing an early release.

An itch prickled under Ford's skin. The thing about Sweeney, not everybody knew how quick he could draw that .45 hanging from his hip. But Ford knew. And now he had one target. Sweeney couldn't be allowed to get close to January.

He swung aboard the roan.

"Hup, horse," he muttered, loosening the revolver in his holster. Sweat gathered under his hat band, even as the day grew brisker.

Ahead of him, the motorcar reached the downed log and stopped.

* * *

ELVIRA HAMMEL, caught with her back turned as she exhorted her troops, went still as the auto's engine died. Her daughter popped up, her head brushing the overhanging hood.

"Mother," Melissa cried. "Behind you."

A cry Elvira ignored even as the suited man snatched his weapon from the low-slung holster.

A typical show-off shooter, January thought, her lip curling with scorn.

From across the log, she rammed her pistol into Elvira's back before Melissa's words could penetrate the woman's rage.

"Elvira Hammel, you are under arrest for murder, attempted murder, and . . . and other charges. You men, put down your weapons. We have you surrounded." January's clear voice rose louder as she addressed Melissa. "Melissa Hammel, you face identical charges, plus several others laid against you. Surrender your guns or face the consequences."

A stupid speech, January thought. Would it work? She almost hoped the woman would ignore it. Almost.

A lack of motion in the dead silence lasted until a mutter arose as Bo Cobb stepped from cover. Then Bent's head rose above the riverbank, and the men at the bridge stood up. Farther back, Ford loped toward them.

"Shoot her," Elvira screeched then. "Shoot her dead."

Faster than January believed possible, the woman spun and leapt at her. Elvira's fist punched out, slamming into January's wounded side.

She'd known just where to do the most damage. The pistol dropped from January's hand as her fingers spasmed. Instantly, Elvira leapt across the log, reaching for the revolver, as January fell on top of it.

If Elvira got to it first, January was done. Shot with her own gun. She couldn't let it happen.

Vaguely, January was aware of Ford shouting. Of gunfire shattering the peace at Kindred Crossing. Of Bo, yelling and shooting. Of cries of pain, of cursing, of the smell of burned gunpowder.

And of Pen, arrived out of nowhere, leaping past her like a black shadow and flinging herself at Elvira. The woman kicked out at January as she fell backward. Drawing that same big knife she'd brandished earlier from a scabbard belted around her waist, she jabbed it at Pen, cutting through the dog's thick curly hair.

"No." January rolled. Found her revolver and forced her grip to close on the butt.

Elvira changed direction, stabbing down at her human target even as Pen's teeth caught in the woman's dress and hung there.

I hate knives! The old dread thought flashed in January's mind as she jerked the gun up and pulled the trigger. A neat round hole opened in Elvira's forehead, her head rocking on her snapped neck.

Dead but still moving, Elvira's momentum carried her

forward. She fell over the log and went still, bent like a child about to be spanked. Ever so slowly, her hand opened and the knife rolled to the ground.

January sat up, the panorama moving all around her. Men shouted, horses squealed, and Pen, lending her voice to the din.

There was Art Langley, taking aim at one of the Hammel shootists, and the outlaw falling back, a stream of red pouring from his chest.

Bent Langley, trying for a man wearing a horsehair vest and missing.

Bo Cobb, firing into the Hammel motorcar, bullet pinging, as Melissa endeavored to crank the engine.

Rand, shooting blindly into the mob of men and horses.

The man stationed at the bridge reloading his rifle.

And Ford, bearing down on the dandy in the black suit who, although she didn't particularly notice, took aim at January.

Didn't they, any of them, realize with their leader dead the fight was over? Should be over?

Except, January saw with astonishment, there was Albert Sims, almost hidden as he huddled on the motor car's rear seat, his face glowing white as a specter's. She saw his fist wave, his mouth open as he screamed something at Melissa.

Sneak around and try to steal Shay's ranch, would you?

Deputy January Billings wasn't about to allow his shenanigans go unchecked for him to bilk other hard-working people. No, sir.

Oblivious to everyone and everything else, she pushed herself off the ground and walked toward the car. Her weapon dangled in her hand.

* * *

"Howard Sweeney!" Ford's shout went unheard amongst the cacophony of horses neighing as riders wrenched them about, men yelling at each other, cries of pain when a bullet reached its mark, the steady bark of rifles and revolvers.

His horse shied as a bullet, possibly from one of their friend's weapons, singed his neck. Ford brought the animal back under control, relentlessly forcing him between a young fellow who'd dropped his gun and was trying to get away, and another man attempting to shove cartridges into a handgun, dropping most of them as his horse pivoted back and forth.

Ford encouraged the one who wanted to leave by swatting at his horse. He knocked the pistol from the other man's hand before he finished loading. Then it was all open space between him and the man whose name he'd shouted.

Something, maybe a highly honed sense of self-preservation, made Sweeney look across the melée and spot Ford coming toward him.

Tervo. Sweeney's mouth formed Ford's name. He turned from January and started walking toward Ford, his old nemesis.

They'd meet, Ford thought, somewhere in the middle as the fighting swirled around them.

Sweeney's full lips smiled under his mustache, his teeth bared like a snarling coyote. Holding his Colt out front, he fired off a quick shot. A ping of dust rose up almost under Ford's feet, the dry odor rising to his nostrils. Sweeney frowned, as though not understanding how he'd missed.

Ford wondered that too, until he saw blood well up on top of Sweeney's hand. When he took his eyes off Sweeney for a fraction of a second, he saw it was January with her dad's .38 Colt pointing at the outlaw.

Quick as a biting snake, Sweeney shifted his pistol to his left hand and came on.

How many times has he fired that gun?

The question shot through Ford's mind as if were one of the bullets, followed by another. *How good of a shot is he with his off hand?*

He hadn't taken his eyes from Sweeney, and he'd seen him fire at January twice, once at the Langley boy lying atop the springhouse, maybe more than once at Cobb. And at Ford himself, just now.

What Ford hadn't seen was the man reloading.

But then, he hadn't reloaded, either.

"Sweeney," he yelled, "lay down your gun and surrender."

The gunman still wore that eerie smile as he took one more step. Then he stopped, so close Ford smelled him, rank with sweat and tobacco. Pointing his revolver, Sweeney bared his teeth and pulled the trigger.

And nothing happened.

All so fast Ford barely had time to blink.

Closing the distance between them in a lunge, Ford slammed his pistol barrel down on Sweeney's gun hand. The outlaw howled as his pistol fell, but Ford wasn't done. He clubbed the man between his neck and his shoulder.

Sweeney dropped to the ground, writhing. "Now what?" He wasn't smiling when he glared up at Ford. "You gonna shoot me?

Ford took a couple steps back in case Sweeney tried to kick his legs out from under him. It was his turn to smile. "Can't," he said. "My gun's empty." And to prove it he dry-fired into Sweeney's face. "So I'll send you back to prison instead of to hell."

* * *

JANUARY, in a bit of a daze, watched her men disarm their prisoners, those who hadn't turned tail and run. But especially she eyed Melissa Hammel. The girl appeared stunned, as if she didn't understand what had happened. And that suited January fine. It made this the best time to pose her question. The single thing that counted the most. Afterward, if Melissa Hammel broke into pieces, she wouldn't care one bit.

Even so, her feet dragged against the dirt as she trod over to the automobile where Melissa sat on the ground and leaned against a tire. January's nose wrinkled at the car's mechanized smell. Gas fumes, grease, hot metal. She preferred horses, manure and all.

Melissa's eyes, as green as her mother's, glared hatred as January stopped in front of her.

The girl lunged to her feet and for a moment January thought she meant to attack bare-handed.

"You shot my mother." Melissa's scream, a mixture of anguish and fury, rang loud as a clarion trumpet "You killed her."

Showing a callousness she didn't feel, January shrugged. "Yes. I did. And one of you killed my husband.

Which of you was it? You or your mother?"

"Mother killed him." Pride snarled behind the words. "She would've killed him twice if she could, because of Eddie and because of Father. But we should've killed you first. I see that now. We tried. I tried. I tried hard."

As confessions went, it was hard to mistake. There were plenty of witnesses to it.

But January had to know just one more thing. She cocked her thumb at Albert Sims, still shivering on the motorcar's seat. "What about him?"

Melissa turned to look. Her lip curled in a sneer. "Oh, him," she said. "He's just a thief."

Just. So, January wondered, did that put murderers in a higher echelon?

* * *

Like any good commander, January made a round to check the welfare of her posse of friends.

Young Art Langley had a nick in his upper arm, she found, of which he seemed inordinately proud. It had bled at a fierce rate for a while but was clotting now. A badge of honor, she figured, grinning a little. He'd probably speak of it, and show off the scar, for the rest of his life. Her grin faded when she thought of Johnny. How much bragging would he do—if he even survived?

Bent, though, hovered over his boy—Or no. Call him a man, after today—like a hen with a single chick. The sight brought back some of her smile.

The others had fared well. Bo Cobb had a nasty scrape

on his face that he said he didn't know how he'd acquired. Rand kept swallowing convulsively, as if struggling to keep the sandwich he'd eaten before the fight secure in his belly. Singling him out, Cobb patted him on the back and went on to talk to his other men. All of them appeared, if not totally unscathed, then with nothing serious to complain about.

Meanwhile, with her big black dog on one side and Ford on the other, January circled the Hammel-Sims people, all of them gathered in a bunch. Her friends held them surrounded and under tight guard. Those alive, she meant. The bodies of two gunmen were laid out on the grass at the side of the road. A few others bore wounds.

"Cobb and some of his men will help me get these yahoos into town," Ford said, eyeing her as if measuring her weariness. "We'll give 'em over for Schlinger to take care of." His gold-flecked eyes flashed. "The least he can do. Him and Dabney, that no-account deputy of his, can escort them to the county seat."

"Including Albert Sims," she said.

Ford nodded. "Didn't figure to leave him out. I've got something special planned for him."

"And Melissa?"

"Her too. Another problem for Schlinger to handle. Make him earn his pay."

"One more thing—" She held up a forefinger, raising her voice and calling out, "Which of you men is Jerry Arnault?"

A stir in a group of three standing apart pushed a man to the front.

"I'm Arnault." Slim, wiry and short. Older than Johnny. Old enough for a little wisdom, at least she hoped so. Johnny had told her about the warning Arnault had given him.

He was also the one who'd said he wouldn't fight for Mrs. Hammel. Ford had pointed him out to her already, but he hadn't known his name.

"I understand you meant to quit Mrs. Hammel," she said.

Arnault's gaze shifted to the group. "Yes, ma'am," he admitted.

"But here you are."

His boots scuffed the dirt.

"Perhaps you'd care to make amends."

"Amends? Ma'am, I ain't hurt you none. I didn't do no shooting. Never pulled my gun." He looked up at her this time, a bit angry and with his face flaming.

Her eyebrows rose as if in question. "And yet, here you are," she said again.

"Honest, ma'am. I meant to draw my pay and go."

"Prove it."

He frowned a question.

"I figure," she said, cool as could be, "that you must've observed them. After hours, in the bunkhouse."

He shifted uncomfortably. "Only enough so they didn't steal us wranglers blind."

"Then you'll know what they're carrying. I want you to check their boots, their back pockets, under their coats. Look for weapons, and I don't mean just guns. Look for knives or anything else that might do harm." She hoped none of them noticed her shudder.

"I seen Crisp has brass knuckles," he said. "Those count?"

"They do."

Arnault started the search with one of the gunmen, grinning as he confiscated the knuckledusters. She had to wonder about that.

"Smart thinking," Ford whispered to her. "You make a good deputy, January Billings."

Deputy? January, on the other hand, would be glad to hand her badge back to Schlinger, her job done. Shay was avenged, justice, though brutal, served.

Funny, though. She didn't feel any lighter or miss her husband any the less.

THREE WHOLE DAYS passed and started on a fourth before Ford returned to the ranch. January had begun to think that with Shay's murder resolved, he'd simply packed up and moved on. Not that she would blame him, exactly, but she did have a strange sense of abandonment.

An odd thing to admit, she thought to herself, on this Thursday morning as she sat on the porch drinking her coffee. The weather was crisp and she enjoyed the fragrant steam rising from her cup and the way it warmed her hands.

After all, her thoughts meandered on, she barely knew him. Him meaning Ford Tervo. Her life was back to what it had been before. Before Shay, when there'd only been herself. Sometimes it was Shay who seemed like a dream. A fanciful dream, where she could love and be loved, and be happy.

But Johnny, at least, seemed to be on the mend. He'd sat up all the way this morning, and eaten a hearty breakfast. Hearty for an invalid, at least, a description he protested.

"I'm no invalid," he'd said, wheezing as he exhaled. "It ain't like I'm sick, ya know."

January figured she had Evie Langley to thank for his rapid recovery. Evie remained with her, helping—actually, doing most of the outdoor chores—and cheering Johnny on.

As for January, her wound, now that she'd entered a period of relative inactivity, only twinged if she stretched too far or lifted something too heavy. As for the other hurt, well, having company helped her deal with the pain of losing Shay.

Enough that she felt a lift of her heart when she spotted the familiar roan gelding lope over the crest of the hill as if he couldn't get to the ranch fast enough.

Setting her coffee cup on the porch rail, she smoothed her seldom-worn skirt over her hips, drew her brown hair forward over her scarred check and pinched the other to bring up the color. She'd looked like an exhausted ghost for most of the time Ford had been around. She wanted to make a better—a healthier—impression.

Worth the effort, to see a grin light Ford's dark face.

"Mr. Tervo, here you are at last," she said as if she'd never doubted he'd show up. "I'm glad to see you. What's the news? I've been anxious."

He dismounted and flipped the reins over the roan's head, tying him to the rail. "Didn't that man of Bo's give you a report? I told him what to say."

It had been a man named Joe Appleton who dropped by and it had been two days ago. An age, to January's way of thinking.

"Wasn't much of a report if you ask me," she said. "I'm sure you can do better. Come on in. Have you had breakfast? Coffee? I can even put a splash of Old Crow in it if you feel the need."

Her chatter took them into the house. She saw him eyeing the wall where she'd ripped down the ink-stained wallpaper. A rag rug lay over the gouged and blue-tinted floor. She'd fixed the easy chair, Evie helping by taking neat stitches in the upholstery. Undecided as to repair or replace, she'd also removed the tambour from the desk. She wasn't sure yet what to do, but the room looked almost normal.

Ford looked in on Johnny before he sat at the table and she heard them laughing. January's impatience grew.

"Well?" she demanded when he finally settled onto a chair. "What happened? What did Schlinger do?"

He took a swallow of coffee, sans the Old Crow, and smiled. "Schlinger hauled the whole kit and caboodle of them to Spokane and jail. He needed help, so Bo Cobb and I went with him. Had Rebecca and Ruth Inman along to guard the Hammel girl. I think any sympathy they had for her disappeared by the time they turned her over to the district authorities." He chuckled. "There'll be another hearing soon, like the one with Marvin Hammel, after which there'll be trials."

"The hearing won't be with Judge Keane, I hope. He's one of Sims's cronies."

"Nah, this is too big for a local court. Banks are held under a federal charter, so anything to do with Sims will go before a federal court. Which means Spokane. Don't worry. The ranch is safe.

When she gave him a nod, he continued, "That's the

property, then. About the murder charges . . .

The murder charges . . . He eyed her and she knew he was wondering if she'd fall apart.

Well, she wouldn't. "Go ahead."

"Everything else will be state courts. They'll put a stiff prosecutor on it. Gonna try to get Sims on that too. Do you agree?"

She didn't have to wonder. "Yes." She hesitated. "What about me? I killed Mrs. Hammel."

"Self-defense. No questions asked."

As though a weight had fallen from her shoulders, January sat straighter although her face was still serious. "What about Melissa Hammel? And the other girl, Allie? What will happen to her? Which of those men shot Johnny?"

Ford was startled. "Hasn't the kid said?"

"He doesn't remember."

"Seems to me he'd better start. He was shot in the lung, not knocked in the head. Do you suppose he's trying to protect that girl?"

"Why would he do that?"

He shrugged. "Might fancy himself in love."

Thinking of Evie Langley, January smiled. "Maybe he does, but it isn't with Melissa Hammel."

She hardly heard everything Ford said next. About Allie Hammel going to live back east with a relative of some sort. Of Melissa facing years in a woman's prison. About the gunmen serving new sentences.

About Sheriff Schlinger thinking he wanted to become a rancher.

About Ford already assigned to a new manhunt and the odd way he watched her disappointed reaction.

* * *

IT WASN'T THE TIME TO SPEAK OF LOVE, Ford knew. Maybe it would never be the time. All he could do is back off, give her the months, maybe even the years, to think about giving another man a chance. But he'd be back, one of these days.

Then they'd see.

A LOOK AT: LIAR'S TRAIL BY C.K. CRIGGER

YOUNG GINCY TATE'S FATHER is murdered before he can fulfill a contract to supply the Army with remounts. In order to pay his debts and save the ranch, she must make the sale in his place. Afraid the lien-holder, whom she suspects of being the murderer, will foreclose before June 7, 1883, she tells no one Morris Tate is dead. Instead, she says he is here, there, or elsewhere. Gincy hires two cowboys to help trail the herd to Fort Spokane. One is on the murderer's payroll, but Sawyer Kennett hires on because he has decided Gincy is the woman for him. With an old Indian, who is her shirttail relative, the group battles storm, stampede, and sabotage to win their way to the fort and sell the herd. Then Gincy must make it home in time to beat the foreclosure and confront her father's murderer - but only if Sawyer is the man she prays he is.

AVAILABLE ON AMAZON

ABOUT THE AUTHOR

C.K. CRIGGER was born and raised in North Idaho on the Coeur d'Alene Indian Reservation, and currently lives with her husband, three feisty little dogs and an uppity Persian cat in Spokane Valley, Washington.

Imbued with an abiding love of western traditions and wide-open spaces, Crigger writes of free-spirited people who break from their standard roles.

Her western novel, The Woman Who Built a Bridge was a 2019 Spur Award winner. Her short story, Aldy Neal's Ghost, was a 2007 Spur finalist. Black Crossing won the 2008 EPIC Award in the historical/western category. Letter of the Law was a 2009 Spur finalist in the audio category.

Made in the USA
Coppell, TX
11 March 2023

14142733R00156